Danielle Steel is one of the world's most popular and highly acclaimed authors, with over ninety international bestselling novels in print and more than 600 million copies of her novels sold. She is also the author of *His Bright Light*, the story of her son Nick Traina's life and death; *A Gift of Hope*, a memoir of her work with the homeless; and *Pure Joy*, about the dogs she and her family have loved.

To discover more about Danielle Steel and her books visit her website at www.daniellesteel.com

You can also connect with Danielle on Facebook at www.facebook.com/DanielleSteelOfficial or on Twitter: @daniellesteel

D0615024

By Danielle Steel

DANIELLE STEEL

Secrets

sphere

SPHERE

First published in the United States of America by Delacorte Press in 1985
First published in Great Britain in 1985 by Michael Joseph Ltd
Published by Sphere Books Ltd in 1986
Reprinted by Warner Books in 1994
Reprinted by Time Warner Paperbacks in 2004
Reprinted by Time Warner Books in 2005
Reissued by Sphere in 2010
Reprinted by Sphere in 2012

13 12 11 10 9 8 7 6 5 4 3

A CIP catalogue record for this book
is available from the British Library.

ISBN 978-0-7515-5067-2

Typeset in New Baskerville by Hewer Text UK Ltd
Printed and bound in Great Britain by
Clays Ltd, Elcograf S.p.A.

Papers used by Sphere are from well-managed forests
and other responsible sources.

MIX
Paper from
responsible sources
FSC® C104740

Sphere
An imprint of
Little, Brown Book Group
Carmelite House
50 Victoria Embankment
London EC4Y 0DZ

An Hachette UK Company
www.hachette.co.uk

www.littlebrown.co.uk

To the best and dearest
gift of my life,
to John,
with all my heart and love

d.s.

The sun reverberated off the buildings with the brilliance of a handful of diamonds cast against an iceberg, the shimmering white was blinding, as Sabina lay naked on a deckchair in the heat of the Los Angeles sun. She lay sparkling and oiled, warmed to a honey-brown by the relentless sun. Later she would go down to the pool for a little while, just to cool off, but there were a dozen rituals she had to perform first. First she lay on her back every morning, her face creamed, her body oiled, the spectacular mane of blonde hair shielded from the sun, her eyes covered with pads dipped in witch hazel, a damp washcloth framing her face so as not to leave the unseen scars of the year before unprotected in the sun. The breasts similarly protected by small, damp gauze pads for the same reasons. The three surgeries she had endured had served her well and didn't show. The first, at thirty-eight, later than she would have thought, just to smooth a small furrow from between her brows, and raise her eyelids to the exact location they had been ten years before. The second at forty-one, to enhance her breasts, and give them a fullness and upward tilt they had never really had, even at sixteen. And the last surgery a year before, a repeat of the first one, with only slightly more emphasis this time, and a few tucks above her ears. On a good day she looked thirty-five, a great one thirty-one, and in the camera's eye, she looked younger than that sometimes . . . sometimes . . . if the cameraman was any good. Sabina Quarles was forty-five years old. And her body was honed to perfection. She exercised every morning for an hour, was massaged three times a week, swam every afternoon, and walked two miles if it was cool enough. Not jogged, walked. She was no fool. She hadn't spent five thousand on her tits to shake them down another three inches jogging along the concrete of Beverly Hills.

She was given to low-cut dresses that revealed the cleavage she was so proud of, the perfect expanse of honey-coloured flesh that showed no signs of age. And she wore her skirts slit up high along her thigh as well. And with good reason. She had the kind of legs most women would have died for. Surgery hadn't given her those. God had. And He had endowed her well. In fact, he had been more than generous with Mary Elizabeth Ralston, born in Huntington, Pennsylvania, almost half a century before. Her father had been a miner, her mother a waitress at a transport cafe lit with a blinking neon sign that flashed all night and was called 'The Cafe'. Her father had died when she was nine, her mother had married three more times in seven years, been widowed twice, and had died herself when Mary Elizabeth was seventeen. There was nothing left to hang around for, there hadn't been anyway. And Mary Elizabeth swung her long, shapely legs onto a Greyhound bus and headed for New York. Mary Elizabeth Ralston, for all intents and purposes, died that day. In New York she became Virginia Harlowe, a name she thought glamorous at the time, as she tried for small modelling jobs and finally wound up in a chorus line in a show that was very much off Broadway. She thought it was the high point of her life, until at twenty-one, someone offered her a part in a film. Her hair was jet black in those days. She carefully dyed it to hide the paler roots so it would set off her wide almond-shaped green eyes. She was not given a wardrobe for this film but told to go to a freezing cold warehouse on the Lower East Side with two other girls and a man. It was a role she no longer ever thought of. Ever. Virginia Harlowe's life was even shorter than Mary Elizabeth Ralston's. There were a few more similar parts, a job in a strip joint on the West Side, but she was smart enough to know a dead end when she saw one. The name Sabina Quarles leapt at her from the pages of a magazine someone had left in the communal dressing room one night, and the money she had managed to save paid for a ticket to Los Angeles. She was twenty-four and knew it was almost too late. Almost, but not quite. She left the black hair dye in New York, and became a blonde when she hit California. Within three weeks, she found herself a rented room and an agent, and there was no mention of the film work she had done in New York. It was part of another life, a life she no longer chose to remember. Sabina Quarles, as she became and stayed after that, had a knack for forgetting whatever it was no longer convenient to remember, the life of the coal mines, the strip joint in New York, and the small budget ugly porn films she had made in the warehouse on the Lower East Side. In Los Angeles she became a model, and was cast in a few commercials, had a screen test at MGM and another at Fox, and in less than six months she had landed a part in a very decent film. There were three more small parts after that, and finally a decent role, and by twenty-six, Sabina's face was one that a number of directors knew and remembered. Her acting didn't set the world on fire, but she was good enough, and her agent found her a coach who helped her over the rough spots. He also helped her to get a few more parts. By twenty-eight, people knew her name and face, and her press agent saw to it that her name appeared regularly in the papers. She was linked with a number of male stars, and at thirty she had an affair with one of Hollywood's hottest stars. And she was more in demand after appearing with him in one of his films. It was a career that had been hard earned, hard won, by the flesh on her back, her willingness to take off more clothes than some of her colleagues were at the time, and the fact that eventually she really did learn how to act. In her early thirties she disappeared for a while, and then reappeared with a bang in a hotly touted film everyone vowed would make her a star. It did not, but it etched her name in people's minds a little more firmly, and won her some better roles than the ones she'd had before.

Sabina Quarles had worked hard to get where she was, and where she was at forty-five was no pinnacle of success, but her name was known in Hollywood, and with a moment's thought, she was known to filmgoers all over the country . . . Oh, I know . . . wasn't she in . . . a moment's blank stare and then a smile, a leer, a look of desire on men's faces. She was the kind of woman men had fantasies about going to bed with, although with age she became surprisingly selective. Sabina Quarles had staying power and a body that just wouldn't quit, no matter how old she was. She saw to that, to all of it, she kept up all her contacts, called her agent every day, worked hard when she got a part, and was surprisingly easy to work with.

Sabina Quarles was not a prima donna, she was a film star . . . more or less . . . one of those second-string bright lights who sometimes outlive the really big names who come and go and die every day in the studios of Hollywood, replaced by younger, fresher faces. Sabina Quarles' face was still well worth looking into, and her name didn't mean money in the box office, but it meant happy men when they left the theatre. She still had the same quality she'd had at twenty-one. Men wanted to reach out and touch her. And she liked that, whether she chose to let them or not. That wasn't the point. Her body was her vehicle to success, and it always had been.

With a glance at the alarm clock she kept on her terrace for exactly that purpose, she turned from her back to her stomach with a graceful flip, and with a familiar, reflexive flick of her wrist towards a large jar of cream, she creamed her face and arms again. They were as young and firm as the rest of her. There was not a millimetre of droop or sag to Sabina.

The phone rang just as she was about to get up anyway. It was almost time for two big glasses of mineral water before she went downstairs to the pool for a swim. She glanced at her watch, wondering who it was. She had already called her agent.

'Hello.' Everything about Sabina Quarles was as smooth as honey. Her voice was deep and soft, a sexy voice that made men want to hold themselves as they sat staring at her in a darkened theatre.

'Sabina Quarles, please.' A twenty-two-year-old secretarial voice chattered at the other end. The voice was unfamiliar to her.

'This is she.' She stood long and tall and beautiful in her living room, holding the phone, as she smoothed the blonde mane off her shoulders with her other hand. No one would have guessed that the colour was not entirely hers. Everything about Sabina was beautifully done, carefully thought out, and well maintained. She had spent a lifetime becoming who she was and she had done it well. It was only too bad that she hadn't gone further in her career. She wondered about it sometimes, but she hadn't given up. She was well known, if not the hottest item in town. She never felt it was too late. There was nothing old or tired or middle-aged or defeated about Sabina. She was still a woman on her way up, even if she had hit a plateau in the last year or so. The lack of important parts was not something that fazed her, as long as the money kept coming in. She had done an ad featuring a sable coat only a month before. She was willing to do any number of things to keep her income flowing at a steady pace . . . as long as it wasn't TV. Television was something she would never stoop to.

'This is Mel Wechsler's office,' the voice said, full of self-importance. Melvin Wechsler was the biggest producer in Hollywood, and whoever worked for him shared in that limelight, or at least his secretary sounded as though she believed that. Sabina smiled. She had been out with him two or three times a few years before. Mel Wechsler, aside from everything else, was an attractive man. She wondered why he was calling.

'Yes?' There was laughter in the golden voice now, as she cast a glance around her living room. The apartment was modern, spare, on Linden Drive, in a slightly less than fabulous slice of Beverly Hills. But the address was good, and the apartment was furnished mostly in white, with two mirrored walls. She saw her naked image now, the breasts high and firm, just as she had paid for them to be, the legs still long and beautiful. She liked looking at herself, there was nothing in her image to worry or frighten her, and if something appeared she didn't like, she knew just how to have it taken care of.

'Mr Wechsler was wondering if you could have lunch with him today. At the Bistro Gardens.' She wondered why he hadn't called himself, and why it was on such short notice. Maybe it was for a part in a film, although he made fewer films these days. In the last ten years, Melvin Wechsler's biggest hits had been on TV, although he did still make films. And he knew she didn't do TV. Everyone knew that about Sabina. Television was crap, and she said so at every chance she got. She was Sabina Quarles, she didn't have to do TV. That was what she told her agent every time the subject came up, and it didn't come up very often anymore. He had better luck talking her into ads like the one with the sable coat. That had some class, as far as she was concerned, television did not. But Mel Wechsler did. And she had nothing to do for lunch. It was ten forty-five. 'One o'clock?' It never occurred to the girl that Sabina would say no. No one ever did. Or damn few people anyway, and never actors.

'One fifteen.' Sabina looked amused. It was a game everyone played in Hollywood, and she was tougher than this girl and they both knew it.

'That will be fine. The Bistro Gardens,' she repeated as though Sabina would forget.

'Thank you. Tell him I'll be there.'

You bet your ass you will, sweetheart, the girl thought to herself as she hung up, and buzzed through to Mr Wechsler. The secretary at the other end took the message that Sabina Quarles would meet him at one fifteen and Wechsler looked pleased when she handed him the note.

At her end, Sabina looked pleased as well. Mel Wechsler. Now that she thought about it, she realised that she hadn't seen him in ages. He had even taken her to the Academy Awards ten years before. She always thought he'd been attracted to her more strenuously than he showed, but somehow they'd never got round to doing anything about it.

She walked into her dressing room, a mirrored cubicle that led into a tiny bathroom, and stepped into the shower, flipping the knobs with practised hands. The tingle of hot water felt good on her well-oiled flesh, and she washed her hair at the same time, wondering what she should wear for lunch with Melvin Wechsler. It all depended what he had in mind, a job, or something more personal. She wasn't quite sure which persona to be for him, hot star on the way up, or sultry woman of the world, and then she laughed. The two were one and the same. She was Sabina Quarles after all, long and lean and blonde and beautiful. He could do a lot for her, in a number of ways, and she knew it.

She ran the water ice cold over her flesh before she stepped out again, and her whole body tingled as she dried herself and then ran a comb through her long hair. If you didn't look too carefully, she decided, she could have been twenty-five . . . twenty-eight? . . . twenty-nine . . . she smiled. She didn't give a damn. Fourteen or ninety-eight suited her just fine. She was having lunch with Melvin Wechsler.

2

Sabina rode down in the lift of her building with a look of relaxation. She pressed the button for the garage and the small metal cage shook as she headed down. Only now and then did she worry about getting accosted or mugged, and the only thing she would have worried about was someone hurting her body or her face. They could have had anything else she had. She rarely carried much cash, and didn't own any jewellery of great value. Whatever she'd got over the years, she'd sold. She had other, more important uses for the money.

Her car was a small silver Mercedes 280 SL, a model no longer made and no longer much in demand. It was racy, but not new by any means, like many of Sabina's things. Her clothes suited her well, and she bought them for what they did for her. She wasn't interested in the latest fashions. She was wearing a white silk skirt slit high up her thigh, and a deep blue silk shirt that set off her tan and the colour of her hair. The first four buttons were left open and the cleavage she revealed was enough to weaken any man and reduce him to near incoherence. Her hair had been dried, well brushed, and swept out behind her in a healthy mane. Her nails were perfectly manicured and lacquered bright red, just like her toes. She was wearing high-heeled white sandals. The car roared into gear and out of the garage, speeding towards the Bistro Gardens.

On Wilshire, she made a sharp right, and then another almost instantly, passing between the tall iron gates of the driveway of the Beverly Wilshire, and she lodged herself between its two buildings like a diamond between two breasts, sparkling in the sun, as she sat waiting in her car for the doorman to come and see her. He did so with a warm smile. He had known her for years. He liked keeping her car for her, she tipped well and she was one hell of a beautiful woman. Just watching her always made him feel good. He opened the door and she unravelled her legs from the tiny car. As usual, she had driven with the top down.

'Afternoon, Miss Quarles. You having lunch here today?'

She smiled the smile that made men forget every word she said. 'Not too far from here. Can you keep the car for me?' It was a rhetorical question. He was always pleased to help Sabina Quarles. And he enjoyed the opportunity he got just to drink the sight of her in.

'Sure thing. See you in a while.' He handed her the ticket stub and she walked away with a smile that made him feel sexy and important. He kept his eyes on her back until she turned right out of the driveway and he couldn't see her any more. It was like watching fine ballet, as he watched her behind undulate in the white skirt. She would have been pleased had she seen the effect she'd had on him and four other men, who had simply stood admiring her, silently staring. Only one of them had recognised her, but that wasn't the point. Men just watched Sabina, no matter who she was, because of the way she looked, and the way she moved, and the enormous presence she had about her. Actually, it was a damn shame her career had been stalled since that last film. All she needed was the right role. And the right producer.

She waited for the light on Wilshire Boulevard, and crossed over to where the Brown Derby had been when she first came to Hollywood. She walked quickly past it, with a destination in mind. It was already ten to one and she knew she had to hurry. But the outfit needed something more, and she knew precisely what. Almost everything Sabina did was by careful calculation.

It was only a few steps from the corner to the yellow-and-white-striped canopy everyone knew on Rodeo Drive, the sacred emporium to all the most glamorous women in Hollywood. Giorgio. She swept into the door on the corner, and walked straight to the hatracks across from the bar, as the bartender eyed her appreciatively.

'Would you care for a drink, madame?' His accent was French, and he should have been jaded by the beauties he frequently saw. But Sabina was among the best of them. She smiled and declined the drink, as she tried on two hats and found precisely what she'd had in mind, just as a salesgirl approached her. She eyed Sabina for a moment, knowing that she should know her name, but not quite sure who she was. She knew she'd seen her there before, but Sabina stayed away from Giorgio's most of the time. It was expensive for her, and she only bought dresses there when something major came up, like the time she'd gone to the Academy Awards with Mel, but they didn't see her there more than once a year, if that. And then suddenly the salesgirl knew who she was. It was exhausting remembering who these women were. Not all of them were faces one recognised, but she knew Sabina now.

'May I help you, Miss Quarles?'

'I'll take this hat.' Sabina looked pleased. It pulled low over her face, just low enough to give her an aura of unbearable mystery, and it enhanced her innate sexiness, but it was not so low as to obscure her remarkable emerald eyes. In fact, it allowed her to play with them. It was a large natural straw hat with a big brim, but its shape suited her perfectly. It was just the accessory she'd had in mind, and that, along with the deep blue silk blouse, the high slit skirt, and the aura of perfume she wore would serve her well. It was now five minutes after one.

'May we show you something else? Some beautiful silks just came in, and some wonderful evening dresses for the autumn.' A mere fifty-dollar sale wasn't what they had in mind, but it was exactly what Sabina had planned. Mel would spend more than that on lunch. And who knew what he had in mind. Fifty bucks was not too much to invest in her career. She could afford that.

'That's all, thanks.'

'Our Jacqueline de Ribes are in . . .' Sabina smiled, easily able to repulse the woman, who would get nowhere with her.

'I just bought three at Saks last week.' Three Jacqueline de Ribes would have represented half her income for the previous year, but the salesgirl looked undaunted by the blow.

'We have a few exclusive ones, just for us. In fact, Fred picked them out of her line in Paris himself.' The illustrious Fred Hayman, impresario of Rodeo Drive's finest emporium, but even the mention of his sacred name didn't impress her. Sabina glanced at her watch. One ten.

'I've got to go. I'll come back after lunch.' Or next year. Or maybe next week, if he has a big part for me in his next film. Her eyes had a look one couldn't argue with. They said, give me the goddam hat or I'll walk out of here. But she wanted the hat for her lunch with Mel, needed it. And the girl knew when not to push.

'Of course, Miss Quarles. Shall I put some things aside for you?' Christ, they never give up, she thought to herself as the girl finally disappeared with the hat to a hidden cash register. It was one fifteen when she returned, and Sabina carefully put it on, set it at the right angle, and shook back her hair. The effect was spectacular, and more than one head turned as she left the store and hurried from Rodeo to Beverly and then one more block to North Canon. It was exactly one twenty-one when she reached the Bistro Gardens, and swept in, looking powerful and beautiful, and her eyes stayed just above the fascinated stares as people turned to look at her. It was a habit people had, to make sure they weren't missing anyone ... Gregory Peck ... Elizabeth Taylor ... Meryl Streep ... look, Jane, over there ... the whispers were constant. But this time, people only stared at her, and then looked away again, as the headwaiter walked swiftly towards her, threading his way through the tables outside. The riot of coloured flowers added to the elegance of the decor, as the brightly striped umbrellas protected each lunch table from the midday sun.

11

'Madame?' It was a question and a statement all at once as he smiled at her.

'I'm meeting Melvin Wechsler for lunch,' she explained, her eyes combing the headwaiter's face, as though testing the effect of the hat. She knew it was working well. It had added just the aura of mystery and panache she had wanted. She looked spectacular. And in the distance, from a quiet table, Melvin Wechsler was watching her. He watched the long legs striding gracefully, the firm breasts in the bright blue shirt, and the eyes beneath the hat. Christ, she had it. He knew she had. He'd remembered it. She was exactly what he wanted. Exactly. And he smiled to himself as suddenly she stood there, looking down at him, as sexy as she had always been, maybe even better-looking than she'd been before, or was he getting soft? Were old starlets finally getting to him? But this was no has-been beauty queen. Sabina Quarles was a woman to be reckoned with, a 9.9 on the Richter scale, he could feel his own guts give a tug as he looked at her and he was pleased. He stood up and held out a hand. His arm was long and powerful, his handshake firm, his eyes an icy blue, and his hair a carefully kempt white mane. Mel Wechsler was fifty-four, and he had the body of a much younger man, like many men in Hollywood. The lucky ones. He played tennis every day, or at least as often as he could and, like Sabina, he had a massage several times a week. But there had been no surgery. He just looked damn good for his age, and aside from the white hair he could easily have shaved ten years off his age if he wanted, which he didn't.

'Hello, Sabina, how've you been?'

'Sorry I'm late.' She smiled, and her voice seemed deeper, sexier than he remembered. And he got a terrific view down her blouse as she sat down. 'The traffic in this town is getting ridiculous.' Particularly if you stop to buy a hat on the way, she smiled to herself. Mel was watching her, suddenly remembering the feline quality about Sabina, like a long, lean beautiful cat stretching in the sun. 'I hope you haven't been waiting for too long.'

12

His blue eyes reached deep into hers. He was always watching, weighing, as though he had something very important in mind. He smiled a smile that had melted women's hearts for years, and if not their hearts, then their resistance. It was a half smile, a smile that touched his lips, even when his eyes were serious, as they often were, as they were now. 'Some things in life are worth waiting for.'

She laughed. She remembered now how much she always liked to talk to him and wondered why he hadn't called her in so long. Their paths crossed from time to time, but not often enough. 'Thank you, Mel.' He offered her a drink and she opted for a Bloody Mary after a moment's thought, and then she noticed he was drinking Perrier. He wasn't in the usual Hollywood mold. There was a great deal of substance to the man, and his success was built on hard work and an absolute genius for their business. He had a magical touch about selecting people for his television shows and films. He rarely went wrong. It was one of the many things she admired about him. Melvin Wechsler was a pro. And he was also a damn attractive man. She knew he had had a long-standing affair with one of the big female stars of Hollywood a few years before. They had been inseparable, and he had put her in three of his films, but something had gone wrong along the line and they didn't see each other any more. Like everyone else in town, Sabina had always wondered why they'd broken up, but he never mentioned her to anyone, and Sabina liked that about him too. He was proud. He had guts. And style. He wasn't one to lick his wounds publicly. Even the major tragedy in his life was something he never discussed. Particularly that. Sabina only knew about it from what she had read, and what she had heard from friends. He had been married to Elizabeth Floyd years before, she had been one of the biggest stars of Hollywood in her day, some thirty years before. They'd met when he first came to town and was still crawling his way up at MGM. He had been their golden-haired boy then, or a few years after that anyway. And she had been 'it', and fallen for Mel. They'd got married a few years after that, and she had retired not long afterwards, ostensibly just temporarily for the birth of their first child. But their first child had turned out to be twins, identical baby girls, who looked just like Liz, and she had stayed home to take care of them.

They'd had a little boy two years afterwards, and once in a while you'd see them all somewhere. He kept them out of the press, even though it wasn't easy to do with Liz. She was so beautiful that photographers had trailed her for years. Sabina remembered her from when she'd first come to Hollywood. She'd already retired by then, but Christ had she been beautiful, a natural redhead with big blue eyes and creamy skin, a dazzling smile, and a figure that made men weep. She'd been involved in women's rights way back then, and she was involved in all sorts of philanthropies. They eventually had a house in Bel Air, and a ranch near Santa Barbara. He had been the perfect family man then, and it wasn't difficult to believe even now, no matter how many young actresses he'd taken out in the meantime. There was something fatherly about the man, and everyone said that working for him was like becoming part of a family. He cared about the people on his shows. Mel Wechsler took care of everyone, and he'd taken care of them. He'd been fabulous, and he'd adored Liz and his kids. They went to Europe together every year, and in 1969 he had taken them all to Israel. It had been an unforgettable trip, and he had been furious when he'd had to go back to Los Angeles for a network conference they'd called and insisted he attend. He had left Liz and the children in Tel Aviv, and promised to be back in four days. He was just going to fly home for the meeting and come back, but once there, everything got more complicated than he expected. There was a major problem with his biggest show, and he hadn't been as secure then. He had finally given up hope of getting back to Israel, and had urged Liz to come home, but she wanted to stop in Paris for a few days, as they had planned for the end of their trip. She didn't want to disappoint the kids.

They boarded an El Al flight, and at the same time they did, Mel had been meeting with the network again, and he had had a strange feeling in his gut. He had looked at his watch, wondering if it was too late to call. He wanted her to take Air France, or another airline, and then he chided himself for foolishly worrying about them . . . until he got the call . . . the State Department called, before he heard it on the news. Seven Arab terrorists had boarded the plane and blown it to kingdom come, taking with them all of the passengers and crew. Two hundred and nine people dead for their cause . . . and Liz and Barbie and Deborah and Jason . . . he had been like a zombie for weeks, unable to believe that it had actually happened to him . . . that if he hadn't left them . . . hadn't come back . . . if he had only called . . . The if onlys of that day haunted him for years. It was a nightmare from which he thought he would never awaken, and all he wanted was to have died with them too. He had nightmares about the flight, and he hadn't flown anywhere for almost ten years. But there was no recapturing the past. There was no turning back. Barbie and Deb had been twelve, Jason ten. It was the kind of thing you read in the news. Only it had happened to him. His whole family wiped out by a terrorist bomb, and in many ways his life had never been the same. He had thrown himself into his work, and the actors who worked for him were like children to him. But they weren't his own . . . and there was never another Liz. Never. There was never anyone like her again, and he didn't want there to be. He lived with their memories, even now. There were other women of course, although it had taken him a long time to come to that. But he had finally, and there had been only one serious affair. He had never married again, and knew he never would, had no reason to. He had had it all, and lost everything. It made him philosophical about life, and wise about the trivia of Hollywood. He couldn't take it to heart, yet he took it seriously. It was a business he cared about, a game he played well. But there was a door to his heart that would never open again. It had slammed shut when that call from Paris came. He wasn't blind to the beauty that surrounded him day after day, and he enjoyed the company of the women he took out, but there was always that moment of truth, when he went home at night, or when they left him the next day . . . that moment when he was alone the next day . . . that moment when he was alone with the memories. It was why he worked so hard. It was an easy escape, and one that worked well for him. But a piece of his heart had died with his wife and children.

'What have you been up to these days?' He smiled slowly at Sabina over their drinks. Sabina remembered the tragedy in his life. But it had been a long time ago, and he didn't wear it on his sleeve. He never talked about his wife, or his children, except to very, very close friends. Everyone had been devastated by their deaths. There had been a memorial service at the Stephen Weise Temple on Mulholland that had been attended by literally thousands. There had been no funeral, there had been no bodies for the airline to return. There had been nothing. Only air. And heartbreak. And broken memories. And regrets. 'I hear you did a very nice film last year.' He had heard more than that. That it had done dismally at the box office, despite decent reviews. But he knew what Sabina was capable of. He had seen her in enough films. He knew exactly who and what she was. And he wanted her. Far more than she knew. She needn't even have bought the hat, but he enjoyed the effect as he sat watching her with a sparkle in his eye. It was work that brought him to life now, work that he loved, and for which he lived. He had lived with the tragedy of his loss for long enough, he had put it aside, he had made peace with it. It no longer ruled his life. But work did, and he liked it like that, and he was thinking of that now. *Manhattan*, the property was called, and Sabina was perfect for it.

Sabina laughed at the kindness of his remark. Only Mel would have put it that way. He was always a gentleman. He could afford to be. He was at the top. The pinnacle.

He owned the world in which he moved, and the network kissed his feet for the sure successes he produced. He made a fortune for everyone, himself, the networks, the sponsors, the actors involved most of the time. And he was generous in the way he dealt with all of them. He didn't need to screw anyone. It made him desirable in every way, and Sabina wasn't only thinking of his career as she looked at him over her glass with a smile that showed the generosity of her lips.

'The film was a bomb. A nice bomb, but a bomb nevertheless.'

'You got good reviews.' He was biding his time.

'That's about it. Good reviews don't pay the rent.' Or her other expenses.

'Sometimes they do.'

'Tell that to the boys who make the films. They want big box office, no matter what it takes. And screw the reviews.' They both knew it was true, to an extent.

'That's the nice thing about TV.' There was no change of expression in his face although he knew the minefield he trod as one of Sabina's eyebrows shot up. 'The ratings mean a lot more than the reviews do in films.' In fact, they meant everything.

She looked annoyed. 'The ratings don't reflect anything real and you know it as well as I do, Mel. They reflect a lot of little black boxes attached to sets in the homes of mindless boobs. And all of you drool or tremble for fear of what the ratings will do. Give me a film any day.'

'Still feel the same way about TV?' He looked mild and relaxed as he ordered another Perrier.

'It's a world of crap.' Beneath the hat, her eyes blazed. She had always hated TV. And she had told him as much every time they met.

He smiled. 'But profitable crap.'

'Maybe. But I thank God I've never prostituted myself for that.' She looked pleased with herself, and he felt mildly dismayed. But she hadn't read the script of *Manhattan* yet. He knew if he could get her to, it would change everything.

'There are worse things, Sabina. You know as well as I do that a lot of the movies being made aren't worth the film they're printed on. And they're no more satisfying than doing a cameo appearance on a sitcom.'

Sabina looked outraged. 'That's ridiculous, Mel. You can't compare films and TV.'

'I can, and probably better than anyone, since I'm involved in both. They're both satisfying and they're very different. There's merit in both. There's nothing better than a really fine, long-running TV series. It gives the actors more satisfaction than Gable probably got doing *Gone With the Wind*.' They both smiled at the comparison. 'Now there's a film for you, Sabina.' She laughed at the thought. She took herself seriously most of the time, but Mel made it easier to laugh at herself. He had a knack for loosening people up, making them comfortable, making them laugh . . . making them important . . . and successful. And he had thought seriously about Sabina before their lunch. She had been around Hollywood for years, twenty years at least, maybe even twenty-five. And having invested that many years in the business, she deserved more recognition than she was getting. That was something Mel Wechsler, or at least *Manhattan*, could give her.

'You ask any actor in the business, Sabina, who's done a long-run show on TV and ask them how they felt about it. You get a chance week after week to come across with some kind of substance, to hone your character, your perform-ance. Hell, half the actors in those shows end up either writing or directing them they get so involved in the guts of the show.'

'They probably do it out of self-preservation.' She eyed him from under the brim of her hat and he laughed.

'I don't suppose anyone's ever accused you of being stub-born, have they?'

'Only my agent.'

'No ex-husbands?' He had forgotten that about her, but as she shook her head, he remembered. She was a solitary

18

soul, but so were a number of women of her ilk and era in the business. They were too involved in themselves and their work and their appearances to have much time to waste on a husband. And if they did, it was seldom for more than a season. It was something that had bothered him about her when they met, the fact that she'd never been married. He always seemed to have a preference for women who had had long-term involvements, and they usually seemed to have children. It filled a need in him that he was no longer able to fill himself. He didn't want another family, he couldn't have lived through another loss like the first one, but he loved being around other people's kids.

'I've never found a man I was tempted to stay with.' She was honest with him. Sabina made no bones about who she was, where she was going, or what she wanted. And the truth was that she was content with her life-style.

'That doesn't speak too well for the men you've known.' Their eyes met and held, and they ordered lunch when the waiter returned, as the conversation turned to easier subjects. He had no plans for a summer holiday. He had long since sold the ranch near Santa Barbara, and when he felt a need for a few days' rest, he rented a house in Malibu on the beach and he spent his time reading scripts and relaxing. But he had no time for that now. He had been in meetings with the network for weeks, and now he had some serious work to do. He was casting *Manhattan*, it was going to be the most important show of its kind, a series like no other before it. 'And what about you, Sabina, no trips in store?'

She shook her head and looked vague as she toyed absently with her salad, and then looked up at him from beneath the hat again. For an instant, she looked vulnerable in a way he had never seen her look before. It was a look that made him want to shout, 'Freeze frame', to stop the action and keep her looking that way forever. But it was gone the moment she smiled and shrugged one of her exquisite shoulders. 'I have to go to San Francisco for a few days. Other than that, I'll be here all summer.' He also knew she wasn't working, and hadn't for all intents and purposes since the film the year before. He wondered if she ever got desperate about the fact that she hadn't made it bigger than she had. Or maybe she was content as she was. That was difficult to believe about a woman like Sabina. And he was hoping that she felt at least a little urgency now about her career.

He waited until their coffee came, and then gently broached the subject. 'I was hoping you'd read a script for me.'

Her eyes lit up slowly, with a warm glow. She had hoped it would be something like that. Either that or that he wanted to take her out again. She would have been open to that possibility as well. In fact, she would have liked it, and wasn't quite sure which she would have preferred, or if she could still have both, Mel, and a part in his next film. His films were rare now, which made it even more flattering that he had thought of her. Either way, she would have been happy, although she needed the work, and wondered if he knew it. Hollywood was a small town, and what people didn't know, they suspected, or imagined or whispered. It was a town filled with gossip and rumours and badly kept secrets. 'I'd like that very much. I take it you're putting together a new film.'

'Not exactly.' There was no point in lying to her. He had the script in a briefcase under his seat, just waiting to hand it to her after lunch, if she agreed to read it. 'I'm putting together a new series.'

Her green eyes snapped shut like twin doors to the Emerald City. 'That leaves me out then.'

'I was hoping you'd at least read it, Sabina. There's no harm in that.' His voice was powerful yet gentle, and there was something very seductive about him. She could feel the pull of the man, just sitting next to him at the table, over their espresso.

'You're a very persuasive man, but I'd be wasting your

20

time and mine.' She attempted to sound polite, but it was obvious that she wasn't interested in his series.

'I can spare the time.' He wanted to say, 'And so can you,' but he didn't. 'How long does it take to read a script? And if it's as good as I believe it is, I don't think you'll regret it.'

She smiled and shook her head with a look of amusement. 'For you, Mel, I'd do almost anything, but I won't do that. I know what you want. You want me to fall in love with it, but I won't.'

'And if you did?'

'I still wouldn't do it.'

'Why not?'

'Maybe it'll sound crazy to you, but principles, I guess. I just won't do TV.'

'You're not acting in your own best interest, Sabina. I wouldn't have asked you here if I didn't know this part is right for you. The character is so much like you that it could have been molded right on your body. I see you and I see Eloise Martin. The series will be called *Manhattan*, and this isn't just any series. It's glamorous, and important, and expensive. It's going to affect the American television industry like no other show before it, and I know that you're right for the part. I could have called your agent instead of inviting you here today. I could have waved dollar signs and contracts at him, but I didn't want to do that. I want you to fall in love with this woman, to see what I do, how much of you she is . . . and then we can talk about the rest. I understand your integrity, believe me, I do . . . but I see something more. I see the long range, and what this could do for you. For your career. A year from now, you could be the biggest name in this country. It's hard to conceive of it now, but I know that the show has that kind of impact. I haven't been wrong too often in recent years, touch wood' – he knocked on the table and smiled at her – 'and I know I'm not this time. I really wish you'd read it. This could put you at the top of your career, and Sabina, you deserve it.' He looked as though he meant every word he said, but Sabina still didn't look convinced when he stopped speaking.

'And if it's a flop?'

'It won't be, but if it is, it's no worse than your last film. So what? You're a survivor, you go on. We all do. But it's not going to be a flop, Sabina. It's going to be a success that will kick the breath out of everyone in this country. It's dramatic and it's tough and it's brilliant. It's not mealy-mouthed or funny, there's nothing halfway about it. And once a week, sixty million people could be watching you, Sabina. Watching you and eating it up. Your life will never be the same again. Ever. I'm absolutely certain of it as I sit here.' He sounded so convincing, so sure, that for a minute she was tempted to read it, just for the hell of it, just to see what he was cooking up that was supposedly so different. Hell, she had nothing else to do except lie on her terrace and go down to the pool and wait for the phone to ring. What harm was there in reading it after all? And as she thought it, she suddenly smiled, and laughed out loud as she looked at Mel Wechsler.

'No wonder you're so damn successful, Mel, you're one hell of a salesman.'

'I don't even have to be on this, Sabina. You'll see what I mean when you read it. *Manhattan* is you, from start to finish.'

'Are you working on a pilot?'

This time he laughed. 'You don't flatter me very much, my dear. Even the network isn't that cruel. No, I'm not working on a pilot.' He was such a sure thing that no one expected Mel Wechsler to do a pilot. 'We'll begin with a three-hour special on opening night, and go on to a sixty-minute show once a week after that. We want to open with a big bang and that'll be it.'

'I might read it. But I don't want to mislead you, Mel. Nothing has changed about the way I feel about TV.'

'All right.' He reached under his seat and the script for the three-hour special appeared. 'That's fair enough. I would just be grateful to you if you would read it.' Grateful. It was a brilliant choice of words, and so like Mel. Grateful. He was grateful, and she was damn lucky. And they both knew it. 'I'll be very interested to know what you think about it. God knows we've both read enough scripts to have a nose for them by now.' He was including her in his expertise and it was no accident. She was suddenly very aware of how skilful he was. In truth, the man was a genius with people and in his field. And she had enjoyed her lunch with him. Enough so to hope he'd call her again. At least if she read the script, she'd have an excuse to see him. 'I also shouldn't tempt you, and you probably don't give a damn, but we're having the costumes done by François Brac. In Paris. Whoever plays Eloise Martin will spend a month in Paris for fittings at his couture house there, and then she gets to keep the wardrobe.' In spite of herself, Sabina could feel a glint in her eyes. It was a hell of an appealing offer, not to mention the money he would probably pay. It would solve her problems for a long time to come. Maybe even forever.

'Don't make it too tempting, Mel.' She laughed her sultry laugh, and he felt a strange little thrill, both at the victory he hoped to achieve in wooing her for the part, and at just being with her. She was a very exciting woman, and that was why he wanted her for his show. He had always sensed that about her, and he felt it again now. But for a moment he had to remind himself that he wanted her for his show, and not just for his entertainment.

'I can make it a lot more tempting than that, Sabina. But I want you to read the script first.' He was teasing her now, but that was a game she was good at.

'And here I thought you invited me to lunch because you suddenly discovered I was the love of your life.' She was teasing, but her eyes held a caress that almost choked him, and for a long moment he didn't answer.

'I enjoyed seeing you again, Sabina.' His voice was quiet, and she knew he meant it. And she enjoyed it too, whether

23

she liked his script or not, and whether or not she ever decided to change her iron-clad position about doing television. For the moment, it didn't really matter. 'Give me a call when you've read it.'

'I will.'

He jotted his home number down on a card for her, and signalled to the waiter for the bill and she was sorry to see their lunch come to an end. She liked being with him.

'By the way, who else have you got for this so far?'

'No one.' He looked her straight in the eye. 'I'm starting with the most important part. I have to fill this one before I deal with the others. But I have some people in mind. I'm thinking of Zack Taylor for the male lead, and I think he might like it. He's free now too. He's in Greece at the moment, but I'll be talking to him in a few weeks when he gets back.'

Sabina did not look displeased. Zack Taylor was one of the best-looking actors in the country, and his credentials were good. He had done everything from theatrical films to television to legitimate theatre. He had even had a major success on Broadway a few years before. He would certainly be a strong counterpart for whoever took the role, and that appealed to Sabina. 'You don't go halfway, do you, Mel?'

'Never.' He smiled and stood up and guided her gently through the tables until they were outside on North Canon Drive. There was a children's shop next door, but he never looked at things like that now. He had no need to. He concentrated his gaze on Sabina. 'I enjoyed seeing you again . . . not just for this. . . .' She had the script in her hand, and he was carrying his now empty briefcase. His car was waiting at the curb, a Mercedes 600, driven by a man who had worked for him for years. The 600 was expensive and important and discreet, like Mel himself. And it had style. Just as he did. 'Call me, Sabina.'

Her green eyes held his for a long moment and she smiled, completely forgetting the script in her hand. For a moment, she had forgotten *Manhattan* and all she could see was Mel, and how appealing he was. He was someone she would have liked to know better. 'I'll call . . .' and then her hand tightened on the script and he offered her a ride, but she declined with a smile that made him want her. There was a quality about her that drove him wild, a sensuality mixed with cool reserve that made you want to tear her clothes off, just to see what the rest of her looked like. He suspected that it looked damn good. And he wouldn't have cared if it didn't.

She waved as she headed back toward Rodeo Drive, and he watched her as his car pulled away from the curb and too quickly turned a corner, obscuring her from his sight. But the thought of her haunted him all afternoon, and he was no longer sure what he wanted from her. If he wanted her for his new show, or for himself, or both. All he knew was that he couldn't stop thinking about her.

3

Bill Warwick had gone to three auditions on the same afternoon that Sabina was strolling back towards the Beverly Wilshire to retrieve her car and go home to swim in her pool before reading Mel's script for *Manhattan*. And unlike Sabina and Mel, he was not in a pleasant mood, nor was he feeling sensual, or as though life had something exciting in store for him, be it a part or an affair. He had been turned down at all three auditions and the last thing on his mind was getting laid. All he wanted was to get work. Anything. All he had left was eight hundred dollars in the envelope in his desk drawer, a dog that ate too damn much, and a wife who hadn't worked in almost a year, although she'd had a good role in a sitcom when they got married the year before. But she'd got canned six weeks later, and she hadn't even tried to get work since then. Nothing. She just sat on her backside day and night, and got stoned all the time. They hadn't made love in almost two months and she was so thin now she looked anorexic. She had started with diet pills years before, gone to uppers and speed, and then downers and heroin, and finally cocaine, and these days she was into speedballs, a mixture of heroin and cocaine that kept her high but gave her the illusion of making sense, but the truth was she didn't. And she was so badly hooked, he wondered if she'd ever be free of it.

He loosened his tie, and prepared to wait an hour for the bus, if he was lucky. They'd had to sell their car, a battered Volkswagen, and if he didn't pay the rent soon, they'd be out on their heels, which might be a relief in some ways. Maybe it would finally shake some sense into Sandy. She was twenty-five years old, and her life was going down the tubes in a hurry. And she'd been so damn cute when they met, all long black hair and big brown eyes, like a puppy. She was like a little girl. He still felt a gentle glow of tenderness when he thought of meeting her at a Hollywood party for the first time. She had looked like a lost child, and his heart melted the moment he saw her. She had seemed so helpless, and so unable to cope with the wolves who abounded in the business. The trouble was, she was still unable to cope with them, and in order to deal with the pressure, she got more and more addicted, and she expected Bill to solve all their problems. And now she expected him to make enough money to pay for her habit.

'What do you expect me to do? Street mime, for chrissake?' He remembered the fight they'd had only that morning, and he was sick of fighting with her. They'd been fighting for so long, and he was beginning to wonder if his parents were right. According to them, acting was for children, morons, and totally unstable people. Sandy was certainly no tower of strength, and he was beginning to wonder if he didn't have what it took. His demo reel, which showed pieces of commercials and television shows he'd acted in, had made the rounds of every studio, producer, director, and ad agency in Hollywood, and he wasn't getting anything from it. He had even shouted at his agent that afternoon. He had wanted to put him on *The Dating Game*, and Bill exploded at the suggestion.

'God damn it, I'm married.'

'So who knows that? You two have kept it such a big secret, no one knows. And besides, you think anyone cares?'

'I do.' But the question was, did Sandy? Did she care enough to clean up? He was beginning to wonder. She didn't seem to give a damn about anything, except her connection. All her money from the show had been blown, and she spent every dime of her unemployment on coke. It was a great life. And Harry was right, no one knew they were married because Sandy's agent thought it would ruin her ingenue image. So would the tracks on her arm, if anyone saw them.

As usual, the bus took forty minutes to arrive, and halfway

home, Bill decided he couldn't face her. Couldn't face the unmade bed, the empty icebox, and last night's half-eaten enchiladas still sitting on the kitchen table. He hated going home these days. Even his dog looked unhappy. And he felt so guilty. That was the worst of it. He kept thinking that if he made it big, he could put her in some fancy hospital and get her to clean up. But for the moment that was out of the question. He was thirty-two years old, married to a drug addict, and he was sick and tired of being an unemployed actor. He had been to every audition he'd heard of for months, and lately no one wanted him. He'd done two commercials earlier that year, big ones, thank God, but even that money had finally run out. There would be residuals eventually, but not for a long time, and in the meantime he was going to have to start borrowing money from his agent. He had done it before, and Harry was always a good sport about it, crazy fool that he was. He was the one who always told Bill he'd make it big one day. But when? Christ, he needed the work now. Desperately. It was a word that was really beginning to apply to him. Bill Warwick was desperate.

He sat staring at the passing traffic as he rode along on the bus, and a mile before he reached the house in the Hollywood Hills, he decided to get off and stop in at Mike's for a quick beer. It was a place where he'd hung out for the last fourteen years, even since he'd come to UCLA from New York, with all his bright hopes. He knew he was going to make it big then, he only wished he were as sure now. The only one who still believed that now was Harry, his agent.

He blinked for a minute as he walked into Mike's Bar. It was the same as it had always been, dingy, dark, reeking of beer, and filled with unemployed actors. Even the bartenders were actors he knew, including Adam, who was on duty now. He had gone to school with him, and they'd been casual friends for years. He knew Sandy too, although only slightly. Four good-looking young men in cutoffs and jeans were playing pool, and there were clusters of them

at various tables, discussing parts they'd either got or auditioned for, or had heard about. There were a few women
here and there, but the crowd was mostly men, and Bill sat
down at the bar and ordered a beer from Adam and told
him about his bad luck trying out for three executive roles
in commercials. As they talked, Bill stretched his long legs
in the khaki suit he was wearing. He felt as though he had
walked miles, and for nothing.

'One of them thought I looked too young, the other
too sexy, and the third one wanted to know if I was queer.
Terrific. I'm beginning to look like a baby-faced sex-crazed
faggot.'

Adam laughed. He had just got a small part appearing
once on a series, and they had promised to have him back
soon. But he had never been as ambitious as Bill Warwick.
Most of the time he was perfectly happy tending bar at
Mike's, but he was amply familiar with the problems of the
business.

'And my agent wanted to put me on *The Dating Game.* I'm
beginning to think my old man is right and I should have
gone into insurance.' He rolled his eyes at the thought, and
Adam set the beer down in front of him.

'Hang in there, kid. The biggest part of your life may be
just around the corner.'

'You know' – Bill took a sip of his beer and looked sobered
by his own thoughts – 'I'm really beginning to wonder. It's
kind of like playing the slot machines, maybe some people
never win. Maybe I'm one of them. I just don't feel like
there's anything out there for me any more.'

'Bullshit.' The bartender looked good-humoured, but
Bill looked exhausted and depressed, and the heat and
rejections had obviously got to him. He still remembered
summers on Cape Cod when he was a kid, and he had never
quite adjusted to the heat of the California summers. Sandy
had been born in Los Angeles and she loved it. Not that
she felt the heat any more. She didn't feel anything. 'How's
Sandy?' It was as though Adam had read his mind. But he

could see instantly that the subject was not going to cheer Bill. He looked even more depressed as he shrugged.

'Okay . . . the same, I guess . . .' He looked bleakly up at Adam then, and their eyes met. 'I think we've about had it.'

'What about methadone?' He also knew she'd been into heroin for a while. He'd seen enough of it to recognise the signs and she'd offered him some cocaine the last time she'd been in with Bill. And Bill had been so annoyed, they left shortly after. Adam was well aware of how much her addiction upset Bill, and he felt sorry for him. He knew what it was like himself. He'd been through it with a girl from Newport Beach several years before, and he'd finally given up on her after a year. Her parents had had her in every sanatorium and hospital in the state, and she'd finally OD'd in a sleazy hotel in Venice.

'I don't know. I've suggested everything. She doesn't want to hear it. The only thing she's interested in is protecting her addiction. She doesn't even go to auditions any more. There's no point anyway. She nodded out at the last one. Made a great impression on the director.'

'She's going to get a rep for that if she doesn't watch out.' Even Adam looked sobered. He knew she already did. And Bill sat in silence, as Adam went to serve someone else. Eventually, Bill ordered a hamburger, and it was eight o'clock before he got on the bus again, and twenty minutes later he was home. He walked in, expecting to find Sandy asleep, nodding out after a fix, or high as a kite after getting some cocaine from her connection. But instead, the house was empty, the usual disorder was everywhere, the bed unmade, the dishes unwashed, their clothes intertwined on the floor and Bill's Saint Bernard exploding with glee as Bill came through the door and he saw him.

'Hi, old guy . . . where's Sandy?' The dog wagged his tail, pushing against Bill's legs with his enormous head, hungry for affection. There was no note to explain her whereabouts, but it was easy to figure out that she'd either gone out with her friends, or alone in search of drugs, or to meet up with her connection. It was the only full-time job she had these days and it was more time-consuming than her acting. His eyes met a photograph that had been taken of them the year before, just before he'd married her, and it startled him suddenly to see the difference in her. She had lost at least fifteen pounds, if not twenty, and there was a glazed look in her eyes almost all the time now. Her hair was always unkempt and she didn't seem to care what she wore. Either she was high, or she was out looking for drugs, too sick to care what she looked like. It was pathetic, and he felt a familiar surge of anger just thinking of her. He began cleaning up the mess himself, as the dog followed him with wagging tail, hoping for something to eat, but there wasn't even dog food in the house, Bill realised as he opened the cupboard where they kept his food. He opened up two cans of beef stew instead and dumped them in the dog's bowl. The huge Saint Bernard lapped them up with relish as Bill piled the dishes in the sink and threw out the rotting food that she had just left sitting in the kitchen.

'Shit . . .' he muttered to himself, but the anger dissipated quickly and by the time he reached their bedroom, he was more depressed than angry. It was dismal living like this, and he had even come to hate the cottage he had once loved. It was a gardener's cottage on a once large estate and it was rented separately for a hundred dollars a month. The owner liked him, and knew he was a starving actor, and it was an illegal rental. It was perfect for them, and he had lived there for three years. It had been spotless before she moved in, but everything was a mess now.

He had got the bedroom relatively in order and even changed the sheets by the time he sat down at his desk and rifled through the drawer looking for the envelope that he'd left there. It had suddenly occured to him to make sure that it was still there. It was all the money they had in the world. Eight hundred dollars, and he hadn't told Sandy he'd put it there, so as not to tempt her, but she'd found it anyway. He found the envelope, and the money was gone. There were tears in his eyes and he stood up and walked slowly to the bathroom, and there he saw a sight that made him feel sick. He'd seen it before, but he hated it even more now. She had left her needle and her cotton and her spoon on the ledge next to the john. She made no effort to hide it. There it was for all to see. The paraphernalia of her addiction. He wanted to cry as he stood there, staring at her needle and knowing that that was where his money had gone. He couldn't take it any more. She had blown the last money they had, and there was no one for him to turn to. He'd be damned if he'd call his father and beg at the age of thirty-two. He'd pump gas or take a job at Mike's before he did that. Plenty of other actors had done it before him and so had he. He was going to call Adam that night and ask if they needed anyone else to tend bar, or wait table, but before he could call, the phone rang, and it was Sandy. She sounded stoned out of her mind, and he didn't even want to talk to her.

'Hi, baby . . .' She was drifting as they spoke, and he remembered all too clearly the needle in the bathroom.

'I don't want to talk to you right now.' He was only glad that she hadn't come home. At that precise moment, he could have killed her. He didn't ask her where she was, or who she was with. He didn't care any more. It was all the same. And it was disgusting. He had a profound feeling of revulsion for her and her friends and everything they stood for. He had seen drugs before, plenty of them, and he'd smoked enough dope in his days at UCLA to be tolerant of other people's recreational indulgences, but what she did was not recreation. It was suicide, and he didn't want to go down with her. That was the only choice one had. He was beginning to suspect that there was no way to save her.

'What do you want?' His voice was harsh. He hated her just then, not that she was lucid enough to understand that. 'I don't have any money left, so I assume you didn't call for that. You blew the last of it in your arm, from what I can gather. I don't know how you think we're going to eat after this, although I realise that isn't a high priority with you these days, but Bernie and I have these insane needs to eat and . . .'

'I . . . uh . . . need you . . . to help me . . .' She was so stoned he felt sick listening to her and he didn't want any part of her. Not now. And maybe never.

'Call someone else. I've had it.'

'Bill . . . no . . . wait . . .' She sounded frightened and a tiny part of him still cared, but the rest of him didn't want to. 'I got busted.' She sounded like a little girl, and he sat down heavily in a chair.

'Shit. Where are you?'

'I'm in jail.'

'Great. Now what? Do you realise that, thanks to you, I don't even have enough money to bail you?'

'Can't you get some, uh . . . from someone . . .' She was having a hard time keeping her mind on the conversation and Bill sighed. He had been this route with her before twice, and once she had almost OD'd. He had had to call the police, and they had sent paramedics to the house to keep her alive till they reached the hospital. She had barely made it.

'What are the charges?'

It would be the usual, of course. Possession. 'Possession with intent to sell and, uh . . . I don't know . . . there's some other stuff . . .' She started to cry. 'Can't you get me out of here? I'm scared.'

'Christ.' He muttered under his breath, and fumbled for a cigarette. He had quit five years before, and thanks to her he had recently gone back to smoking. The tension of living with her was unbearable. There were days when he wondered if he'd survive it. That and no work and no money. 'Maybe it would do you good to sit on your backside in jail.' But he knew that it was only a matter of time before somebody figured out who she was and called the papers, 'Ex-star of *Sunday Supper* gets busted for possession of cocaine', or whatever it was, and then the photographers would arrive

33

and start taking pictures. He didn't want to expose her to that, or himself, in case one of these days someone figured out that they were married. She was becoming an embarrassment to him and it made his agent nervous.

'Bill . . . I have to go now . . .' He could hear voices as she hung up the phone, harsh voices, voices of cops, and suddenly it came home to him, where she was, and what it would be like for her. And he couldn't stand it. She was so helpless, and he was so tired of rescuing her, but he felt as though he had no choice. He took a drag on his cigarette and dialled his agent.

'How'd you do at the last call?' The agent sounded surprised to hear from him at home, but not very. Lots of actors called him at home and he didn't really mind it.

'Like shit. Look, I'm sorry to call you like this but something's come up . . . can I borrow some money?'

There was a startled silence, but the agent recovered quickly. Bill was someone he had the utmost confidence in, he would have done anything for him. And he knew for certain that one day he would repay him. 'Sure, baby, how much?'

Bill almost groaned. He had forgotten to ask her how much the bail was, but it couldn't have been too bad. 'Say five hundred bucks to be on the safe side?'

'The safe side of what? Sandy's not fucked up again, is she?' He knew about Sandy and he didn't like her. As far as he was concerned, Bill Warwick didn't need that headache. No one did. She was bad news, and getting worse all the time, from what he heard. She was poison in Hollywood, and Bill hadn't looked happy for months. It was easy to see why. But Bill was not in the mood to confide in anyone, least of all his agent.

'No, she's okay, the damn dog had to have an operation, and I just need some money, that's all.'

'Okay . . . sure . . . no sweat. Come by the office tomorrow.'

'Could I come by tonight?'

From the tone of his voice, Harry knew it was Sandy, but

there was no point arguing with him. They'd been over it before, and he had all these stupid chivalrous ideas about what was expected of him, as her husband. Besides which, Bill was still half in love with her, actually he was in love with the girl she'd been when they met, a girl who no longer existed. But Harry had learned years before not to argue with his clients about their women. 'Okay, okay, man. I've got some money at the house. Come over whenever you want to.'

Bill heaved a sigh of relief and stubbed out the cigarette. He glanced at his watch. 'I'll be there in an hour.' It was difficult to play knight in shining armour when you had to depend on public transportation to get anywhere, particularly in Los Angeles. But Bill tore out of the house and walked down the hill to stand at the bus stop. It took him less than an hour to get to Harry's house on the fringes of Beverly Hills, and another half hour to get to the Hollywood station on North Wilcox, where he discovered that Sandy had been busted with two black men and another girl, for possession with intent to sell illegal substances, and she and the girl had been additionally charged with prostitution. He stood white-lipped and stunned as he peeled off Harry's money to bail her, and she looked frightened and sick as she stumbled towards him and he caught her.

He said nothing at all to her, but walked outside and hailed a cab, and once in the cab he saw that she was shaking, and she started to cry. She was heavily drugged, and she looked filthy and sleazy. He suddenly saw her as she was, sick and broken and degenerate and dirty, and the idea that his wife had been arrested for prostitution hurt him more than the rest of it. She would have done anything to get drugs, including steal from him, and sell her body to a stranger. He said not a word to her as he walked into their cottage and she followed him. The dog bounded towards them, and Sandy collapsed on the couch, as he went into the bathroom to run a bath for her. He picked up her needle, and the rest of it, and dropped it in the wastebasket.

He crushed it with his foot, and came back out again when the tub was full.

'Go take a bath.' It was as though he wanted her to wash the filth off her, but they both knew she couldn't. He wondered how often she'd done that before, how often she'd slept with him after sleeping with a john to make some extra money for a fix. As he had too often that night, he felt tears burn his eyes as he looked at her. She had nodded out on the couch, looking more than ever like a broken child. It hurt him just looking at her, and he marvelled that no one had called the papers before she left the jail. At least they'd been spared that, although it was on page 4 of the Los Angeles *Times* the next morning. SANDY WATERS ARRESTED ON DRUG CHARGES, the headline on the piece read. The charges were all listed and Bill cringed as he read the paper over the last of their coffee. He had already called Adam earlier that morning and arranged to go in and work at Mike's Bar that day. He was damn lucky that one of the waiters had got work the week before, and they were looking for someone new to replace him. At least he'd eat and to hell with the auditions for a while. He wasn't in the mood anyway. Sandy was standing looking pale and fragile in the kitchen doorway as he read the paper. She looked deathly ill, and Bill would have felt sorry for her if he weren't feeling so sickened by everything that had happened the night before. He was determined not to play the game with her any more. It was all over.

'Does it say anything?' She walked shakily to the kitchen table and sat down, looking like a twelve-year-old child with a terminal disease. She was thin and pale but she had beautiful eyes and a face like a cameo, and long black hair that lay matted and tangled around her shoulders, like a widow's shawl, and there was the sorrow of aeons in her eyes as she looked at the man she had married. 'I'm sorry, Bill.' Her voice was a whisper and he avoided her eyes.

'So am I. And in answer to your question, yes, the paper got all the charges right.' The only thing they'd left out was the fact that she was married to Bill, because they didn't know it.

'Christ. Tony'll kill me.' Tony was her agent, and Bill looked up at her in disbelief. Was she kidding? She'd been arrested for prostitution, among other things, and *Tony* would kill her? What about him? What about their marriage vows? But he didn't say anything. He lit a cigarette and went back to reading the paper. He could hardly wait to get the hell out, but he wanted to settle some things with her first, and there was no time like the present.

'What are you going to do now?' He forced himself to look into her eyes, no matter how much it hurt him.

'Hire a lawyer, I guess.' She shrugged, tossing the tangled hair back off her shoulders.

'Really, with what? Or will your new career pay for that too?' She flinched visibly at the harsh words, and for once he didn't care. 'I think you ought to put yourself in a hospital, before you do anything.'

'I can do it myself.' He had heard it all before. And he was tired of it.

'Bullshit. No one can. You need help. Now put yourself somewhere where you can get it.' He couldn't commit her. No one could. She had to do it herself, or the hospitals wouldn't accept her. He'd been over it with her before, a thousand times, and got nowhere.

'What about us?' She looked searchingly at him, and he looked away for an anguished moment. 'I get the feeling you've kind of had it.' Kind of . . . sort of . . . the eternal ingenue . . . at twenty-five, she was still a baby.

'How would *you* feel after last night?'

'You mean about my getting busted?' She looked help-less and frail, and he fought not to feel sorry for her.

'I mean about the nature of the charges, Sandy. Or have you forgotten?'

He saw her squirm in her chair, but he also realised that it was not only guilt. She was probably in need of a fix. These days he knew she was using first thing in the morning. 'That doesn't mean anything . . . you know that. I just needed some money . . . that's all . . .'

'Guess what, so did I, but I didn't hop down to Sunset Strip to sell myself to the first john who came along. Somehow that isn't exactly how I envisioned our marriage.' He was suddenly angry at her. Just thinking about it made the hurt and the rage course through him again. He had always thought of her as an innocent child, a child with a terrible habit. But it was much worse than that, it was a life-style based on a suicidal obsession.

'I'm sorry.' The words were barely audible, a breath in the still room as the dog panted in his bed in a corner of the kitchen. 'I'm sorry about everything.' She stood up nervously, as though suddenly facing a stranger. And she looked as though she were going out. He had seen that look before. That look that says I need it now . . . no matter what you say. . . . The look that had destroyed their marriage.

'Where are you going?'

'I have to go out.' She was still wearing her clothes from the night before and she hadn't combed her hair or brushed her teeth. She just picked up her handbag and looked around, and Bill had the feeling that she was going for the last time and he was suddenly frightened. He stood up and put down the paper as he looked at her.

'For chrissake, Sandy, you just got busted last night. Will you lay off?'

'I just have to see someone for a little while.' He took two quick strides and crossed the small kitchen to grab her arm and hold her there.

'Don't feed me that shit any more. I'm taking you to the hospital *right now. Right now!* And I don't give a damn if you never see me again, but you're not going to go on like this until you OD in some stinking shooting gallery or someone sticks a knife in you somewhere. Do you hear me?' She was suddenly crying, with regret, with the sickness, with all she felt for him, and the terrible pull of the drugs, and he was

38

crying too, as he pulled her into his arms and began to sob, wondering where the girl he had loved had gone to.

'I'm so sorry, Billy . . . I'm so sorry . . .' No one had ever called him that before, and it tore at his heart now. He wanted so badly to save her.

'Please, babe . . . I'll stay with you all day . . . I'll stay at the hospital with you. We'll do whatever we have to.' But she only shook her head as the tears coursed down her cheeks.

'I can't . . .'

'Why not?'

'I'm not strong enough.' Her words were the merest whisper, and he pulled her closer to him. There was nothing left of her but bone, but he didn't care. He knew that deep down he still loved her.

'Yes, you are. I'll be strong enough for both of us.'

'You can't.' She pulled slowly away from him, their tears mingling on her cheeks, and she reached up and smoothed his hair away from his eyes with a pale, trembling hand. 'I have to do it myself . . . when I'm ready. . . .'

'When will that be?'

'I don't know . . . not yet . . .'

He felt a hand clutch his heart. It was like watching her die. 'I can't wait any more, Sandy. . . .' He had never regretted anything so much in his life, but he knew that he couldn't help her.

'I know . . . I know.' She nodded and then stood on tiptoe to kiss his lips, and as she turned from him, he saw that she was no longer wearing their wedding band. And he suddenly realised that she must have sold it. She stood looking at him for a moment, as the dog whined softly behind him, echoing how Bill felt, and then quietly, she was gone, and this time, he didn't stop her. He knew he couldn't have anyway. There was nothing he could do. Nothing. He wiped the tears from his cheeks, and fought back waves of fresh tears as he went to brush his teeth, remembering how it had once been . . . how pretty she had been . . . how crazy they were about each other . . . they had met only two years before, and now it seemed a lifetime ago . . . a lifetime in the depths of hell with a woman he had once loved, and still did, although she was long gone. The woman who had been arrested for prostitution the night before was no one he knew any more . . . she was no one . . .

4

The house in Pasadena was a long white shingled L shape, with stone fireplaces at either end, rosebushes in tidy rows in the front, and a vast expanse of green lawn leading to a huge rectangular pool filled with shrieking children. They all appeared to be in their late teens, and they were throwing a volleyball amid screams of outrage and delight, shouting each other's names, and hurling friendly insults, as a woman with a body that would have stopped traffic anywhere appeared oblivious to them. She lay, as though dead to the world, in a black bikini, her fair skin heavily oiled and tanning lightly in the morning sun, with a large straw hat over her face and a stack of towels next to her. Her breasts were very large and full, spilling from the black bikini top, and then her torso narrowed sharply to a tiny waist only to move outward again to round, sensual hips that tapered into long, thin legs. She had the body of a beauty queen, which was how she had begun after arriving from Buffalo almost two decades before. Jane Adams was thirty-nine years old and her body showed no signs of having borne three children.

She opened one big blue eye and peered out from under her hat to make sure the children were all right and then went back to dozing in the sun. She wore no jewellery save a narrow gold wedding band and simple gold hoop earrings, yet the house had a definite look of substantial suburban opulence and there was a Mercedes station wagon in the garage, which she drove, a Volvo for the maid and kids to drive, and her husband had left for work in his Mercedes sedan. And the pool was large, even by Pasadena standards.

'Hey . . . over here . . . you guys! . . . come on! . . .' The ball flew out of the pool, landing near her chair, and she bounded up with almost childlike grace, adjusting her bikini top with one hand as she ran to get it, and the young men in the pool found themselves staring at her as they always did, while her son glowered at them. It always annoyed him when his friends stared at her as though she were one of them. Thank God she wore enough clothes to cover herself most of the time. She wasn't given to low décolletés, or slits in her skirt. Most of the time she looked respectable, in old Oxford shirts and wraparound skirts and espadrilles. She appeared unconscious of her striking looks. And once her body was out of sight, the rest of her looked quite unremarkable. She was a nice-looking woman with a pretty face and a warm smile she shared with everyone. She had red hair and freckles on her chest and arms, and big blue eyes that seemed filled with innocence, as she threw the ball back to the children.

'Ready for lunch?' she called out to them, but they were already involved in the game again by the time she sat down. She always made trays of sandwiches for them, and kept the refrigerator filled with the sodas they liked and ice-cream sandwiches. After eighteen years of motherhood, she knew the things they liked best. Jason was going to UC Santa Barbara in the fall, and both girls would be in high school that year. Alyssa would be a freshman finally, after what seemed to her a lifelong wait, and Alexandra a junior, angling heavily for her own car. She claimed the Volvo was too big and too old and she wanted something racier, like the car Jack Adams had given his son the month before when he turned eighteen. Jason would be driving a Triumph to Santa Barbara in September. Alexandra thought that might be a nice car for her too. And their mother smiled to herself as she stretched out again. They were such typical teenagers, and it was such a far cry from her own youth in Buffalo. She had almost frozen to death getting to the high school, until she turned sixteen and ran away. She got to New York and was terrified, and worked there just long enough to make the money she needed to get to Los Angeles . . . Los Angeles . . . Hollywood . . . land of her dreams . . . and it was there that she had won her first crown as beauty queen. She had been seventeen . . . there had been modelling jobs . . . and a thousand different jobs serving hamburgers at drive-in eateries . . . and finally a small part in a horror film. She had honed her screams to perfection and she was doing well, she thought, when she met Jack Adams. She had been only nineteen and she had fallen madly in love with him. Mr All American. He had gone to Stanford, and was working for his father in his brokerage firm, and he had been twenty-three. She had never seen a man as beautiful, she thought, or so clean-cut. He had taken her home to meet his folks on their fourth date, and he had told her what to wear and what to say and how to act. It was better than acting in horror films, and a lot more fun. They had a beautiful brick house on Orange Grove, and Jane had been in awe of them, and of Jack, so grown up and mature, and wonderful in bed. He was the sweetest man she'd ever known, until he started pressuring her to give up her acting career. Acting was everything she'd always dreamed and she knew that if she hung in long enough she'd get somewhere and really make it. But Jack wanted no part of it. He hated the place she lived, her friends, the films she made, hated everything she did, except the way she made love to him. He had never known anyone like her, and as he buried his head between her legs in the golden nest of curls she shared so generously with him, he knew he'd never give her up, no matter what his parents said. They thought she was a tramp, his mother even dared to call her a whore, but only once. And he refused to give her up. He forced her to give up her dreams instead. He made her careless in a way she'd never been before, and she was not quite twenty-one when she found out that she was pregnant. And that was the end of it. Jack wouldn't let her get rid of it. She had got the name of an abortionist in Tijuana, and she sobbed the whole story out to him. He proposed to her that night, and they were married two weeks later at a small church near his parents' home, and that was the end of the horror films and her career. She became Mrs John Walton Adams III, and Jason was born six months afterwards, a bouncing, smiling baby boy with a shock of her red hair that stood straight up for the first year. He was so sweet, and Jack was so good to her that she barely missed the world she'd given up. She hardly had time to miss it for the first five years. Alexandra was born when Jason was two, and Alyssa two years after that. Alexandra looked like Jack, and Alyssa like no one at all, except, Jack's mother thought, an aunt of hers. They were the perfect family, and Jane was happy taking care of them. They kept her busy all day long, and Jack kept her busy all night. He never seemed to get enough of her. He hungered for her night and day, and sometimes took her in the bathroom for just long enough to come between her breasts while the children were watching TV at night, or eating dinner. He could hardly wait for her to come to bed, and they made love every night even if she was too tired to think or talk or eat after a day of running around with the kids and satisfying him. She sometimes felt as though she had no time for herself, but she didn't really care. She wanted to be the perfect wife, perfect mother and keep everyone satisfied and happy. She rarely, if ever, thought of herself. She was just grateful to have come so far from Buffalo, and she loved being Mrs Jack Adams. It was the best role she'd ever had, and it was only when the children went to school that she began to long for all that she'd given up for him. She was twenty-seven by then, but she didn't look much different than she had ten years before, especially when she swam naked in their pool. Jack would watch her there, late at night, and he would turn off the lights, and slip in after her. She didn't have to worry about the children seeing them then. She didn't have to worry about anything. He took care of everything for her, their bills, their life, he told her who to see, what she could do, what to wear. He moulded her into his perfect fantasy, and the only thing that wasn't part of it was the love she had for the work she'd done. Sometimes she'd talk longingly about going back to work again, but he would hear none of it.

'You don't belong there any more. You never did.' His voice was harsh when he spoke of it. 'That's a world of tramps and leeches.' She hated when he talked like that. She'd loved the world of Hollywood, she still missed some of her friends, and he never let her see them. All of her old room-mates had drifted away, and when he saw her writing a Christmas card to her agent once, he threw it out. 'Forget it, Jane. That's all over now.' He wanted it to be. Desperately. He wanted her to forget all of it . . . even the parts she'd loved . . . the people she'd known . . . the dreams she'd had . . . Alyssa was only three when a man in a supermarket had handed her a card. He was a talent scout for some agency, and it was like the old days of Hollywood. He invited her to come to his office for a screen test, and she laughed. She'd heard plenty of that in the old days, especially when she first got to Los Angeles. She was surprised at how insistent he was, but she never called him, and threw away his card eventually. But he had stirred forces in her she had quelled for too long. She called her old agent one day, just to say hello, to 'see how he was', and he begged her to come back. He said he could find work for her. And six months later, when she was shopping in Los Angeles, she dropped in to see him, just for the hell of it. He threw his arms around her, and begged her to let him take some photographs. She even sent him a few other snapshots after that, and then the big decision came, four months afterwards. He had a part for her. On a soap opera, he said. It was perfect for her. She tried to laugh it off, but he wouldn't let her off the hook. He begged her to audition for it, just for practice he said, for old times' sake, for the hell of it . . . for him . . . for yourself . . . for all that hard work you did ten years ago . . . She lay in bed at night, thinking about it, wishing she could try out, worrying about what Jack would say. She tried to mention it to him, but there was nowhere to start, no way to explain the emptiness she felt, the loneliness with the children at school. But all he wanted from her was between her legs. He wouldn't listen to her. He never talked to her. No one did. And ten years later, he was as hungry for her as he had been when they first met, and she knew she should be grateful for it. Her friends complained that their husbands paid no attention to them, never wanted to make love, had no interest in them sexually . . . and here she was with a man who was insatiable, he whispered things like 'I'm gonna fuck your brains out tonight . . .' over the children's heads, and she was always terrified they would hear. But she couldn't talk to him. He had no idea what was in her head, her heart . . . her soul . . . but her agent knew too well. He had seen it all in her eyes the day she'd dropped in on him in Los Angeles, and he wasn't going to let her go again. She had something he knew he could sell, always had had, and it was more than sex appeal. There was a humanity to Jane, a decency, a warmth, she was motherly and yet the sexiest broad he'd seen in years, like Marilyn Monroe with kids, she appealed to women and men, and he'd never met anyone who wasn't drawn to her. She had a kind of inner warmth that drew people like babies looking for a teddy bear . . . and what a teddy bear, she made the term 'tits and bum' sound bleak. There was so much more to her.

She went to the audition, finally, on a hot day in June, although they were trying out for a different part by the time she went. And she insisted on going in a black wig she'd bought. When Lou saw her afterwards, he whistled and then erupted in a big happy grin. She looked like a sexier, richer, younger Gina Lollobrigida. And she got the part. They didn't even question the black wig. They wanted her. Immediately. And Jane sat in Lou's office in tears.

'Now what am I going to do?'

'Go back to work. That's what.' He could feel his heart pounding, just looking at her, not with desire, but with the excitement of having got her the job. He knew that, given the chance, he could do great things with her. She had an appeal like no one else in Hollywood, if he could just get her to get rid of that jerk she was married to.

'What'll I tell Jack?'

'Tell him you want to go back to work.' But it wasn't as easy as that. She had lain in bed, sleepless, for over a week, and finally turned down the part. There was no way she could explain it to him. None at all. He wouldn't listen to anything she said. He just cooed and groaned as he made love to her, and every time she tried to say something, he turned her over, and made love to her again. It was almost like a joke. It was his way of not listening to her. All he wanted was for her to sleep with him, take care of his children, and entertain his clients over dinner. But the producer of the show just thought she was being coy. They doubled the money, and Lou called her five times a day. She was terrified Jack would answer the phone, and once he did. Lou was smart enough to say it was a wrong number and hang up, and finally she gave in. Trembling, terrified, she put the black wig in a bag and went to the studio in Burbank to talk to them. She signed the contracts that afternoon, terrified at what she'd done, at what Jack would do to her. He had said, more than once, that if she ever went back to acting, he'd throw her out. And she knew he would. He said he'd keep the kids, the house, everything. And the only thing she gave a damn about were the kids . . . and the show . . . the worst of it was that she fell in love with it. She played Marcia on *Our Secret Sorrows* in a black wig. She worked from ten to four thirty every day, and got home every afternoon in time to listen passionately to what the children had done all day in school. She cooked at night, baked for them, drove them to school before she went to work. And everyone, including Jack, thought she was doing volunteer work in a hospital. She even told them stories about it. The 'hospital' became her life . . . but in truth it was the show. She loved the people, the excitement, the atmosphere . . . and everyone was crazy about her. She worked under the name of Janet Gole, her real name from long ago from Buffalo before she

47

came to Hollywood, and miraculously no one ever knew. She shunned all publicity, and although the show got top ratings every year, no one she knew ever seemed to know or care how much she looked like Janet Gole, on *Secret Sorrows*. It came on live at noon every day, and she had never been happier. Other roles came up, and some important opportunities, but she turned them all down. She couldn't afford to lose her anonymity, and she knew on other shows she would. Not everyone would cater to her idiosyncrasies about no press, no interviews, no publicity. And for ten years on *Secret Sorrows* she managed to hang on to both her anonymity and her black wig. She even paid her taxes under the name of Janet Gole, and had a separate social security number, so Jack never knew anything. No one did. The secret was perfectly kept.

Until the phone rang as she lay by her pool, watching the kids play volleyball. She had just lain down again, after throwing them the ball, when she heard the phone ring. They were on hiatus for two months, which worked perfectly for her. She could hang around with the kids, and they were all going to La Jolla for two weeks, as they did every year. She walked into the house and picked up the phone.

'Hi, beautiful.' It was Lou. He often called her, sometimes just to say hello. He took good care of her. He was sixty years old and he had always been kind to her. She respected him a great deal, and he respected what he called her 'craziness' about keeping her career from Jack. He was as careful as he had to be. He didn't want to screw up what she had. But the new director on the show had done that anyway.

'Hi, Lou.'

'Enjoying your holiday?' His voice sounded strange to her, but she figured he was under a lot of pressure. He was most of the time, working with a handful of stars, and an army of hungry actors desperate for work, and badgering him night and day.

'I always love the break. It gives me a chance to be with

48

the kids.' Jane and her family. It was all she talked about. That and her house, and her cooking. Christ, it was just as well she didn't give interviews, he always thought. With that body of hers, no one would believe she was for real. 'What's up?'

He paused, searching for the words. He knew it was going to hurt. A lot. But he had to tell her before she found out on the set. 'Not such great news.' He decided to plunge right in. He hated doing it to her. 'They're going to write you out after the break.'

'What?' It was a joke. It had to be. Her face went white beneath the tan, and the big blue eyes filled with tears. 'Are you serious?'

'I'm afraid I am. The new director wants a new look for the show. He's writing out four of you in a car crash on the first day. They're giving you a gorgeous severance, of course, I saw to that, but it looks like . . .' He didn't have to say more, as tears coursed silently down her cheeks. It was the worst news she'd ever had. *Sorrows* was her whole life, that and Jack and the kids. She'd been on the show for almost eleven years . . . eleven years. . .

'It's been ten years of my life and he's going to . . .' It happened all the time, particularly on soaps. But it was devastating to her. They were like her family. 'Can't you change his mind?'

'I tried everything.' He didn't tell her that they were bringing in a younger girl to take her place, and three of the director's gay friends. There was no point in telling her that. All that mattered was that she was out. 'They want you back for the first day after hiatus and then that's it.'

'My God! . . .' She sat crying openly at the kitchen table when her oldest daughter walked in and looked at her in surprise.

'Something wrong, Mom?'

She shook her head silently, smiling valiantly through her tears, and Alexandra shrugged and helped herself to a 7-Up before going outside again to rejoin her friends, with

49

never a backward glance towards Jane, as she started to cry again.

'I just can't believe it.'

'Neither can I. And personally, I think he's a damn fool, but there's nothing we can do. It's their right, and I guess you should be happy you were on for ten years.' Yeah, but now what? She knew she'd never find anything like it again. No other soap would let her keep her anonymity, and she couldn't let Jack find out.

'I feel as though someone died.' She laughed sadly. 'Me, I guess.'

'Screw 'em, we'll get you something else.'

She began to sob, and at his end, Lou cringed. 'I can't do something else . . . you know that . . . this was perfect for me. . .'

'So we'll find you another daytime soap that needs a sex bomb in a black wig.' She had twelve of them by now, in different styles and lengths from the last ten years. But she was inconsolable, as the tears flowed and she blew her nose in a paper towel she found near the sink. 'I don't know what else to say, babe. I'm sorry. I really am.' And he was. He hated seeing her hurt. She didn't deserve a rotten break like that.

'What am I going to do?' She blew her nose again, as the tears dripped from her cheeks to her chest, and were absorbed by her bikini top:

'Give in gracefully. There's nothing else you can do. Go to work for one day and say goodbye.' He knew it would be a ghastly scene, and as he talked to her, he jotted a note down on his calendar. He wanted to send her flowers that day, anonymously, as he always did. 'And I'll see what else is around.'

'I can't do anything else, Lou.'

'Don't be so sure. Leave it to me. I'll call you in a day or two.'

She hung up and blew her nose again, feeling as though the world had come to an end. And in a sense it had. And just as she hung up the phone, the teenagers came thundering in, eleven of them. Jason, Alexandra, Alyssa, and their friends.

'What's for lunch?' Jason smiled at her, seeing no evidence of the tears she had just shed. He looked almost exactly like Jack when they'd first met. And Alexandra looked a lot like him too, although they both had her red hair. But other than that, none of them looked even remotely like her.

Turning her back to them, so they couldn't see her damp eyes, she took the tray of sandwiches she'd made out of the refrigerator. There was ham, bologna, turkey, several combinations, and half a dozen BLTs, and carrying handfuls of them and three six-packs of Coke, they all disappeared again, as she sat down at the kitchen table with a sigh. It was all over. All over for her. Jack had won in the end, and he didn't even know it. And then, as though just thinking of him had made him materialise, she heard a car in the drive, and glanced out the window to see his familiar silver Mercedes grind to a halt as he bounded out. He still looked like a very young man, and his blond hair hid the grey she knew was there. He was athletic and in good shape, and looked far less than his forty-three years, but there was something unkind about his eyes, and a hardness to his mouth, that hadn't been there years before. He had good looks, but he lacked warmth, and even now, as he came through the kitchen door, he didn't smile at her, didn't see the grief so obvious in her eyes. In fact, he never really even looked at her.

'Hi, honey, what brings you home?' She smiled, as he turned his back and reached into the refrigerator for a beer.

'I had a meeting nearby and thought I'd come home for lunch.' He turned and seemed to eye her from the neck down, his eyes never meeting hers. He loosened his tie, and took a sip of the beer right from the can. He had tossed his jacket on a chair, and she could see the muscles ripple beneath his shirt. He played tennis almost every day when he got home. He and Jason were lethal on the courts. Jane

51

had never learned to play well, and they hated playing with her. 'You're not working at the hospital today?'

'I'm off for the summer. Remember?' She smiled again, and this time he smiled back.

'Yeah. That's right. I always forget.' He eyed the ripe luscious body, and seemed to lose interest in all else. 'Been out by the pool?' He provided well for them. He provided everything. Pool, cars, clothes for her and the kids, rented house in La Jolla every year, holiday in Hawaii over the Christmas holiday, yet it always seemed to her that there was so much he didn't share, so much he couldn't give. Like himself. He was always so distant, and he never talked to her.

'I was keeping an eye on the kids.' They always exchanged banalities, and little more. He never told her about his work, never had, and he seldom talked about his friends at work.

'Did you get the stuff I wanted for La Jolla next week?' He had given her a precise list of fishing gear he wanted replaced.

'I haven't had time. I'll do it this afternoon.' But suddenly it felt as though the world had come to an end. Hadn't it, she wondered, as he approached, and stuck two fingers down the front of her tiny black elastic pants. He found what he was looking for and plunged in, hurting her, but she said nothing to him.

'Got time for something else?' It was a rhetorical question. She had never said no to him. He had already set down his beer and grabbed her breast with his other hand. His mouth crushed down on hers and he bit her lips. 'Wanna fuck?' She was used to the way he said it by now. After twenty years, the brutality of the way he made love to her no longer shocked or surprised. It was simply the way Jack was these days. It had been different when they first met. He was gentler then, but once they were married, things had gradually changed, and it was as though he were crazed to possess her sometimes and couldn't go deep enough or hard enough. He'd been that way even when she was pregnant, and it had scared her sometimes, but no harm had ever come of it. She'd been embarrassed to tell her doctor what they did. And he pulled her towards him now and ground against her, chewing on her lower lip, and then he pulled away and smiled. 'I'm glad I came home after all. This beats lunch downtown.'

She laughed, but her eyes weren't smiling today, and he grabbed her by the arm and hurried down the long hall with her, around the L shape that surrounded the sunken living room. Their bedroom was at the farthest end, he had planned it that way, and she often wondered if he had done that so the children wouldn't hear the noises he made. He slammed the door behind them, and locked the door. He never bothered pulling the window shades but the kids couldn't see them from the pool anyway, and she liked seeing the trees as he pulled her roughly to the floor and yanked off her bathing suit. He unzipped only his fly and forced himself inside her with no prelude, no gentleness, his hands milking her breasts as roughly as they always had, until he bent down and bit her nipples too. Sometimes he bit them till they bled, but not this time, this time he worked them until she was aroused too, and began to moan softly beneath his hands, and then he startled her by pulling away, and fondling her with his lips, pulling her wide with both hands and then plunging inside her again and this time for the last time as he gave a loud shout and then a long soft moan, as he lay on her, satisfied, pleased with himself, smiling to himself as he touched her breasts for a last time, never seeing the tears that ran slowly from her eyes as she looked at him.

5

Jane walked onto the familiar set with a knot in her stomach the size of Boulder Dam. She saw the faces of the carpenters she knew so well, the sound men, the gaffers she had known for years. And all of them were dear to her. She baked cakes for them, brought biscuits, knitted for their babies when they came. She cared about everyone, and she needed all of them. Needed them for her well-being. They were her family, as much as her children were. These people were her only friends. And now she was losing them.

The atmosphere was sombre, no one said hello to her that day. Everyone knew what was coming. Word had got out. The victims had been warned. And Jane had to fight back tears when the director spoke to her. He described the scene, the 'carnage' afterwards, and made no mention of what he was doing to her, in real life. That he was taking a role from her that she had cherished for ten years. In fact, this was the first day of her eleventh season on the show. Her first day and her last. She didn't even want to think back to when it all began. She couldn't bear the thought of it.

She went to her dressing room upstairs and packed her things into the suitcase she'd brought. Four more black wigs, a sweater, a jumpsuit and a pair of shorts to wear between scenes sometimes. She had left a pair of slippers there and dozens of little jars of makeup, a dozen bottles of nail polish. She packed it all while praying she could do the last scene without getting hysterical. She knew what a shock the scene was going to be to the audience, and like Lou, she thought the director was making a big mistake. And word was out, by Christmas, all the old faces would be gone.

The stand-ins were in place while the light men worked when she got downstairs. They were being used so the lights could be adjusted properly, and suddenly Jane envied them. She would have loved to stay on as one of them, as anything . . . she felt as though she were leaving home for the first time. It had been easier leaving Buffalo than it would be leaving this show.

There were twenty-five or thirty people around, and the walls of the set were being slid into place, and it seemed an eternity before the warning bells sounded for the last time, the air conditioning was turned off to eliminate the noise, and the sign flashed on to tell them they were on the air.

The scene was even more devastating than Jane had feared, and as they shot her face in the fatal car crash that would end her career, her tears and sobs were genuine, as was her last ghastly scream. Jane fainted as they went off the air.

The director had disappeared when the rest of the cast helped her to her dressing room. And there was no cast party for them. There were tearful goodbyes, last hugs and final promises to stay in touch, as Jane drove the Mercedes slowly off the lot for the last time, crying all the way home, and trying to concoct a suitably awful 'hospital' story for her family to justify the way she looked when she got home. Lou's flowers were waiting for her there, and mercifully all the kids came home late from school. Jason was living at UC Santa Barbara, and the girls had hockey practice that day. Even Jack gave her a break. He called to say he had an unexpected meeting to attend and he wouldn't be home till nine.

She lay on her bed and cried for hours, and never even answered the phone that night. There was no one she wanted to talk to. Her life on *Our Secret Sorrows* was a thing of the past, her career was over at last, just as Jack had wanted so long ago, and life looked bleak to her as it stretched ahead. Bleaker than it ever had before. And mercifully, she was asleep, still wearing her clothes, when Jack came home that night. And having had too much to drink, he passed out before he had a chance to begin the nightly sex ritual

55

with his wife. He left her alone, dressed, heartbroken, and exhausted by the rigours of the day. He had no idea what she'd been through, what she'd done for the last ten years, or even who she was.

6

Bill Warwick was tired by four o'clock in the afternoon, after waiting on table all day at Mike's. There was a lull, with the only customers sitting at the bar, or playing pool, and he was chatting with Adam when the phone rang on the bar.

'It's for you.' Bill looked surprised as Adam handed him the phone, and suddenly wondered if it was Sandy. He couldn't remember whether or not he had told her he'd be working there. And he'd been worried about her all day. He wondered where she was, and how stoned she was. But it wasn't Sandy. It was Harry, his agent.

'Hi, kid.'

'How'd you find me here?'

'Your answering service gave me this number. Where are you?' He'd forgotten he'd left the number with the service after all.

'I'm working, for a change. I'm waiting table at my favourite bar.'

'Tell them you just quit.'

'Any particular reason? A starring role in a film perhaps?' He was kidding as he sat down at the bar.

'Would you settle for Mel Wechsler's new series?' There was a pause as he gloated silently at his end, and Bill stared into space, wondering if it was only leading up to another disappointment. 'He's casting for it now, and it's going to be a biggie. A real hot one. I heard about it last week, and heard he was looking for a guy about your age. We sent him your reel, and he wants to see you.'

Bill whistled and looked at Adam with a grin. 'Think I have a chance?' He didn't dare hope, he had built so many castles in the air, and they had all fallen at his feet like so much sand. But maybe this time . . . that was the beauty of the business. There was always hope, always another chance, always tomorrow.

'I think you have a good chance. He wants to see you at ten tomorrow morning, and I have a copy of the script. I want you to read it tonight. And, baby, you're going to love it.' He would have loved a dog food commerical at that precise moment, but a Mel Wechsler series was too much to hope for. 'Can you come by the office and pick it up?'

'I'm working till ten. Can I pick it up at the house?'

'I'll drop it off at your place on my way home. And I want you to promise me you'll read it. I don't give a damn what Sandy pulls on you tonight, or if she OD's. Lock yourself in the bathroom and read it.'

'I'll read it, I'll read it. Believe me, you don't have to beg.'

'Good. And call me after you see him.'

'You got it.' He hung up with a boyish grin, and looked pleased with himself as Adam smiled.

'Something new?'

'That was my agent.'

'I figured.'

He didn't even dare tell his friend about the Wechsler series they were casting. He didn't want to do anything to jeopardise his chance. Hell, maybe one of the guys at the bar would overhear and want to try out for it too, and he didn't want to lose the part. He felt as though he were walking on air for the next six hours, and he wasn't even tired when he got home at eleven that night. There was a moment of dread as he opened the door, fearing that Sandy might be in bad shape, and would cause a scene. He just wanted to be left alone to read the script Harry had left in the mailbox for him. It was there, just as he'd promised it would be. And the cottage was empty when Bill walked in, except for Bernie, the Saint Bernard, waiting for him and the scraps he had brought home from Mike's. He let him out in the garden, put the scraps in his bowl, and helped himself to a beer from the fridge before sitting down with the script. He was still worried about Sandy, but it was a relief not to find her at home. He just didn't want to have to deal with her problems. Not tonight. He wanted to read the script, and prepare for his meeting with Mel Wechsler the next day.

It was one o'clock when he finished the script, and his heart was racing he was so excited. It was the best part he'd ever read, and it was tailor-made for him. He knew he could do a hell of a job, if he could just convince Wechsler of that. He couldn't sleep when he got to bed. He just lay there thinking of the script, and the kind of series it would be. Just thinking about it made him want it so badly he could taste it. It was four o'clock when he rolled over in bed, still half awake, and he thought he heard a noise outside, and figured it was Sandy. But it wasn't. It was probably a racoon, foraging for something to eat in the dustbins. Sandy never came home that night, and he was half relieved and half worried about her as he shaved the next morning. Life was a hell of a lot simpler without her, but that was sad too. He remembered what they had once shared, and thought of what it could have been like, if they had ever had a chance at a real marriage. He wondered if they ever had, or if the relationship had been doomed from the beginning. He hadn't wanted to believe it then. He still remembered their honeymoon at the Mauna Kea in Hawaii, and how sweet she had been to him. She was always sweet to him, but that wasn't enough any more. It didn't compensate for the agony she caused him, worrying about her day and night. But he couldn't afford to think about that now, neither the good times, nor the bad. He had to concentrate his whole being on his meeting with Mel Wechsler. That was all he could think of now.

He waited for the bus, thinking of the script again, and the trip to Wechsler's offices in Burbank didn't seem long at all. He was so excited he could barely breathe as he gave the guard his name. He was expected and was told which building to go to. He walked across the car park and into a building, down a long hall, and into an anteroom with four secretaries in it and a wall of books and paintings. He gave the nearest secretary his name, and was told to take a seat, and he suddenly wondered why he had come. He would never get the part. It was just too big a break. And he probably wasn't ready for it.

'Mr Warwick.' They announced his name just as he was deciding that he should probably never have come, and he stood up, feeling like a small boy waiting to go into the principal's office, but his fears began to dissolve as he was ushered into Mel Wechsler's inner sanctum. He reached across his desk with an outstretched hand and a warm smile, his brilliant blue eyes taking in every inch of Bill Warwick.

'Hello, Bill. Thank you for coming.' Bill wondered briefly if he was kidding. He would have walked over ground glass and rusty nails to get to this meeting. 'I like your reel.'

'Thank you.' He felt suddenly tongue-tied and very frightened, and he couldn't think of what to say, but Mel took care of it for him.

'Have you read the script?'

'I have.' Bill's eyes came to life, and he smiled a smile that would have melted a million women's hearts. It was precisely the look Mel wanted for Sabina's son on the show. The female lead in *Manhattan* was going to be the head of a corporation, aided by her son, detested by her daughter, adored by her lover and colleague, an older actor, a role Mel hoped to offer to Zack Taylor. And the other strong woman's role would go to the sister of the lead, a woman who has no interest in the corporation, at first, and then eventually fights her sister for it, her children, and her lover. It was a story of power struggles, and the inner wars of a corporation, led by strong, greedy, glamorous people. And Mel could see Bill perfectly as Sabina's son. The script called for a man in his late twenties, and Bill looked close enough.

'I loved it.' Bill's eyes shone with sincerity as he said it. 'There's a lot of meat in all the roles, and particularly the one I liked.' He beamed like a little kid, and felt shy in the gaze of Mel Wechsler. It was like seeing the Wizard of Oz, knowing how powerful he was with networks, and how successful with all his shows.

'I'm glad. We love it too. I think it's going to be the biggest show on any of the networks next autumn. We want to start shooting in December.' Bill stared at him as though listening to God, and afterwards felt stupid for not having said more, but he couldn't think of a thing to say to him. He just kept thinking of the show and how badly he wanted to be on it. 'How would that work with your schedule?'

'Uh . . . my schedule? . . .' His mind went blank. What schedule? Working at Mike's, or *Dating Game*? Or bailing Sandy out of jail? There was that too. 'I . . . uh . . . fine . . . I don't have any commitments at the moment.' It was like being nine years old and he could have kicked himself for being so tongue-tied. 'I'm fairly free, in fact, at the moment.'

Mel Wechsler smiled, the brilliant blue eyes taking all of him in. He was young and nervous but he liked him. He had seen what he was capable of on his reel, and he was pleased. He didn't want any half-baked actors on this show. He wanted only the best for *Manhattan*. And he thought Bill was. He was handsome, sexy, young, and a damn fine actor. 'You're good, Bill. Very good.' He mentioned the bits that had pleased him most. He had also seen him in a film made for TV the year before. It had been cheaply made and poorly directed, but Warwick's performance had been flawless.

'Thank you. I haven't had as much opportunity to show my stuff as I'd like. I've been doing mostly commercials lately.'

'Everyone goes through it.' Mel smiled. 'This is a tough business. How long have you been at it?'

'Ten years.' It seemed amazing even to him. Ten long years of auditions and minor successes and failures, summer stock and commercials, and any part he could get as long as it didn't sacrifice his professional integrity. It had been a long hard climb, but even as he sat here, in Mel Wechsler's office, it suddenly didn't seem all that long. It was worth it.

'That's a respectable length of time.'

'I went to UCLA and majored in drama before that.'

'And you're . . . ?' He was fishing for his age, most actors didn't tell the truth, but he was young enough that he might. In any case, he looked the right age for the part, and that was all that really mattered to him.

'Thirty-two.'

'Perfect. Eloise Martin's son, Phillip, is twenty-eight, possibly twenty-seven. We haven't quite pinned it down yet, but thereabouts. That's fine for you.' It also depended on how old Sabina was willing to be in the role, if she took the part, but he figured to have her play pretty close to her age. 'You also look the part. There are going to be a lot of women in love with you once we're on the air, teenagers, grandmothers, women your own age. There will be the usual madness, or maybe even more so. Posters, pinups, press coverage, God knows what else in this case. You're going to be a big star after this, Bill.' He wondered if that meant he had the part, and he held his breath as he waited. 'I take it you're unencumbered. Publicly, in any case.' Mel had made inquiries, and he liked what he heard. He was clean-cut, hardworking, and well liked by almost all the directors he worked for. Mel Wechsler didn't like drugs, dropouts, or headaches with his cast. He didn't like people showing up late for work, staggering around the set drunk, or screwing everything in sight, so that it interfered with shooting schedules and people's attitudes once they were on the screen. He ran a tight set, and he intended to keep it that way for *Manhattan*. 'You're not married, are you, Bill?'

Bill Warwick felt the opportunity of a lifetime slipping through his fingers, with a drug-addict wife hanging on his coattails. 'No, I'm not.' He prayed that Mel would never find out about Sandy. But there was no reason why he would. No one had ever known they were married. And if she cleaned

62

up, they could always stage a big wedding. She was in no condition for that now, but he felt traitorous anyway for the lie he had just told.

'Divorced?'

'No, sir.' That much was true anyway.

'Fine. Your fans will love that.' And he knew he wasn't gay, at least that was what he had been told. Two of Mel's sources thought he had a regular girl, because he didn't go out much, or hadn't in a while, but they were sure he was straight, and that was good too. Mel Wechsler wanted Phillip Martin to become America's heartthrob, and that meant Bill Warwick. 'I'd say you're our number one man for the job, what do you think?'

Bill's heart was racing . . . it was almost in his hands . . . almost . . . 'I'd love the part, Mr Wechsler . . . I know I would . . . and I could do a hell of a job.'

Mel Wechsler extended his hand across his desk. 'I think so too. I'll call your agent with a definite answer in the next few days.' He stood up, and Bill had no choice but to do the same, praying that he'd made a decent impression. He wanted to beg him to give him the part. He knew how often people had left meetings like this one, convinced that a part was theirs, only to find out later that they'd lost it to someone else.

'I hope I get it, Mr Wechsler.' It was all he could say as their eyes locked, and Bill quietly left the office. He didn't know what to think when he left, and he was a nervous wreck by the time he got to Mike's and called his agent. At the bar Adam told him to be cool, worrying wouldn't change anything anyway. He had finally told him that he had auditioned for Mel Wechsler, but he didn't say for what. He was still terrified that someone else would get the part. But Harry was encouraging when Bill called.

'Relax, baby, it's in the bag.' But he had said that before, and it had been in someone else's bag, not Bill's.

'I made an ass of myself, Harry.'

'What'd you do? Kiss him?'

'No, I mean it. I was just so damn scared I could hardly talk. I probably didn't even make sense.'

'So what? You're an actor, not a debutante. You got a script, you'll read it, you'll learn it, you'll make sense. Listen, he's been asking all over Hollywood about you. He means business.'

'What's he asking?'

'If you're clean, how you work, the usual bullshit. And you're in good shape. Everyone loves you.' They both thought the same thing at the same time.

'Think anyone's told him about Sandy?'

'No one knows except me and Tony Grossman, right?'

'Right.'

'Well, I'm sure as hell not going to say anything, and Tony never wanted anyone to know she was married. That was when she was on *Sunday Supper* of course, maybe now he doesn't give a damn, but I don't think he'll say anything. He wants to book her as a virgin again next time.' Harry hated Tony Grossman, and Bill knew it, it went back to their early days as agents and Bill had never heard the full story but he knew there was no love lost between them, and in the beginning of his romance with Sandy it had almost turned them into Romeo and Juliet, escaping the Montagues and Capulets, in this case their agents.

'He asked me if I was married.'

Harry swallowed. 'And what did you say?'

'I said I wasn't.'

'Good boy. He wants to cast you as America's hero, and he wants somebody single and free.'

'That's what I figured, but I felt like a jerk anyway. What if he finds out?'

'He won't. You did the right thing. Now shut up and go and do something relaxing till he calls.'

'I'm still working at Mike's.'

'You won't be for long.'

He borrowed one of Harry's own favourite sayings. 'From your mouth to God's ears.'

'I'll call you.'

'Thanks.' He hung up the phone and got busy immediately afterwards with the lunch crowd. It seemed years since he had sat across from Mel Wechsler, and it was five o'clock before he had a chance to sit down with a cup of coffee and a hamburger of his own. He sat down at the bar during a break, and watched the news on the television over Adam's head. But he stopped eating very quickly. They were flashing a picture of Sandy as she had looked when she started on *Sunday Supper* three years before, and it reminded Bill again of how different she looked now, and then they went on to announce that she had been involved in a major drug bust that morning. That morning . . . while he was talking to Mel Wechsler . . . it made him feel sick again. He sat riveted to his seat, watching the TV, anxious for more news, but they only said that she was being held at the Los Angeles City Jail with five other suspects and this was not her first arrest. It said also that she had been released from the series the year before for breach of contract relating to drug abuse. And then they went on to the next item.

Adam had seen it too, and he said nothing as Bill went to the phone. He figured he was going to try to call her. And he was right. But they told him at the jail that she'd already been bailed, and they couldn't tell him by whom. The next five hours seemed more like fifteen. He had called the cottage five or six times but there was never any answer there. And when he got home, he expected to find her passed out on the couch, or lying on the bed, fully dressed and filthy dirty, stoned out of her gourd, with a needle lying nearby. Instead, he found only the mild disorder he had left himself that morning, and Bernie waiting anxiously for his dinner. It was obvious that Sandy hadn't come back to the cottage. And he had a sudden sense that she felt she had gone too far and she was keeping it away from him now. In a way he was glad, and in another way he was sorry. He was so used to rescuing her that he didn't know what to do now. He couldn't just

65

forget her. Her clothes were still hanging in the closet, and stuffed in all the same drawers. Her toothbrush was on the rack next to his, and all her makeup in the case she took to the set. But she didn't use any of it any more. She didn't care. The clothes no longer fit, and she no longer wore makeup, or even brushed her teeth half the time. All she did was get loaded all day long.

He sat down pensively on the couch, thinking of her, wondering where she was, and the phone rang. It was almost midnight. He was sure it was Sandy. But it wasn't.

'Bill?'

'Yes.' His voice was terse. Maybe it was the cops. Maybe she'd been hurt or . . . and then he recognised Harry's voice.

'Sorry to call so late. I had to go out, and I wanted to call you myself. I figured you wouldn't mind if I called you.'

'What's up?' Bill was frowning. All he could think about was Sandy. He wondered where the hell she was, and in what condition. And then he hated himself for worrying about it. He didn't want to think about her any more, yet he did . . . too damn much, hating and loving her all at once, resenting the misery she brought to his life.

'You got it, kid.' Harry sounded as happy as he knew Bill would.

'Got what?' His mind was blank and then suddenly he understood. 'Oh my God! . . . You mean . . . I . . . I did?'

'You bet you did, baby. Wechsler's secretary called at six o'clock. They'll send the contracts over next week. And you start shooting in New York December 6th. You report for Wardrobe on October 19th, and that, my friend, is that. A star is born. How do you like that, Mr Warwick?'

There were tears in Bill's eyes. It had been ten years of hard work and broken dreams, and four years of hope in college before that, and now here it was . . . the part of a lifetime. 'Son of a bitch . . . I never thought it would happen.'

'I did. I sure as hell did. I never doubted it for a minute.' And then he remembered something else. 'I saw the news tonight, by the way. I guess you know . . .' Bill knew he meant Sandy.

'Yeah.'

'Is she with you?'

'No. I haven't seen her in two days. We had kind of a blowout a couple of days ago. She got busted then too.'

'Look, do yourself a big favour, Bill, and keep your mouth shut, and keep her away. All you need is for this whole thing to blow up in your face because of her. That girl is trouble.'

'She's all messed up, that's all.' Defending her was second nature to him.

'That's enough. And it could cost you this part. Is that what you want?'

'No.' But he couldn't betray Sandy, if she needed his help, he knew he would help her. But he'd be discreet. He had to be now. He had lied to Wechsler about being married. 'Don't worry about it. I'll be careful.'

'You'd better be, or he'll sue you, for embarrassing him, and lying to him. And he'll can you so fast your head will spin and I don't blame him. Keep away from her, Bill.'

'For the moment, it's not a problem.'

'Keep it that way. And congratulations. You're gonna do great.' He sounded moved. 'I'm proud of you.'

'Thanks, Harry.' He hung up with a smile and a feeling of disbelief, wishing there were someone to share it with. But there was only Bernie, wagging his tail, and waiting for his next meal. And Bill had no idea what had happened to Sandy.

7

Sabina was standing on her terrace in a bathing suit. She had just come up from the pool, and was thinking. She had had lunch with Mel the day before, and since then she had read the script seven times. Seven. If she wanted to do TV, it would have been exactly what she wanted. And Mel was right. The part of Eloise Martin read as though it had been written for her. They could have been twins. Sabina Quarles and Eloise Martin. In fact, they were the same woman. And if Mel got what he wanted, and Zack Taylor took the male lead, it could be one hell of a show. She knew that was what Mel was counting on, but was it enough? Enough to make her change her mind? It would make her a laughing stock to go back on her word now. Even though she would be doing all the laughing. She had heard from her agent that morning, and they were offering her three million dollars for the first season. Three million. There were other considerations in her life. And three million dollars would take care of all of them, for a long, long time. The truth was, she couldn't afford to turn it down, and the funny thing was she didn't really want to. Yet she still felt she had to think about it. And suddenly as she stood there she laughed, wondering who she was kidding. For three million dollars, there was no decision to be made. She had to do it.

She called Mel at four o'clock, and he was in a meeting at the network. He called her back shortly after six and she had just come out of the shower. She was lying naked on the couch, reading a magazine, her hair wrapped in a huge white terry cloth towel.

'Sabina?'

'Yes.' Her voice always gave him the same thrill deep in the pit of his stomach, and he could just imagine what it would do to male viewers all across the country, if he could talk her into doing the show.

'Sorry I wasn't here when you called.'

'That's all right.' She smiled the feline smile that was so perfect for the voice. Everything about her fit together, everything was right. There were no pieces misplaced or mismatched or mistaken. 'I've been doing a little reading since our lunch.' She had never called to thank him for lunch. She had wanted to be left alone with the script and now she had her answer.

'Should I ask what your reaction is, or should I be polite and wait till you decide to tell me yourself?'

She had an idea she liked better. 'Why don't you come over for a drink and we'll talk about it?' At least she wasn't turning him down cold. That was something. 'How does that sound?'

'It sounds delightful. What about dinner afterwards?'

She was pleased. She liked Mel Wechsler, and she liked being seen with him. And she was going to be seen with him a lot if she took the part. She suspected they'd be seeing a lot of each other. 'That sounds very nice. In fact, why don't we have the drink here afterwards?'

'Perfect. I'll pick you up at eight. All right?'

'Fine. See you then, Mel.' It was a purr that made his heart race as he set down the phone. He went home to change and had his secretary make reservations at L'Orangerie. He picked Sabina up at exactly eight o'clock, and he was driving the Mercedes 600 himself, which he liked to do at night. It was a little less awkward, if he was spending the evening with a lady, and you never knew how or where things were going to end. He preferred using his driver only in the daytime.

The restaurant was jammed, and he had chosen it on purpose. Everyone in Hollywood was there, and all heads turned as they walked into the room. There were plenty of people who recognised Sabina, and more who recognised Mel. He was one of the most important men in Hollywood, and together they made an impressive pair, and she looked spectacular as they waited briefly for their table. They waited just long enough for the headwaiter to make sure that everything was the way 'Monsieur Wechsler' liked it, and for everyone to admire the tight white satin dress Sabina had worn. He was sure she was wearing nothing under it, though you couldn't tell, but it clung to her like a second skin and he had the urge to run his hands over her from the moment he picked her up at her apartment. She had also worn long diamond drops hanging from her ears, and sexy white satin very high-heeled sandals. Her blonde mane was swept up on her head, and her deep tan set off the white dress in such a way that everyone stared as they made their way to their table.

'And this is now,' Mel said in a soft voice after they sat down, commenting on the stares they'd gotten on their way in, 'can you imagine what it could be like a year from now, with everyone in America watching you on *Manhattan*?'

She smiled noncommittally, torturing him, a cat with her prey, and she loved it. He ordered champagne, and they quickly graduated to dry martinis, followed by an excellent dinner. He was remarkably able at tossing the conversational ball with her, and they talked about everything but the show, until he could stand it no longer.

'You have to admit, I've been very good. I haven't even asked for your reaction. But I can't stand the suspense any more, Sabina. What did you think?' He looked like a small boy for a minute and she leaned closer to him and smiled, looking him in the eye.

'I loved it.'

He waited for more but she said nothing. 'That's it?' He looked disappointed.

'It's perfect. Just as perfect as you said.'

'But? . . .' He could already tell she wasn't going to do it, and he was bitterly disappointed. The part was so perfect for her, and she was too blind and stubborn to see it.

'But what?'

'It's perfect "but"?'

'But nothing.' She looked perfectly calm.

'Sabina Quarles' – he gently grabbed both her wrists and looked deep into her green eyes – 'will you please tell me what you're saying, you are driving me crazy.'

She threw back her head and laughed. She loved it. She was torturing him and she knew it, but it was all in good fun. She knew it was only foreplay.

'Are you going to do *Manhattan* or not?'

'Of course I am. I'd be crazy to turn it down . . . do you really think I'm that stupid?' She looked at him as though it had been obvious from the start and he looked as though he would have liked to strangle her, and then suddenly he threw his arms around her and kissed her. Interested stares made due note of the gesture, and he signalled the waiter and was about to ask for champagne when she stopped him and spoke to him in a low voice that only he could hear. 'Why not go to my place for a drink to celebrate?' He looked at her for a moment and then nodded and asked the waiter for the bill, and a few minutes later he was leading her out of the door to the waiting 600. He still couldn't believe what he had heard. He felt like a little boy having won the grand prize. Sabina Quarles was going to star in *Manhattan*.

'I still can't believe it, Sabina. You're wonderful! You're terrific!'

'Thank you, Mr Wechsler, so is your script. The first one anyway. The others had better be just as good.' But they both knew they would be. Mel hired only the best writers, and in this case, he was even more anxious for a great show than he usually was. This was *Manhattan*.

She looked just as beautiful as she had when they walked in to L'Orangerie and he drove quickly to where she lived. When they arrived at her apartment the doorman greeted them both and they went upstairs. Mel sat down on the couch, still feeling a holiday air, and Sabina went to get one of the two bottles of champagne she always kept on ice, in the event of a special occasion. And this was, a very special one. It was the beginning of a whole new life for her and they both knew it.

She brought in the bottle and two glasses and Mel opened it as the cork flew through the air and he turned to her with a smile. 'I can't tell you how pleased I am, Sabina. It's going to be a wonderful show.'

She smiled at him, looking deep into his eyes. 'I know I'm going to love it.' But she wasn't speaking only of the show, and he felt the thrill that he got every time he looked at her. He had seen a lot of women come and go in his life, since his wife had died, but none quite like Sabina.

He poured their champagne and toasted her. 'To you, Sabina . . . and Eloise Martin.' Eloise Martin was the character she was going to play, and Sabina had never looked lovelier as she took a sip of champagne and quietly watched him. She felt a powerful attraction to the man, and sensed that it was mutual. It was going to be a very interesting show for Sabina in a number of ways. Not just the part . . . but Mel . . . He reminded her that she would be leaving for Paris in about a month, for fittings with François Brac, and Sabina smiled with delight. She suddenly had a lot to look forward to. 'Have you been to Paris before?'

'Once. A long time ago. Actually, I was there on location. Will we be filming any of the episodes there?'

'I don't think so. Although maybe the second year . . . There's room for almost anything in a format like that, and we're always open to suggestion.' She liked everything he was saying to her, but even more than that, she liked the way he looked at her, as though he cared about her, more than anyone had in years. It touched her, and she reached out and touched his hand with her own.

'I'm grateful for the opportunity, Mel. I know that sounds corny, but I am . . .' The words were in sharp contrast to Sabina's image as a self-possessed star, but she knew just how lucky she was to get a part like that, at her age. And he was right. A part like that, on a series like *Manhattan*, could make her the biggest star in the country. It was a hell of a big break to get at the age of forty-five, no matter how good her plastic surgeon was, or what kind of shape she was in. She was damn lucky and she knew it. And she knew it was all thanks to Mel, and she wanted him to know that.

'Don't thank me, Sabina. I wouldn't be here if you weren't someone very special. You'll be good for the show.' But they both knew it was more than that, and before he could say anything more, she leaned forward and kissed him. It was a gentle kiss at first, but it was rapidly warmed by the passion she felt, and the fact that he took her in his arms and held her fast. His grip was strong, and his lips pressed hard against hers, and she was breathless when she pulled away at last. She said nothing but the look in her eyes said it all, as he kissed her again, and then stood up with a look of regret. But he knew his limits, and he had already reached them. Another kiss like that and he would have torn off the white satin dress, and he didn't think he should do that.

'I think it's time for me to go.' He smiled down at her with a tender look that warmed her heart.

'Any special reason?'

He laughed softly in the dim light of her apartment. 'A very good one. You're driving me crazy, Miss Quarles. And if I'm expected to behave myself, I'd better go, before I attack the star of my new show.'

She smiled in the catlike way that drove him to distraction. 'I thought we were going to celebrate.'

'I thought we had.'

'I thought we were just beginning to.' She gently pulled him down next to her again and nestled close to him, and then suddenly he laughed.

'I don't want to be accused of using the casting couch. I want it known right here and now that you've already accepted the part, Sabina Quarles, and this is purely a celebration.'

'So stated, Mr Wechsler.'

'All right then.' He kissed her again, and this time the heat of passion was his as she seemed to melt into his arms and he could feel the satin of her dress come away from her flesh beneath his fingers, and a moment later she stood before him, statuesque and perfect, in all her naked splendour, reflected from every angle by the two mirrored walls in the room. She was remarkable-looking, and taking his hand she beckoned towards the bedroom. As he followed her, it was the last time that night that Sabina led the way. From the moment they reached her bed, it was Mel who took over, leading her to heights she had long since forgotten and never dreamed of feeling again. It was a night of passion worthy of the two most important people of *Manhattan*. The producer, and the star.

8

It was after Labor Day when Zack Taylor finally returned from Greece, looking tanned and very debonair in the new clothes he'd had made in London. He looked more like a polo player on holiday than a film star. He had the aura of the upper classes about him, which had always been part of his appeal, and which was part of what made him so perfect for *Manhattan*. He had been away for three months, after finishing a film, but he was happy to be back in Bel Air. He had a beautiful home there, and, like everyone else, a house in Malibu, and he owned several racehorses, which he kept in Del Mar near San Diego. He was a man of many pursuits and numerous passions. And he was intrigued as he listened to Mel. He liked the sound of the show, and he especially liked the idea of Sabina Quarles. He had worked with her once before, and although she wasn't a big star, he knew she worked hard and performed well, and having her on the show still left him top billing.

He ran a hand across his slightly wavy hair, greyed at the temple in recent years, and smiled at Mel. They had been having lunch at the Hillcrest Country Club. 'I'm curious to read the script, Mel. If it's as good as you say, you've got a very big winner. But then again, you always do.'

'Thank you, Zack.' He smiled and told him about Bill Warwick, and about the other actors and actresses he had in mind for the show. There were two in particular he wanted to pin down, but Sabina and Bill were the only sure ones. 'And the network is behind us all the way.' He always worked with the same one, and he had no problem with them. They knew that anything Mel did was a sure thing, and so did Zack. And he had no quarrel with doing TV. He liked doing television in fact, and he welcomed the idea of an important series. He knew how valuable it was in terms of the numbers of viewers who would see him. It was a point Sabina had only recently acknowledged. But Zack had liked doing TV for years.

Mel handed Zack a script, just as he had Sabina two weeks before, and he felt certain that Zack would be as impressed as they all were. Impressed and excited and anxious to get going on the show.

'I'll call you tomorrow, Mel.' Zack never fooled around, never played games, never played 'Hollywood', and Mel had always liked that about him. 'I have nothing to do tonight, and I'll give it a good read and tell you what I think in the morning.'

'I appreciate it, Zack. I think you'll like it.'

'I can't see how I could do otherwise, after all you've said.' The two men exchanged a smile and Mel wondered about him, as he had before. Zachary Taylor was a likable man, someone he would have wanted to be friends with, yet there was always a discreet distance, an invisible wall. He never seemed to get close to anyone, and Mel wondered why. Perhaps he was shy, or just very reserved. It was difficult to believe, given his enormous success. But Mel had no idea who his friends were.

The two men parted company outside, and Zack climbed into a convertible dark blue Corniche that was waiting for him outside. It was a fabulous-looking car, and he looked even more so, in his blazer and open blue shirt driving off towards Bel Air, with a last wave at Mel, as two women pointed and screeched, having recognised him at the wheel. And just wait till next year, ladies, Mel thought to himself with a smile as he got into the 600 and went back to the office.

There was a message waiting for him from Sabina, and he smiled to himself as he looked at it. They had been together almost every night for two weeks and she had awoken a passion in him that he had never known before. They were dining together again that night. And he enjoyed showing her off, although they had decided to cool it. They were

76

staying home for a while. He didn't think it was wise to let on publicly that they were having an affair. It was all right for the producer to take out his big star, but more than that would create problems for her with the rest of the cast when they started shooting.

And he was still at his desk that afternoon, when Sabina answered the intercom in her apartment. The doorman said there was a package for her and only she could sign for it, which she did, with a questioning air, as the man handed her a robin's-egg-blue box tied with white satin ribbon. She signed the stub, and closed the door, wondering who it was from, and she saw the lettering TIFFANY as she took the ribbon off. Suddenly she wondered if it was from Mel. She opened the box, and gave a startled gasp as a heavy diamond bracelet emerged. She put it on and it fit perfectly, but it was a remarkable piece of work and she was so startled she could barely read the card, which said only 'Welcome to Manhattan'.

9

Jane Adams felt as though life had ended for her with the last day on the set of *Our Secret Sorrows*. There seemed to be nothing left to live for any more, and once the children were back in school it was so depressing she could hardly stand it. She read novels, lay by the pool, let Jack push her around constantly and make all the unreasonable demands he chose, as he had for twenty years, and she didn't give a damn. About anything. And she refused to read any of the scripts or go to any of the auditions her agent mentioned to her. There was no point. There was nothing available on any current daytime soap, he had checked them all out, and she couldn't do prime time TV, even if she could get a part. There was no way she could keep it from Jack if she did that.

And she was furious when her agent mailed her the script to *Manhattan*. He sent it right to the house, and Jack could have opened it just as easily as she had.

'Do you know what he'd do to me for that, Lou?'

'What?' He really couldn't imagine that the guy was as uptight as Jane said. No one was. Not in Lou Thurman's world.

'He'd divorce me.'

'Read it anyway. It's terrific, and you don't know what I had to go through to get it.'

'Why? What's so special about it?' She sounded unhappy and bored and irritable with him, as she had for weeks. Once she had stopped crying about the lost part, she had become bitchy. But he knew how unhappy she was and what a crisis it was for her to lose a part she'd had for almost eleven years. It would have been rough on anyone.

'What's so special about this is that it's a new Mel Wechsler series, and he's casting. I want to submit a few tapes of *Sorrows* for him to see, if you'll let me.'

'Is this daytime?' For a minute, she sounded hopeful.

'Prime time.' He was proud of it and she almost hung up on him.

'God damn it, Lou. I told you, I can't do that.'

'Just read the script for chrissake, and we can fight about it later.' He didn't tell her he had already sent a series of tapes to Wechsler's office, but he did call the next morning to tell her that Wechsler had called him.

'Why?' She didn't understand. She had read the script the night before, after Jack went to bed, and it knocked her right out of her seat, but she also knew she couldn't touch it. Not on prime time TV.

'Why? He called me because he liked the tapes of you on *Sorrows*, that's why. Did you read the script?'

'Yes.'

'And?' It was like pulling teeth.

'I loved it, but that doesn't make any difference. I still can't do it and you know it.'

'Bullshit. If you get a part on that show, it will be the biggest break of your career you'll ever get, and I will kill you if you don't take it.'

'He's not offering me a part anyway.'

'He wants to meet you.'

She felt her heart skip a beat. 'When?'

'Tomorrow. At eleven.' He didn't ask her if she could do it. She had to.

'Can I wear a wig?' Maybe she should go, just for the hell of it, just so she could tell Lou she'd done it. What harm was there in that anyway? Jack would never know. . . .

'I don't care if you wear all your wigs and a hat, just do it, Janie. For me . . . please God . . .'

'All right, all right. But I can't take a part on the show, just so you know that.' She knew there was no danger of his offering her one anyway, but she was dying to meet Mel Wechsler. And when Jack came home that night, horny and a little drunk, she didn't care how disagreeable he was, how much he complained or how often he wanted to make

79

love, all she could think about was Mel Wechsler, and her meeting with him the following morning. And when Jack finally fell asleep, she got up and read the script again. It was the best thing she'd ever read, and she hid it in her closet before going to bed and she lay there awake, thinking of what it would be like being at a studio again, only for a visit.

The next morning Jack got up, as always, at five o'clock and left for his office at six. Jane made coffee for him, and she had an hour to herself before making breakfast for the girls. And by eight o'clock she was alone again, and had two hours to get ready for her big meeting with Mel Wechsler. She did her makeup carefully and selected a pretty beige dress she'd bought only the week before. It wasn't glamorous but it looked expensive and she didn't bother fixing her hair because she was going to put on the wig on the way into Los Angeles. She had chosen one of the shorter curly ones, and she planned to put it on in the ladies' room of a garage on her way to the meeting.

She was so nervous driving in that she almost forgot to stop, but she finally did, at a garage off the Pasadena Freeway, and when she looked at herself, she almost decided not to go. She looked tired, there were tiny new lines next to her eyes, and the black hair suddenly didn't look right. She even toyed with the idea of not wearing the wig, but she didn't dare go with her own bright red hair. She completely forgot the voluptuous body poured into the beige cashmere dress, the sensational legs in high-heeled pumps, or her basic talent as an actress. She'd been good on *Sorrows* for almost eleven years. They hadn't kept her because she was sleeping with anyone. She had stayed on the show for as long as she had because her performances were good, and sometimes they were even terrific. And viewer response to her had always been excellent. She got dozens of letters every week telling her how much she meant to them. But that seemed different to her. Mel Wechsler's shows were in another league, and she was so terrified her mouth was dry when she reached the gate. But the security guard smiled appreciatively at her. She was a pretty girl, except for the harsh black hair, and Mel noticed it too as she sat down across from him, crossing and uncrossing her legs, and clutching her purse as though it were a shield that would protect her from him. He was touched by how frightened she was. There was something so vulnerable about her, so innocent despite her age. It made you want to put an arm around her and tell her everything was going to be all right. But he also knew that it was exactly what the viewers were going to do. They were going to want to protect her from 'Eloise', and they were going to root for her. Jane Adams was exactly the counterpoint he wanted for Sabina Quarles. She was exactly what he'd had in mind, except for the black hair . . . he kept staring at her as they talked and then it suddenly came to him, and he smiled to himself as he leaned toward her with a gentle smile.

'May I ask you something very rude, Jane?'

'What's that?' Oh God, she thought to herself, even more terrified, he's going to ask me to take off my clothes, he's going to do something to me . . . he's . . . she blanched as he went on.

'Is that your own hair?'

She had forgotten about the wig. 'This?' She looked blank and then reached up to the touch the stiff black curls. 'Oh.' She blushed beet red. She was just like the girl next door, only a little older. 'No, it's not. I always work in . . . that is, on *Sorrows*, I . . .' How could she explain it to him as tears stung her eyes? That her husband had forbidden her to work years ago and she had had to have two identities so he wouldn't find out. . .

'Would you mind terribly taking it off?' He wondered if there was something wrong with her own hair, but he was startled as slowly she took off the wig, and sat in front of him, her own hair uncombed but beautiful, in what he could see was a beautiful and surprisingly natural red. 'Is that your own colour, Jane?'

She grinned at him. 'Yes, it is. I always hated it when I was a kid.' She shrugged, looking fourteen instead of thirty-nine and he wanted to whoop with joy. He had found his Jessica. She was perfect, Sabina, the sensual, powerful blonde, and Jane the sweet redhead everybody would love. The women would identify with her, because there was nothing threatening about this girl, despite her incredible figure and bright red hair, and the men would all want to go to bed with her, even the kids would fall in love with her, she was so damn likable. And he knew she could act, he had seen that on her reel. He had seen twelve of her shows in all, and she was good . . . she was better than that. . . . He was beaming at her, and she was smiling at him. He wasn't what she had expected at all. He wasn't tough or rude or mean to her, she wasn't even frightened of him now. She could imagine being friends with him. She could imagine a lot of things. She could even imagine being in love with him . . . if it weren't for Jack, of course . . . he looked as though he would have been great with kids . . . she thought of a lot of things as she sat looking at him, and he sat back in his chair, admiring her hair.

'You know, you're absolutely beautiful, Jane.' He was admiring her professionally, seeing what they could make of her on the show. There was nothing personal about the remark but she blushed anyway.

'I've always thought of myself as plain.' And she was, in a way. She had a clean, all-American-beauty face with beautiful even teeth, and big blue eyes, and a pale stardust of freckles that even her makeup didn't hide. And on her they didn't look incongruous, they looked nice. That was the thing about Jane Adams, she looked nice, and sexy, and as though you wanted to be her friend, but she looked as though she could have been fiery too. He was going to bring that out in her. He was going to do a lot of things with Jane. Including have her dressed beautifully. François Brac would know just what to do with her, and although her wardrobe wasn't going to be as extensive as the one they'd planned for 'Eloise', François was committed to dressing the other women too, and Jane would look fabulous in his clothes . . . in a fur . . . in an evening dress . . . Mel was squinting as he looked at her.

'How did you feel about the script, Jane?' He smiled at her again. He had no real qualms about that, but he wanted to hear what she thought of it. She was a pro in the world of soap opera, and daytime was not so totally different from night, except for a little more melodrama perhaps.

'I fell in love with it.'

'Zack Taylor is going to be the male lead.' He saw the look in her eyes, and knew every woman in America was going to look just like that, as though she would fall out of her chair at the sight of him. 'We settled it last night. And Sabina Quarles has agreed to play Eloise.' A private look came to his eyes that Jane didn't recognise. 'We have a young actor, Bill Warwick, lined up as Sabina's son, he's very good.' His eyes questioned her, and this time she paled. 'And what about you, Jane? How would you feel about playing Jessica?'

She couldn't tell him . . . but she had to . . . but then he would want to know why she had come. And why had she? He would think she was playing games with him and he'd be furious. That kind look in his eyes would disappear, and the very thought terrified her. 'I . . . I don't know . . . I . . . I'm not sure I'm ready for it.'

'It's not very different from what you've done, and I think you are ready, Jane. So does Lou. We had a long talk this morning before you came in to see me.'

Lou was pushing her. The bastard. And he knew she couldn't take the part. Why had Lou let it go this far? 'I'll have to think about it.'

'We want you very much, Jane. Very much.' He quoted the figure he had mentioned to Lou and she got so pale her freckles stood out. Half a million bucks . . . my God . . . what she could do with that . . . and Jack crying all the time that they spent every dime he made . . .

'I . . . I'm very flattered, Mel.'

'Don't be. You're worth every penny of it.' Oh God. Her name would be mud when she turned him down. 'Now, you give it some thought, and I'll expect to hear from you.' He smiled at her and stood up, and walked out of his office with her, his arm around her shoulders, feeling brotherly, warm. He was amazed at the effect the woman had on him. He wanted to tell her to go home and he would take care of everything. 'I'll give Lou another call.' And when he did he added another two hundred thousand. But Jane didn't even care. She was so blinded by the experience of meeting Mel and all he had said to her that she hit a parked car on her way out of the studio and crumpled her front fender. She left a note on the windshield of the other car with trembling hands and drove home, grateful that no one was there when she got in. She wasn't even thinking about the car. She was just thinking about Mel and the series she couldn't do. She hated answering the phone when it rang, she knew who it was going to be and she was right. It was her agent.

'He was crazy about you. He even upped the price.'

She was near tears as she sat down, her black wig in her hand. She had almost forgotten it on the seat of the car. 'I can't do it, Lou. But it was wonderful.'

'Screw wonderful. It's the biggest offer you'll ever get, the biggest show anyone's ever going to do.' He didn't remind her that she was thirty-nine years old and this was a hell of a break for her. 'You've got to do it, Jane.'

'I can't.'

'God damn it, why not?' But he knew. And he was sick of hearing it. 'I know, I know, because of Jack. Christ, tell him about the money, no man can resist that, no matter how he feels about Hollywood.'

'He won't care.' Although for once she wasn't entirely sure. Seven hundred thousand dollars was a hell of a lot of money to turn down, for anyone, and he didn't make anywhere near that in his father's brokerage house. He made a hundred thousand every year, and he thought that was a lot. But her old salary had been easier to conceal, she had explained it as investments she made on her own. But this was impossible. No one could make that much on investments. Not even Jack.

'I won't let you give this up.' Lou was firm.

There were tears in her eyes when she spoke again. 'I don't have any choice.'

'If you turn this down, you're out of your mind. Now I want you to talk to him. Tell him you want to do this . . . tell him I'll kill you if you don't . . . tell him anything, and then call me tomorrow. I told Wechsler we'd get back to him by the end of the week.'

She knew there was no point arguing with him, and she was dying for the part, but she couldn't imagine explaining it to Jack. She could imagine it even less when he came home that night and yelled at her for what she'd done to the car. He'd had too much to drink and he was furious. He even threatened to take the car away and make her drive the Volvo wagon they had for the kids.

'Christ, you can't even do that right, can you, Jane?' He was always belittling her, but lately he did it in front of the kids, which made it even worse. And they joined in the attacks these days, as though it was all right to yell at her, because their father did, but she could never convince him of that. She had tried explaining to him that it destroyed the girls' respect for her when he treated her like that in front of them. And Alexandra was proving it now looking at her with eyes of ice, and then she turned to her dad. 'Can I have Mom's car?'

'That's not a bad idea.' He was always spoiling her, and making a fool of Jane, as though she weren't as bright as her own kids. She hadn't noticed it as much when she was doing *Sorrows* every day. She got so much satisfaction out of that that somehow the rest of her life didn't matter as much, the problems anyway. But now everything stood out in sharper relief. 'You drive better than your mom any day, Alex.' He smiled at their youngest child then. 'And Alyssa does too.'

He complained about the dinner after that, and asked

her why she didn't cook something he could eat, and he stormed out of the house afterwards, furious, supposedly to play tennis with a friend while it was still light, but she suspected that he was doing something else. He smelled even boozier when he got back and he wasn't wearing his tennis clothes. There were times when Jane even wondered if he cheated on her, hard as that seemed to believe, given what he did to her. But he didn't lay a hand on her, he just berated her again for the damage she'd done to the car, and called her a 'dumb cunt', and as he said the words she could feel something snap inside. She had taken enough abuse from him over the years, and the truth was that that was what he thought of her. He thought of her as a piece of meat he had bought years before and could use as he chose. And she didn't want to be used any more, not by him, or by anyone. Not even by her girls, who had treated her like dirt that night after listening to Jack do the same.

'Don't talk to me like that,' she snapped. It was the first time she had said that to him.

'Like what?'

'Don't call me names.'

'What, a cunt?' He smiled evilly. 'That's what you are, isn't it?' He was drunker than she'd realised and she decided not to argue with him. She went into the bathroom and closed the door, and got into the shower, thinking of the show, and Mel, and everything Lou had said, when suddenly Jack yanked open the shower door and stood staring at her. 'Get out of there.' She looked stunned, wondering what had got into him. He was worse than usual, as though he was trying to prove a point to her.

'I'm taking a shower.' Her voice sounded calm, but she was furious with him. He was keeping her from the only thing she wanted in the world, and he had for years. She had had to sneak around for close to eleven years while she worked, instead of being proud of it, and now if she listened to him, she'd give up the opportunity of her life. 'I'll be right out.'

'Get out now.' He grabbed her arm, and his shirt was instantly drenched but he didn't seem to care.

'Let go of me.' Her voice was dangerously calm, and he yanked her so hard she almost slipped, and pulled her arm away. 'Stop it, Jack!'

'Fucking cunt!' He said the words again, and pulled her out of the shower, slamming her into the sink, holding her arms wide in his tight grasp, and grinding his knee into her crotch. 'You owe me one for smashing up the car today.'

'I don't owe you anything.' She spoke in a quiet, even voice, which belied the way she felt. 'Leave me alone.'

He laughed and grabbed her hard where her legs joined. 'I own you, and don't you ever forget that, bitch.' And with that he turned and walked out, and she stood trembling in the bathroom watching his retreating back. She wanted to scream at him but she didn't dare. He didn't own her. No one did. But the truth was, he thought he did. He thought he had bought her with his respectability, and his gift of life as the wife of a stockbroker. He didn't understand anything.

Jane dried herself off, and slipped on a robe before walking into the bedroom. He was sitting in bed, watching TV, his clothes in a heap on the floor. He always left his things like that. She did everything for him, that was what perfect wives did, she thought, and for the first time in twenty years, she admitted to herself that she hated it. She was tired of being a perfect wife, perfect hostess, perfect lay. She was suddenly tired of all of it.

'I have to talk to you, Jack.' He clicked to another channel and paid no attention to her. She sat down in a chair across the room from him, far from his grip, from his hands, and she watched, terrified at what he would say, but knowing she had to say it anyway. 'I have to talk to you.'

'What about? You going to pay for the car?' He never even looked at her.

'No. I've been offered a part on a television show.'

'So? Big deal.' It was almost as though he didn't hear.

'I want to do it.'

He didn't answer for a long time, and then he looked at her. 'What did you say?' There was nothing but contempt in his voice, and she noticed that his blond, good looks had faded over the years. He was not as handsome as he had once been. And he looked mean so much of the time now.

'I've been offered a part in a television show, a very important one.' She repeated for him.

'How do you know? Who offered it to you?' He had forbidden her years before to even call Lou any more.

'That doesn't matter.' She suddenly felt her heart quail at the thought of facing him. He was frightening sometimes. 'I want to do it, Jack . . . it would mean a lot to me . . .'

'Are you out of your mind? I told you, all that ended when you married me. Or do you want to go back to sleeping with directors and producers again?' It was an unkind blow and they both knew it wasn't true. At least she did, she always wondered what Jack had believed.

'I never did.'

'Well, you're not going back. You can't have that crap and be married to me.'

'This isn't crap. It's a big show. Mel Wechsler is producing it.'

'When did all this come about? What have you been up to, Jane?' He spoke to her like a truant child, but at least he was talking to her.

'Today.'

'Then how do you know so much about it?'

She didn't dare tell him she'd been to see Mel. 'My old agent called.'

'I told you not to talk to him.' Jack's eyes went back to the TV. 'Just forget it. That's all. Tell them to go to hell.' There was no talking to him, and she sat wondering what to say next when their daughter knocked and walked in.

It was Alexandra, holding an armload of laundry with a look of disdain. She dumped it on Jane's lap and almost spat her words at her. 'You didn't do any of my ironing today.'

'I had other things to do.' Jane rolled it up and handed it

back to her. Things were suddenly changing in Jane's mind. She wasn't going to take any more abuse from any of them. 'I'll get to it when I can.'

'I have nothing to wear.' It was an angry whine and Jane stood up. Enough was enough. It was the first time she had felt that way in years, instead of beaten down by all of them.

'You have a closet full of clothes. I'm sure you'll find something in there.'

'Why don't you iron the kid's clothes? You have nothing else to do right now.' It was eleven o'clock at night and she still wanted to talk to him, not that there seemed much hope of it now.

'I'll do it tomorrow.' Jane suddenly looked tired and depressed. It was like living among enemies sometimes, especially when they all ganged up on her, as they so often did, as they were now. Why did they do this to her?

Jack looked at her angrily. 'Do it now.'

'Thanks, Dad.' Alexandra looked at him adoringly. 'Can I take Mom's car to school tomorrow?'

'I have to get it fixed.' He looked annoyed again, and then glanced at his wife. 'But you can have it as soon as I get it out of the shop.' It was another slap in Jane's face, and she'd had all she could take from him. She took the bundle of Alexandra's clothes and went out to the kitchen alone. She got out the ironing board and the iron. They had a cleaning woman three times a week, but she didn't iron as carefully as Jane did. She had spoiled them all and now she was paying the price, but she was suddenly sick of it. All of it. And all of them.

It took her an hour, and when she got back to their room, Jack was asleep with the television on. She turned it off and stood staring at him for a long time, and then slipped quietly into bed, thinking of Mel and how kind he had been.

The next morning Jack left before she woke up, and Alexandra took the Volvo wagon when she went to school. Jack had taken her car to the shop, and the keys to his own car and she was trapped at home, like a naughty child. And she was suddenly sick of that too. She was sick of everything, and suddenly the money Wechsler was offering sounded wonderful to her. And so did the show. She decided to take her life in her hands, and call Lou. It meant too much to her to give it up. And for what? To take more abuse from her family? Maybe once they got over the shock, they'd respect her more. There was always that possibility, and Lou was right, Jack would get over it. He had no choice.

With trembling hands she picked up the phone and dialled, and in a moment Lou came on. She was so nervous, she could hardly get out the words.

'Well?' He held his breath.

'Tell Wechsler I accept.'

Lou Thurman gave a shriek. 'Hallelujah, baby! You had me scared for a while.'

'Me too.' She smiled. Her hand was still shaking like a leaf.

'You're going to be the biggest there is, you know that, don't you?'

'I'm just looking forward to the work.'

'I'll call you this afternoon.'

He didn't have time, but his flowers arrived, and so did Mel's, two huge bouquets. One that sat in splendour in the dining room, the other devouring most of the front hall. They were beautiful, and she was scared out of her wits about what she would tell Jack, but for the first time in her life she felt sure of herself, and strong, and very, very good.

10

Mel Wechsler looked at his watch as the intercom buzzed. He was expecting someone, and he was in a good mood. Jane Adams' acceptance of the role of Jessica put the show in even better shape, and he had a feeling this girl was going to be good too. She didn't have a great deal of experience, but he had seen her reel, which consisted mostly of commercials and a few small parts, but with a little coaching she would grow, and she had exactly the look he had in mind for Tamara, Sabina's daughter and Jane's niece. And he was startled by her when she walked in. She was strikingly beautiful, with long, silky jet black hair, and big green eyes. She was also smaller than he had expected her to be, but she had a presence about her that one couldn't miss. According to her bio, she was twenty-four, but she didn't even look that, which was perfect. The role of Tamara Martin called for a girl of nineteen. She had been an afterthought in Eloise's life and she hated her mother and had gone to live with her aunt, and she would make trouble for all of them eventually. She looked capable of it, as she sat down across from him. She looked capable of a lot of things, and her voice was rich and smooth as she sat back in her seat with poise. She was excited to be there, and she was much more composed than Jane had been. Mel suspected this girl would go far, and he was willing to help her along, with the biggest role of her career.

'Miss Smith, tell me something about yourself.' He didn't have to be gentle with her as he had been with Jane. This girl could take care of herself, but she also had a sparkle in her eyes, and he liked that. She looked as though she could be funny and mischievous, and that pleased him too.

'I'm an only child, I come from the East, and I've been out here for two years.' He hadn't realised that, and given that, she had done quite a lot of work.

'What training have you had?'

'I studied drama at Yale.' That impressed him more than he showed. He had always been impressed by people who went to important eastern schools, and he suddenly began to wonder who she really was, beyond Yale, beyond the two years in Los Angeles. One sensed a lot more about Gabrielle Smith and he wanted to know it all, but she was cautious about what she said. There was very little personal information in the data she gave.

'Where in the East before that?'

She hesitated for a beat. 'New York. I went to school there.' She didn't tell him she had also gone to school in Switzerland too, and spoke perfect French, and had gone to one of the best prep schools in New England before attending Yale. There was a lot she didn't tell Mel, a lot she didn't tell anyone in Los Angeles.

'What's your family like?'

She smiled, and wondered why he asked her that. 'Very nice. I get along fine with them.'

'They must be very proud of you.'

She smiled again, noncommitally. She didn't tell him that her parents had been heartbroken over her choice. Her father had hoped she would go on to law school after all, her mother wanted her to get married. But she had her own dreams, and she had been firm with them.

'Have you read the script, Gabrielle?'

'I have. It's the best thing I've ever read.' She grinned, the mischief peeking through. 'And I'm so glad you called me instead of someone else.' He told her who the rest of the cast were and she was visibly impressed. 'I did a commercial with Bill Warwick once, and he's good, very professional.'

'So are you. I liked your reel very much.'

'Thank you, sir.' There was something about the way she

said the words, and he wondered about her as he looked at her, and decided to try again.

'Gabrielle, who are you really? I get the feeling you're holding out on me. You don't fit into the classic mould out here.' And he liked that about her. He liked it very much, but he wanted to know more.

'Does it matter?'

'It might. Are there any secrets you want to share with me?' Only if the job rested on it. That was the bitch of it. She had never told anyone. And she wasn't going to tell him now.

'No, sir.' She looked pleased, and he liked her. She was a nice girl, wholesome and beautiful. She was perfect for the show. They all were. He had the perfect cast now. Sabina, Zack, Jane, Bill, and now Gabrielle. She was still praying she'd get the part as he smiled at her.

'We go on location in New York on December 6th. Any problem with that Gabrielle?'

'Not at all.' And she knew her parents would be thrilled. She could spend Christmas with them. If she got the part. The big if. 'How long will you be there?'

He smiled. 'Four to six weeks.' And then he decided to share the good news with her. Why wait and play games? 'And it's not "you", Gabrielle, it's "we". I hope you'll be there too.' Her eyes grew wide and she really did look like a child as she suddenly leapt to her feet and stared at him.

'You mean I've got the job?' She looked incredulous, as though it couldn't possibly be happening to her.

He laughed. 'I do. You're a fine actress, Gabrielle, and you got the part because of it.'

'Wow!' She came around his desk and threw her arms around him, giving him an enormous kiss on the cheek and then standing back as he grinned. 'Thank you, Mr Wechsler. Thank you!' She pumped his hand, and he walked her to the door, assuring her that they would be calling her agent by the following day. And he watched her go, as she bounded down the stairs. He couldn't hear her, but as she'd reached

93

the pavement outside, she gave a leap in the air she learned in ballet, and let out a victorious whoop of joy. She'd done it! She had the biggest part of her career! Gabby Thornton-Smith was on her way.

11

'Who are those from?' Jack Adams eyed his wife suspiciously as he walked in the front door and saw the arrangement sitting there.

There was a long pause as Jane looked at him. She had been rehearsing the words in her head all afternoon, and suddenly she couldn't remember any of them. She knew what she had to say, but it was even harder than she had been afraid it would be.

'I asked who they were from.' She never got flowers from anyone but him, and he hadn't given her flowers in the past ten years.

'They're from Lou.'

'What for? Did you tell him to go screw himself about that part?'

Slowly, she shook her head. It was the hardest thing she'd ever done, but she also knew, deep in her heart, that she was doing the right thing. They would all treat her differently after this. Jack, and the kids. They'd respect her now. She was sure of it. And more importantly, she'd respect herself.

'That's what you told him, isn't it?'

'No, it's not.' She looked beautiful as she said the words, but Jack didn't care, and Jane herself wasn't aware of it. 'I told him I would.'

'You did *what?*' He looked as though he'd been slapped.

'I told him I'd take the part.' Her voice was stronger now. 'I know how you feel about it, Jack . . . but it's important to me. Very important to me, in fact.' With every word, she felt victory, and he looked at her in disbelief, as though unable to believe what he was hearing from her.

'Do you remember what I told you about that?' They were still standing in the small entrance hall, and the perfume from the flowers seemed to envelop them. Jane could hardly breathe as he looked at her angrily. 'Do you remember my telling you that it was either Hollywood or me? Do you remember that?' As always, he spoke to her as though to a very stupid child.

She nodded miserably. 'I do but . . . Jack, this isn't like that. This is an important part on a major show—'

He cut her off. 'Who'd you screw to get it, Jane?'

'No one.' She looked at him unhappily. 'They called me out of the blue.' It was almost true, though she knew that one day she'd have to tell him about her part on *Sorrows* too, but there was time for that later on.

'Why did they call? Because they heard you were an easy lay?'

She started to cry and turned away from him. 'Don't say things like that. Jack . . . please let me do this.' She turned imploring eyes up to him, and he pushed her away from him and shoved past her into the living room, only to see another enormous bouquet in the dining room beyond. He stalked into the bedroom then, yanked open the closet door and threw a suitcase on the bed, as Jane hurried after him. 'Jack, please . . . please listen to me.' She knew she had to tell him she'd give up the part, but it wasn't fair of him. And it was too high a price to pay for the little happiness he gave her in return. 'Please . . .' She started to sob and he was shouting at her, as the girls came out of their rooms to see what was going on.

'Your mother's going back to Hollywood, to sleep with all the producers and directors there, and I'm leaving her,' he shouted at them, as they both began to cry. 'I'm leaving her because I refuse to be married to a Hollywood whore.' And yet he expected her to be a whore to him, any time of night and day, without a kind word, after all the indignities and brutalities he'd put her through, and twenty years of taking it because she thought she owed him that, because he gave her a nice house and three kids and respectability. Well, to hell with him. She slammed the bedroom door so the girls

96

couldn't hear what was going on, but they could anyway. And Jane was livid now.

'Stop saying things like that! I've been faithful to you for twenty years, and I was never an easy lay, *never!* Do you hear me, Jack? I want my career again, some recognition, a little respect . . . a feeling of accomplishment before I'm too old to care and you drive me into the ground for the last time . . . is that so much to ask? Is that so wrong?' He didn't even answer her, he just threw an armful of ties and shirts and underwear into the bag, grabbed two pairs of shoes and his tennis clothes, and slammed the bag shut again, zipping it up and then scooping an armful of suits out of the closet, before yanking the bedroom door open again. He looked at her with complete disdain and she wondered if he'd been drinking again as he spoke to her.

'I'm calling my lawyer, Jane. And since you have your own career, you won't be needing anything from me.' How could he think of that? What did it matter now? He was flushing twenty years down the can, their whole life, their marriage, empty as it may have been. But it meant nothing to him. None of it. The girls clinging to him as he made his way down the hall with his clothes in his arms, they begged him not to go. Alexandra even went so far as to ask him to take her along, as he turned back to Jane with a vicious look. 'See, that's what they think of you. They don't want to live with a whore any more than I do.'

'Stop calling me that!' She advanced on him, but the two girls were between her and Jack, and Alex screamed at her.

'Stay away from him! . . . stay away from all of us! I hate you! . . . I hate . . .' She was still sobbing when Jack slammed the front door and drove off. A moment later both girls locked themselves in their rooms, and Jane was left alone again, with her own thoughts, her broken dreams, and a trail of ties and socks that Jack had left behind him down the hall. She picked them up as she walked slowly back to their room, thinking of all that had happened there. The times he'd ravaged her, the abuses she took from him constantly . . . and now he'd walked out on her . . . all because of the part in *Manhattan*, or was there more to it than that? She wondered if he'd been waiting for the opportunity for a long, long time.

The girls didn't come out of their rooms again that night, even though Jane pleaded with them, knocking softly on their doors at regular intervals. She left their dinner wrapped in tinfoil in the oven, and went back to her own room alone. There was no one to talk to, no one to call, and there was no comfort from the girls. He'd seen to that. Just like he'd seen to everything. She sat wondering if what she was doing was worth the price she was paying for it. She thought of calling Lou and telling him she couldn't take the part. But she had a right to it . . . didn't she? . . . She lay down on her bed in all her clothes that night, and sobbed herself to sleep, wondering what the answers were.

12

The invitation reached each of them on precisely the same day. The main body of the card was engraved at Tiffany on creamy white, with a narrow edge of gold, and a simple script. *Mel Wechsler requests the pleasure of your company for . . . on . . . at . . .* with the address of his home in Bel Air. And his secretary had carefully written in each name, and eight o'clock, and at the very bottom in small script, just as he had instructed her to, *to meet your fellow members of the cast.*

She had called Chasen's at the same time, and ordered his favourite menu for them. Steak, chili, small roasted potatoes, asparagus with hollandaise, with hors d'oeuvres first, and plenty of caviar. There was a rich chocolate fudge cake for dessert, with ice cream and chocolate sauce. It was good, simple fare, and it appealed to everyone. In all, there would be five guests and Mel. He had briefly thought of inviting a few friends, and then decided not. It was best to let them get to know each other, without outsiders looking on. They were the five main stars of the new show, and he wanted them to make friends. It would be important to the show, and he wanted everything to go as smoothly as possible. He had been meeting with the network all week, and everything was set there. All of the contracts had been signed, there were no more wrinkles to work out with the stars, François Brac was expecting Sabina in Paris in two weeks, and everything was set to go. The supporting actors were being hired, the auditions were in full swing, and an item had been leaked to the press, mentioning who the stars of *Manhattan* would be. And Mel was pleased with all of it. Extremely pleased, he acknowledged to himself as he left the office that day. He wanted to go home to oversee the dinner arrangements himself. He wanted to make sure the house looked just right, and the atmosphere was what he had in mind. He had had his secretary invite everyone in black tie, just to set the mood for them, besides it was always more fun to get dressed up, especially for the girls.

And when he got home he was satisfied with everything. Chasen's always did a bang-up job, and his housekeeper had organised everything. He even had time to take a swim and lie by the pool for a while. And he knew that if he fell asleep Maria would wake him up in plenty of time to dress.

He wasn't the only one sleeping that afternoon. Bill had been so nervous all day that he'd gone jogging in the hills, come home and taken a shower, and fallen asleep lying stark naked on the bed in the little cottage, with Bernie stretched out on the floor nearby, panting in the warm September afternoon, and standing guard over him. He only wagged his tail when Sandy came in; he never greeted her with the same enthusiasm he greeted Bill. But he felt no need to bark, he knew who she was and that she was welcome there, although she hadn't been back since the morning she had come to take her clothes several weeks before. She stood for a moment, watching them, not sure whether to wake him or not, and then gently he stirred. Then, as though he realised there was someone in the room, Bill sat up suddenly and stared at her, not sure if he was dreaming or if she was really there.

'Hi, there. . .' She looked even worse than she had three weeks before, and his heart went out to her. There was an ugly bruise on one cheek, and a fresh scar that ran into her hair.

'Where've you been?' Wherever it was, it hadn't been good, and he wondered for a horrified instant if someone had been beating her. 'Are you okay?' It was a foolish thing to ask. She was anything but, but at least she didn't appear to be completely loaded for a change, a little high perhaps, but no more than that, and she smiled at him and sat down on the edge of the bed. She was wearing clothes he didn't recognise and he wondered where she was living now, and he suddenly felt self-conscious as he realised he wasn't wearing anything. He reached for the towel he'd left on the bed and covered himself as she smiled at him.

'I hear you got the big break you've been waiting for.' He nodded, more concerned with her than himself. 'I'm happy for you, Bill.'

'Thanks.' She'd had her big break too, and screwed it up, but neither of them mentioned that. 'Where are you living now?'

'With friends on South La Brea. I'm okay.' It was difficult to believe, looking at her. She looked dirty and tired and ten years older than she was.

'I wish you'd put yourself in hospital.' He refused to give up on her. He felt as though he owed it to her, in memory of the good times, and also out of guilt because his life was going so much better now.

'I will one of these days, when I get the chance.'

'How about like right now?' He would have taken her there, anywhere, to any of the drug cures they both knew about. He just wanted to know she was all right before he moved on with his life. She'd been his wife, after all.

'I've got to be somewhere in a little while.' He knew she was lying to him and there was no point arguing with her. He had no control over her any more, in truth he never had. 'I just wanted to tell you how happy I am for you. Will you be moving to New York?'

He shook his head. 'We're just going on location for a month or six weeks, but not for a while. I'll be around.' He wanted her to know she could still call him, if she needed to. He was scared for her. She had entered a world that frightened him, and he was afraid of what would happen to her there.

'I guess you want to get a divorce one of these days.' But the truth was he didn't want that. He was afraid of the publicity now.

'There's no rush. I'm not going anywhere. Okay?'

'Sure.' She looked sadly at him, as though he represented

everything she'd lost and it tore his heart out just looking at her. She looked like a frightened, broken child. But he knew he couldn't make it right for her any more, he had never been able to do that. 'I just thought that now . . . with the show . . .'

'Never mind.'

She looked at him sorrowfully. 'I didn't want to take you down with me. I figured you were better off this way, that's why I haven't called.' She had wanted to explain that to him, and he understood. He figured that was why she hadn't been back. He wrapped the towel around his waist and stood up, and the contrast between them was pitiful. She was so thin, so sick, so pale, and he looked so young and healthy and strong and alive.

'Can I fix you something to eat?' She shook her head. She was living on candy bars and cigarettes, she had no appetite any more. All she needed was a fix, she didn't care about the rest. Food didn't even look good to her. And the irony was that his fridge was full now. They were paying him a quarter of a million dollars for the first year. He had never dreamed of making anything like that. His fridge was going to be full for a long, long time. And it saddened him that she wouldn't be around for the good times. It was all over between them now, but he had to remind himself of that as he looked down at her, sitting on the corner of his bed. 'Do you need anything? I can . . .' He started to offer her money, and then realised it would only wind up in her arm, and knowing the same thing and not wanting to take it from him, she forced herself to shake her head, and then slowly she stood up.

'I told you . . . I'm fine. . .' His eyes filled with tears as he looked at her, and then gently, he reached out to her.

'Sandy, stay here . . . I'll help you clean up. I swear. You can do it if you want.'

'No, I can't.' She smiled sadly at him. 'Not now. It's too late for me. This is your time, not mine.' She was twenty-five years old and she acted as though her life were over. It was terrible, and he had to turn away so she wouldn't see him cry. He didn't want to lay that trip on her. There was no point guilt-tripping her out. She had her own life to lead. That was the way she wanted it, and maybe she was right.

'It can be your time again, anytime you want it to be. Just remember that. All you have to do is clean up.' *All* you have to do . . . no small task . . . they both knew that . . . but not impossible . . . she knew that too. The trouble was she didn't want to clean up any more.

She walked over and touched his arm, so gently he barely felt her hand, like a little bird, lighting on his arm. 'Take care of yourself.' She reached up and kissed his cheek, and then walked quickly out the door. He could hear her beat-up shoes on the pavement outside, and he forced himself not to go after her. He stood alone in the cottage, tears rolling down his cheeks, terrified he'd never see her again, and whispered softly, 'Goodbye, sweetheart.' And after she left, he was in no mood to go anywhere.

In Pasadena, Jane spent the afternoon at the hairdresser. This was a big day for her. She was going to meet the rest of the cast. She had been looking forward to it since the invitation arrived, and she had gone to Saks and bought a white beaded gown, and then almost returned it, deciding it was too showy after all. But it looked so fabulous on her that the saleslady had talked her into keeping it.

The girls weren't home from school yet when she got in, with her hair impeccably done, and her nails lacquered bright red. She took the dress out of the closet and looked at it, worrying about it again, as she did about everything, but to hell with it, she thought as she ran her tub. She still had hours before she had to leave, and Mel was sending a car for her so she didn't have to drive all the way in. This was just the beginning, she knew. It was like being Queen for a day, only it was for a year, and maybe more, if the ratings were good. It was so exciting she could hardly stand thinking of it. And the only thing that dimmed the excitement for her was what Jack was doing to her. He was poisoning the girls' minds, and he had gone up to see Jason at UC Santa Barbara, and told him the same things. Jason had called her himself and begged her not to do the show, that it was just too upsetting to Dad. And Dad had called his attorneys and not only filed suit for divorce but offered to sell her his half of the house. He said she could afford it now, and since they had community property, she owed him that after all these years. And if she didn't want to buy the house from him, she'd have to get out. She had ninety days' 'grace' according to the letter she'd received, and he was refusing to take any of her calls when she tried to reach him, and she had finally given up. She had called an attorney of her own, it was difficult to believe it had come to this in a few short weeks. But Jack was serious. If she wanted to do the show, he wanted a divorce. She had thought more than once of giving it up, but she knew that if she did, she'd hate him forever afterwards, so there was no point to it. The marriage was irreparably blown. She was no longer willing to play the game with him any more, and she was looking forward to her new life. She hoped that eventually the kids would come around to understanding that she was a human being too, with feelings and needs. And all the things Jack said about her weren't true.

She didn't hear the front door open and close, or the footsteps in the hall as she stood in her underwear, waiting for the bath to fill, and she jumped when she saw him, as she turned around and turned it off.

'Jack . . . what are you doing here?' She hadn't seen him in weeks, since he'd come back for the rest of his clothes, and suddenly there he was, just standing there, staring at her, as though he had something to say to her.

'I came back to get something.' But she knew as well as he did that there was nothing left to get. He had taken it all weeks ago, and she wondered why he was there.

'Is everything all right?' She stood nervously watching him. There was an odd look in his eyes.

'I guess. I was going to call and talk to you anyway.'

'I haven't been able to get through to you.'

'I've been busy.' He shrugged, looking at her breasts as thought they were her eyes.

'I thought we ought to talk about things sometime, but . . .' She hated to say it to him, but she wanted time to get dressed peacefully, before the girls came home. 'Tonight isn't such a great time.'

He looked at her suspiciously. 'Why not?'

She hated to tell him, but there was no reason now to lie to him. 'The cast dinner is tonight.'

'What do you do? Try each other out and then see who does it best?' His eyes glittered evilly, and she realised then that he was a little drunk. That was a new one with him, this business of drinking all the time. He was impossible to deal with.

'It's just a dinner, that's all. Why don't I call you in the office tomorrow?'

'What for? To tell me how it was? What do I care? I know what you're like. . . .' He advanced on her and she took a step back, tripping over her shoes on the bathroom rug.

'Jack . . . stop . . . let's not start that again. We need to sit down and talk.'

'I don't need to sit down with you. I don't sit down with tramps.' The man was sick, and it was the first time she'd ever thought of it. His obsession with whores and tramps had gone too far finally.

'Why don't you just go now?' She spoke quietly. There was no point talking to him. But he didn't want to go anywhere.

'Why? Expecting someone?'

'Only your daughters. And I have to get dressed.'

'Don't bother. I've seen it all before.'

'Fine. Then why don't you just leave now?'

'I want to stay and see the girls.' He stood belligerently in front of her, his eyes hard with deeply etched lines on either side.

'You can see them some other time.'

'You can't throw me out. This is still my house. It's still *mine.*' He took a step toward her and she held her ground. 'And so are you. I can take you anytime I want.'

'Let's not talk about things like that.' She was suddenly afraid of him and she didn't like being alone with him. He was like a crazy man. And he had sensed her terror now. He took another step closer and grabbed her arms.

'It's true, you know . . . I own you . . . just like I always did . . . my very own little cunt . . .' She hated it when he talked like that. She hated everything about him now, and wondered for how long she had. But just as she thought of it, he yanked her arms and pulled her into the other room towards the bed.

'Come on, Jack . . . please . . .'

'Please what? Please give it to you like I always did, you little tramp? That's all you ever were, just a piece of skirt I kept around for the convenience of it . . . I never cared about you, did you know that . . . did you, you bitch?' She wondered why he hated her so much, as he slammed her onto the bed, and laid his full weight on top of her, pinning her down as he tore off her bra, and then forced down her pants. It was crazy, she had been married to him for twenty years and he was raping her. It didn't make any sense.

'Jack, *stop!*' She was crying now, and she could hardly breathe he was so heavy on top of her, pushing at her breasts, as he unzipped his pants, and forced himself inside her. She wondered how he could always manage that. Maybe it excited him to know how unwilling she was. 'Please . . .' She was begging him and he was biting her, she could feel blood in her mouth as he bit her lip, and then moved backward to bite her breast until she felt a trickle of blood there too, and he was pushing into her, riding her, hurting her, and at the same time squeezing her breasts, and then suddenly with tremendous force he slapped her face, and started beating her, and all at once he was howling with ecstasy, coming at the same time. He pulled away from her roughly, and looked down at her, sobbing on their blood-smeared bed.

He stood back, zipped up his pants and sneered at her and the only word he said to her before he left was 'Whore.' He left her crying on the bed, and she heard his car speed away, but she didn't care about anything any more.

13

Bill Warwick was the first to arrive, looking as handsome as Mel remembered him, but sombre somehow, as though he had a great deal on his mind. He was perfectly groomed in his rented tux, and his blond hair looked like a golden crown, but there was something about his eyes that troubled Mel, as though he had seen the sorrows of the world. He made easy chitchat at the bar, asked for a Scotch on the rocks, and looked around with obvious awe. It was a beautiful house and Mel was happy there. It was tucked in high on a hill, looking out over Los Angeles, with a spectacular view and a huge living room with stone columns and stone floors. There were large modern paintings everywhere, a vast swimming pool just outside, and a formal dining room with a roof that could be electrically removed on warm nights, as it had been now.

'This is quite a place,' Bill said admiringly, thinking of his own tiny retreat, and then thinking, just as quickly, of Sandy's visit only that night. He wondered where she had gone, where she was living . . . who had given her the bruise and the scar . . . it was all so ugly and so sad. He could hardly keep from crying as he talked to Mel and waited for the others to arrive.

'You're looking very serious tonight.' Mel was a perceptive man, and his stars were always important to him. They meant a great deal to him, and everything to the show.

'Just excited I guess.' Bill passed it off. 'Seems like there's an awful lot to think about these days.' He smiled and Mel thought of the millions of women who would fawn over this young man in a year when they went on the air.

Zack Taylor arrived next, having driven himself in his open Rolls. He looked at ease and elegant and debonair, and very much at home. His own house was much larger than Mel's, and equally beautiful. They got into discussing gardeners, workmen, and contractors they had known, like old friends, as Bill stared at the view.

Gabrielle came next, wearing a peach-coloured chiffon dress that made her hair look like shining ebony as it hung down her back. Mel kissed her on the cheek when she arrived and escorted her down the steps, introducing her immediately to Zack, who stood nearby. They chatted for a moment about Greece, and how pleased they were about the show, and then Mel led her outside to meet Bill, who was standing admiring the view, and when he turned around, Mel was the first to see the look of sharp anguish in his eyes. Gabrielle looked much as Sandy would have, and had once before, when she was clean, only Gabby was much more beautiful, and infinitely more sophisticated and poised. But it was like a vision seeing her standing there, and it hurt him just looking into her eyes.

'Hello, Bill.' Gabrielle smiled at him, her eyes warm, her face a perfect cameo, with uplifted nose, and huge green eyes, sweetly carved mouth, and everything about her so delicate and beautiful, and her breeding having endowed her with such poise. 'I gather we're going to be brother and sister on the show.'

He barely spoke to her, and answered her in monosyllables before going back inside for another Scotch. She seemed unaffected by the slight and went back inside to talk to Zack. They had a long chat about a hotel they'd both been to in the Dolomites, when finally Jane arrived. She stood for a moment, at the top of the stairs as Mel chatted with Bill, and Gabrielle was engrossed with Zack. Jane looked like an exquisite bird about to take flight, her exotic bright red hair was in sharp contrast to the white beaded dress, and the richness of her figure took one's breath away. But it was the expression in her eyes that made one stare at her, and Mel was once again taken with the inexplicable desire to put his arms around her and tell her everything would be all right. She looked frightened and sensual and beautiful, and it was almost an act of sex just looking at her, and at the same time, he felt sinful looking at her like that. And then slowly, hesitantly, she came down the stairs, looking for Mel, and there was such relief in her eyes as he came to her side. None of her earlier torments showed, except for an ugly bruise on her left breast, which she had treated with ice before covering it with the spectacular dress she had worried about so much.

Her eyes were warm as she spoke to Gabrielle, almost as though she could have been a mother to her, and Mel congratulated himself silently for the choices he had made. She turned to Zack, who looked bowled over by her, almost too stunned to speak, and then he laughed at himself.

'That's quite a dress.'

'Thank you . . .' She blushed. 'I was afraid . . . I thought . . . I wasn't sure . . .'

Mel gently put an arm around her. 'You look fabulous, Jane. Except I miss the black wig of course.' They laughed and she felt more at ease, and he introduced her to Bill, and her warmth even brought him out of his shell a bit. The group grew more comfortable, sitting on his large white couches, all of them drinking champagne, except Bill, and then the door opened again, and there was no question at all who was the star. Sabina slinked down the stairs in a grey satin dress with her blonde mane framing her face, her eyes like those of a tigress on the prowl, and Mel's new diamond bracelet on her arm.

'Good evening,' the voice purred and she looked slowly around the room, as Mel smiled. She was already taking the role to heart, but it wasn't even that. The role was made for her. She looked down at Zack and held out a hand as he smiled at her.

'Miss Quarles . . .' He knew just how to handle her and they had met before.

'Hello, Zack.' She turned to Bill. 'I don't believe we've met. I'm Sabina Quarles.' She didn't need Mel for this, she was in full control, just as she always was, the entrance calculated, the dress perfect for the part, the eyes, the hair, the face. Jane felt like a bumpkin next to her and Gabrielle was fascinated. Sabina dismissed her with one glance, and then turned to Jane. 'So you are the sister I will love to hate.' All five of them laughed, and Jane smiled nervously at her.

'I've admired your work very much.'

'I'm afraid I don't know yours.' She turned to Mel, dismissing Jane, and accepted a glass of champagne. Her eyes were warm, but they gave nothing away. She wasn't foolish enough to let the others know she was sleeping with him. That was too important to her, and she was on stage now, for all of them.

They went in to dinner at exactly nine o'clock and he had seated them carefully. Sabina at his right, Jane at his left, next to Bill, Gabby beside him, and then Zack on Sabina's right. Zack played the game expertly. He was charming to his co-star, but Mel noticed that he was watching Jane for most of the night. He seemed fascinated by her, and her glances were warm. She seemed the only one able to draw Bill out, and he ignored Gabrielle almost totally, as did most of them. Only Zack was polite enough to speak to her, whenever Sabina was chatting with Mel. It was an interesting group, and he was curious to know what Sabina would have to say about all of them. All in all, despite a few tensions that arose, the evening went admirably. They would up drinking more champagne by the pool, as Sabina stood with the city like a glittering backdrop behind her, chatting with Zack, and occasionally watching Bill. She was barely polite to Gabrielle the few times they spoke, and Mel noticed that Gabby's attempts to talk to Bill were always rebuffed. Only Jane seemed able to talk easily with all of them. Despite her nervousness her innately motherly way warmed each of them, except Sabina, who commented cattily about her dress, causing Jane to apologise for it again. But Zack rescued her that time, artfully and deftly, while complimenting Sabina on the handsome bracelet on her arm. She seemed pleased that he had noticed it, and Mel was amused. He liked watching the interactions between each of them, and it worked, the only thing he was sorry about was that he sensed Gabrielle was not going to have an easy time. She was the ingenue, the least proven member of the team, and like vicious children, they were going to make her pay for it. He was also not upset about the friction between Sabina and Jane. Jane would learn to cope with it in time, as she gained self-confidence, and it would be good for the show to carry over a little of the story line that way. And Zack was enough of a gentleman to handle both of them. He wasn't quite as sure of Bill, but the boy could act, and that wasn't negligible. Whatever was bothering him would blow over eventually. Sabina seemed to like him, and that was important, and Jane liked everyone.

It was after midnight when they left, and Sabina was the first to go. She had got Mel's message just after dessert. He would meet her at her place after everyone was gone. She showed no sign of it as she kissed him on the cheek, whispered something to Zack and laughed, smiled interestingly at Bill, nodded at Jane, and ignored Gabby totally. And then, with a sweep of silver fox covering the grey satin dress, she left in Mel's car, as she had come. The star. It was fitting. The Queen is always the first to leave. And the last to arrive. And she had done both to perfection.

'My God, she's fabulous,' Jane whispered to Mel after she left. 'It's like watching royalty.' He laughed. Sabina played her part well, poor Jane, she needed a lot of self-confidence.

'That's the whole idea. Don't worry. The viewers will be just as taken with you. There's something for everyone in this show.' He smiled at all of them, and Gabrielle looked like a dark-haired angel standing near the pool. He wondered that Bill wasn't more taken with her. Had he been Warwick's age, but . . . to each his own, he thought to himself.

Zack was the next to leave, having offered both ladies a ride, but Mel had provided a limousine for each, so they were fine. They left on their own shortly after that, and Bill followed them, after shaking Mel's hand twice and thanking him for the opportunity to be on the show.

'Just relax and enjoy it, Bill. Is everything all right?' He was worried about him, but Bill insisted that he was fine. And he slid into the Porsche he had bought with his first check from the show, and heaved a sigh of relief. It had been an interminable evening for him. All he had been able to think about was Sandy and how she had looked that night. And that damn girl on the show . . . she looked so much like her . . . it could have been Sandy in her place, going to New York with him, if she had been clean. Just thinking about what she'd done to herself depressed him again. They could have had everything.

Jane leaned her head back on the seat of the limousine on the way home, thinking of all of them . . . Sabina . . . Zack . . . Gabby . . . Bill . . . they were all such strong, interesting people, she wondered how she'd ever fit in with them. Her breast throbbed where Jack had torn her flesh, and she found herself thinking of Mel, and those kind eyes of his. He looked as though he had seen a lot of life, and she felt as though they could be friends. She wanted to be friends with all of them. She liked Gabby a lot, Bill . . . and Zack was fabulous, but he'd probably fall madly in love with Sabina. God, she was incredible, that figure . . . those eyes . . . she closed her eyes as she thought of them, and when they reached Pasadena, and the driver opened the door for her, she was sound asleep in the back of the limousine.

14

'Well, what do you think of them?' Mel sat back against her white couch, and looked pleased. It was one o'clock, he had paid the caterers and locked up when they left, and then he had driven himself to Linden Drive where Sabina lived.

'They're quite a group.' Sabina was stretched out on the couch in the grey satin dress, still looking as she had at his house, only a little more relaxed. Her eyes danced as she reviewed the cast, and Mel laughed as she told him what she thought.

'Poor Jane is a mouse.' She laughed. 'And she'd better watch out, or I'll eat her alive ... grrmmpphh ...' She gently gobbled his neck and he laughed.

'Be nice to her. She's scared to death of you.' He wagged a fatherly finger at her and Sabina laughed evilly.

'I know. My God, she's got some figure. How old is she?'

'Thirty-nine.'

'I wonder how much she paid for it. All that can't be real. What's she done up to now, anyway?'

'Daytime soaps. She was on *Our Secret Sorrows* for ten years.'

'Oh my God. Not one of those.' She dismissed her with one hand. 'Bill Warwick is interesting. Wounded about something. A broken heart, I suspect. He's one of those brooding, passionate types, and probably very good in bed.' Mel looked less than pleased and she tweaked his cheek as she laughed at him. 'Don't worry, little boys aren't my style. He's too young for me, but that little ingenue looks like she has the hots for him. She's hiding something.' She said it with an instinct straight from her gut, but Mel shook his head. He was sure she was wrong. 'I doubt that very much.'

'Take my word for it. She is. I can tell. Maybe she's been sleeping with someone she shouldn't be.' She glanced up at Mel and frowned. 'It better not be you, my friend.'

This time he laughed. 'I'm not into the nursery school set either, my dear.'

'Good. And Zack Taylor is queer.' Mel almost fell off the couch as he stared at her.

'You mean as in homosexual?'

'Yes.' She looked smug.

'Now there, you're all wet.'

'The hell I am.'

'He's the hottest male lead in Hollywood, and I have never heard any rumours about him.'

She looked unimpressed. 'Then he's discreet. Believe me, I can tell. There's no chemistry there. No vibes. Nothing. He is polite, charming, and gay.'

'Sabina, you are full of hot air.'

She laughed at him and shrugged. 'Maybe I am, but I'd lay you odds I'm not. He's just very careful about who knows.'

'There's no such thing in this town. If he were, *everyone* would know.'

'Maybe I'm wrong, but I don't think I am.' Not that she cared. She was happy with Mel. Happier than she'd been in years.

'I hope you're right about Bill. I was worried about him tonight. He looked like a volcano about to erupt, and I don't want problems on the set.'

'Gabrielle will keep him in line. Either that or drive him nuts. Who is she anyway? She seems to have done an awful lot for a kid.' She'd overheard her talking about trips, Europe, archaeology, Palm Beach . . .

'She's probably just showing off, or maybe you're right. Maybe she's been travelling with someone.' He was amused at Sabina's analysis of everyone.

'Can she act?'

'Would I have hired her if she couldn't act?'

115

'No, my darling.' She kissed him generously on the lips and they both forgot Gabrielle. 'Now what about me?' she asked. 'How do I fit in all this?'

'You're the star. They were all dazzled by you tonight.' She loved hearing it and he didn't mind telling her. He was used to stars and the reassurance they needed constantly. Sabina needed less than most, but still . . . 'I thought they were all going to drop when you walked in.'

She threw back her head and laughed. 'I thought that poor woman was going to pee in her pants.' She meant Jane, and Mel understood.

'Sabina,' he chided her gently, 'be nice to her . . . she won't do you any harm. You can afford to be generous with her.'

'I don't have the patience for people like that.'

'She could be any of us. She's unsure of herself, and shy, and desperate to please.'

Sabina tossed her golden mane. 'I can't even imagine it. I told you, she's a mouse. I eat mice.' She kissed him again. 'Among other things.'

'You're a bad girl.' But he liked her just the way she was, tantalising him with her lips, and her body, and her eyes.

She set down her glass and unbuttoned his evening shirt. 'I missed you tonight.'

'What do you mean?'

'I felt silly playing games, pretending I barely know you . . .' But they both knew it was for the best, as her tongue darted across his bare chest and he closed his eyes, swept up by desire for her. He easily unbuttoned the grey satin dress. It undid on her shoulders, and with the release of the four buttons, he slid the evening gown down to her thighs, as he opened his eyes to look at her.

'My God, you're beautiful . . .' He spoke in hushed tones, wondering if he'd ever get used to her, or if he'd ever have the chance. He was hungry for her all the time, and as she stood up and the dress fell to the floor, he saw that she had been wearing nothing underneath. The very thought of how she had been sitting next to him all night suddenly made him feel weak, all that exquisite naked flesh so close to him, and now as she spread her legs to tantalise him, he leaned forward and expertly enchanted her with his tongue. She pressed his face between her legs, and moved rhythmically as she moaned, and he gently caressed her buttocks as he excited her more and more, darting his tongue in and out, making her beg for him, and then as she screamed, he undressed hurriedly, and lay down next to her on the thick fur rug in her living room. They lay there side by side as he excited her again, with his fingers, with his tongue, and then entered her, driving her to new heights until he met her there, and together they sailed into space as she screamed again, seemingly endlessly this time, until finally she lay spent in his arms, and he looked down at her, pleased, running his hands through her long, blonde hair.

Her voice was even deeper than usual when she spoke to him and looked up at him with a limp smile. 'They're going to ask me to move out, if we don't stop doing this.' He smiled.

'You can always move in with me, if they do.' He was hoarse with pleasure, and they lay together on the rug for a long time. They were a good match physically as well as in other ways. He wanted nothing from her, and she wanted very little from him. She already had what she wanted, the starring role in the show, and she would have had it anyway. But they enjoyed what they gave each other, and neither of them wanted anything more. No promises, no dreams, nothing to last an eternity. Just right now.

'Will you come to Paris with me, Mel?' She rolled over on her side to look at him, and she looked amazingly young.

'I'll try. I can't stay there with you for the whole three weeks, but I'll do what I can.'

'Good.' She smiled and closed her eyes. Life was being so good to her these days, and they lay side by side until the dawn, when he drove back to Bel-Air again.

15

Mel sent her to Paris on Concorde, and Sabina boarded it in Washington, D.C., with all the fanfare imaginable. Photographers, press, a new mink coat over her arm, a private gift from him. And she was met in Paris by a Rolls-Royce limousine, which drove her to the Plaza Athénée on the Avenue Montaigne, where he had rented a suite of rooms for her. There was an international press conference the next day, and then she was whisked away to her first series of fittings with François Brac. He was an intense little man with a moustache and grey hair and he had been dressing duchesses and film stars for thirty years. The wardrobe he had planned for Sabina was fit for a queen. She was delighted with almost all of it, and what she didn't like, she changed. Mel arrived the following week, also on Concorde, and he had rented his own suite of rooms, but he stayed with her every night. Only the chambermaids knew but there was no reason for them to tell anyone and, anyway, they were used to such things.

They had lunch at the Relais-Plaza or Fouquet's, and dinner at Maxim's, and the Tour d'Argent, and two nights in a row they stayed in bed making love and ordered dinner in their rooms. It was the most fabulous three weeks in her life, and she hated to go back to Los Angeles, but the fittings were done, and Mel insisted he had to get back. He had a lot of work to do, and so did she. Rehearsals were due to begin the following week, and in a month they were all leaving for New York. Life was very interesting these days. For Sabina anyway.

For Jane, it was sheer hell, and mostly drudgery. It was difficult to believe that she was going to be one of the stars of the biggest show on the air the following year. Waiting for rehearsals to begin, she had almost nothing to do. François

Brac's assistant had flown to Los Angeles to take her measurements, make sketches of her, take photographs, and then had gone back to Paris to create a wardrobe for her. But all of her fittings were scheduled to be in Los Angeles once rehearsals began and, in the meantime, she had nothing to do, except take care of her house and attempt to make friends with her daughters again. Which was to no avail. They wanted none of it. They didn't want to hear about the show, and they were threatening to move in with Jack, but Jane wouldn't hear of it. They were her daughters and they belonged with her. She wanted to work things out with them. And she also wanted Jack to calm down. But that was hopeless these days. He had come to the house to see her, and she had been prepared for him. She had found the pistol he had forgotten in his desk. He had always liked to have a gun around 'just in case' and he had forgotten it. But Jane had not. When he had come after her again, she had pulled the gun on him.

'And if you ever touch me again, I'll kill you. Do you hear that?' She had been crying, but calm, gulping sobs with each word, and he was furious, but he hadn't come back again. After that, she'd changed the locks. The papers had been filed, and she had three months left to stay in the house. She had refused to buy it from him. She didn't want anything from him. She didn't need him any more, and she was tired of being treated like a tramp. She wasn't a tramp, and never had been, and that was what she steadfastly continued to tell the girls. But he had poisoned their minds, and they didn't believe anything she said, although she was totally honest with them. And her son wouldn't even talk to her now. She even told them all about the show she had done for almost eleven years. And they were shocked. How could they not have known? How could she have lied to their father that way? She tried to explain that it was because she was afraid of him, because he didn't understand what was important to her. She tried to explain it all to them, but they were determined not to understand, and to torture her. They barely spoke to her, and after dinner every night they went to their rooms. She felt like an outcast in her own home, and it was a huge relief when Zack Taylor called and invited her to lunch one day. It felt like a reprieve, and a reminder of a better life in a different world. He offered to pick her up, but she said she would meet him in town. He suggested La Serre in the Valley for lunch, and Jane was thrilled as she hung up the phone. She bought a new dress, a sexy-looking knit dress in a flattering shade of green, and her figure looked remarkable as she put it on with brand-new high heels. She had had her hair cut recently, and she felt like a new woman as she walked into the restaurant, and almost laughed out loud as she saw people stare when he kissed her hello. Everyone knew who he was, and suddenly everyone wanted to know her. Zack introduced her to the headwaiter as his new co-star, and they both ordered white wine instead of drinks, and then they chatted about the show. She made him laugh with tales of Brac's assistant, his accent and his quirks, and his complaints about Americans.

'I wonder how Sabina fared over there with Brac himself!' He laughed at the thought and then shook his head. 'Although I suspect that she can take care of herself.' And so could he, he was so smooth that Jane couldn't believe he had invited her to have lunch with him. He was charming and elegant, he seemed to know everyone, and everyone knew him. She felt like Cinderella in a fairy tale. One day she was washing the kitchen floor and ironing for the girls, and the next here she was with one of the biggest stars in Hollywood.

'Some days I just can't believe this is happening to me.'

'You deserve every bit of it. You know I used to watch that crazy soap opera of yours. I just never realised it was you.'

Her eyes grew wider at what he said. 'You did?'

'I never would have recognised you without the wig.'

'That was the whole point.' She told him about Jack, and his refusal to let her work.

'How has he adjusted now? Pretty well?'

Jane hesitated for a moment and then decided to tell him the truth. 'He walked out on me when I took the part.'

'Are you serious?' Zack looked shocked.

'Yes.' She looked chagrined, but she was no longer as upset as she had been at first. It was beginning to dawn on her that she might be well rid of him. 'After twenty years. Maybe it's just as well. But it's kind of screwed things up with my kids. They all hold me responsible, and sometimes I feel guilty as hell for doing this, but I couldn't live a lie anymore for him. And, well . . . there were other things . . .'

'There always are.' He seemed to understand everything, and she was touched by his gentleness.

'Are you divorced, Zack?' Everyone was in Hollywood, at least once if not more. But he shook his head.

'No, I'm not. I've never been married. I'm a forty-six-year-old virgin.' He grinned and she laughed. That he clearly was not. He was the most desirable man in town. And she supposed that had made it too easy for him not to get tied down. She couldn't blame him. Why not? 'How old are your kids?'

'Jason is eighteen and at UC Santa Barbara, the girls are fourteen and sixteen' – she sighed – 'and very difficult these days. Jack has poisoned them against me.'

'They'll get over it. Wait till their mom is the hottest thing on TV. Their friends will be crawling all over them, and you'll start looking pretty good to them again. Kids are very vulnerable to that.' She wondered how he knew, and hoped he was right. It was unbearable living with them the way things were. But she refused to give them up.

He asked if she had seen the rest of the cast since their dinner at Mel's, and she said she had not. When Zack said he'd had lunch with Gabby the week before, Jane was disappointed. She realised that he was only trying to make friends with the rest of them, and probably not attracted to her. It had been foolish to hope that he was, a man like him after all. But he invited her to lunch again the following week, and asked where she was staying in New York. They had given him a choice between the Carlyle and the Pierre, and he thought he might prefer being uptown, and wanted to know what she thought.

She laughed. 'It all sounds good to me.' She told him she was going to have the girls meet her over the holidays, although her son refused to come. He was going skiing with his father. But she had insisted about the girls.

'Then stay at the Carlyle.'

'Will you be staying for Christmas too?' They were getting four days off, and she had no reason to come back, but he was vague and said he probably thought he would come home. She watched him carefully as they had lunch, he was incredibly good-looking and she wasn't sure why he had asked her out, to make friends, or for something more. But he didn't invite her out at night, and she was just grateful to have lunch with him. As she waited for rehearsals, life continued to be pretty bleak. And then suddenly, everything started to happen all at once: she was packing for New York; her wardrobe arrived from Brac; Mel and Sabina came home, although separately. And the girls went to stay with Jack for the duration of her trip.

The next thing she knew, she was on the plane with the rest of them and they were flying to New York and shooting was about to begin. There were sixty of them flying east, on a chartered flight, production assistants, technicians, actors, cameramen. There would be additional crew hired on in New York, but this was approximately half of them. They drank gallons of wine, and people sang and talked and began making friends, as Sabina chatted with Mel and Zack, ignoring the rest of them, while Jane talked to Bill. Gabby sat by herself despite Jane's attempts to draw her into their conversation. Bill was almost rude to Gabrielle as they flew east, and eventually Sabina borrowed someone's guitar and began singing filthy songs that made everyone laugh. This was a side of her they had never seen before. And when they landed they were all a little drunk. There were two buses for the crew, and three limousines for the rest of them. Jane was pleased to discover that she and Zack and Gabby and Bill were all staying at the Carlyle, while Mel and Sabina had opted for the Pierre.

Zack had dinner with Gabby and Jane in the hotel dining room but Bill preferred room service. He said he was tired and everyone forgot about him. After dinner they went to the Bemelmans Bar and chatted until almost one o'clock and then Zack urged them to get to bed. They had to be on location the next morning at six fifteen.

Gabby said she needed some air, and insisted on walking around the block alone. She said she knew New York, and finally Zack let her go, and rode up in the lift with Jane.

'Tired?' He looked solicitous and she smiled. She was crazy about him. As a friend. She no longer hoped for anything more than that from him. He obviously had other women in his life, and she liked just being his pal. He was someone who cared about what she thought, what she felt. For the first time in twenty years she was with a man who cared about her, even if he was only a friend. He made her feel good anyway.

She smiled up at him. 'I'm too excited to be tired. I'm not even sure I can go to sleep.' For them it was only ten o'clock, but she knew she'd regret it when she got up the next morning, if she didn't go to bed soon.

The call sheets had been distributed that day on the plane, telling them what scenes they'd be shooting the next day, and which actors were playing in what order. It was all new and exciting to Jane, she'd never been on location before.

'I think we're on first,' he reminded her. But they'd rehearsed the scene several times in Los Angeles, and they were both comfortable about it.

'Yeah, then you and Bill, Sabina, me and Gabby . . .' She had memorised it all and he smiled down at her and gently touched her cheek.

'You can relax . . . it's not going to go away . . . probably not for a very long time, knowing Mel. He only knows how to make hits.'

'I hope you're right.'

'You know I am.' The lift stopped on her floor and he got out with her and walked her to her door. 'This is just the beginning for you, Jane. Of a whole new life you deserve more than anyone I know.' She stopped outside her room and looked seriously up at him.

'You're the nicest man I know, Zachary.'

'No, I'm not.' He looked sad, and she was troubled by the look in his eyes, wondering what could cause him to look as unhappy as that. It was the first time she had seen him that way.

'Yes, you are. You've been there for me, when I needed a friend desperately.'

'I'm glad.' He looked gently down at her, then opened the door for her with her key. 'Now get some sleep, beautiful, or the Dragon Lady will eat you up tomorrow.' He laughed and Jane groaned. Sabina still scared the hell out of her.

'Don't say that. She'll hear you all the way down at the Pierre.'

'Never fear. She's got bigger fish to fry.' He had long since figured out that she was having an affair with Mel, but he wasn't one to talk. He had his own problems to worry about. And why not? If that was what she wanted, why the hell not? 'Good night, sweet girl.' Zack kissed Jane's cheek and a moment later he was back in the lift again thinking of people far away, and a distant time when choices had been made. But Jane kept coming to his mind again, and again, and when he got to his room, he called room service, and ordered a drink.

16

The first day of shooting was fraught with activity and everyone's nerves were taut. Horoscopes had been read. Superstitions were being catered to. Sabina had refused to make love with Mel the night before, for fear that it would leave her looking tired. Everyone had done all the quirky little things actors did when they first began shooting. In time they'd all relax, but not for a while yet.

The call sheets had been distributed the day before, showing that only four scenes were being shot, although some days there would be six, or even seven, or eight. But they had to get started. They were shooting at headquarters for IBM, in the lobby and on the twenty-seventh floor, and the view of New York stretched out behind them from upstairs was incredible. The first scene was to be shot in the lobby, between Zack and Jane, and she was terrified as she rehearsed her lines with him again. She had been over them a hundred times the night before, and she and Zack had rehearsed plenty of times in Los Angeles, but she was afraid she would freeze and forget everything.

'Relax,' he whispered, on his way to one of the trailers outside to have his makeup done. It was just after six thirty, and they had all arrived on time in three limousines. Even Sabina had come looking very professional in a black sweater and jeans. All the clothes for her scenes were hung in a separate trailer. She had her own wardrobe room, unlike Jane, whose clothes were hung from a pole that stretched between two windows in her trailer dressing room. Jane was wearing a white dress in her first scene, her hair had already been done, and she was wearing a huge plastic smock to protect her dress as the makeup woman finished her face. Zack had stopped in just for a minute to drop her a word of encouragement, and it cheered her just seeing him. He was always there when she needed him. He seemed to be there for everyone, which was rare for a star. Always friendly, always polite, never complaining, and yet somehow keeping his distance from everyone. Even after their lunches in Los Angeles, Jane felt as though she barely knew him, yet she liked him very much. And he was always so kind to her.

'More coffee, Miss Adams?' A production assistant came through to make sure everything was all right, and Jane could almost feel a hum in the air. She had caught a glimpse of Gabby and Bill. Gabrielle looked serious, and Bill, as usual, looked handsome but surly. She wondered what his problem was. It was obvious to everyone that he had one. He was getting to be known as the loner in their midst.

The actors were all listed by name and number on the call sheet, and Jane checked it again after she read her lines. She was number three, and she appeared in two of the four scenes, once with Zack, and once with Sabina and Gabby. That would be the toughest scene, it called for a confrontation, establishing who the three women were. Everything they were shooting that day was for the three-hour special the first night, but as the weeks progressed they would be shooting scenes from different shows, and always out of sequence. It was so different from shooting *Sorrows*, which aired live. There everything made sense, everything was always in order, and after all her years on the show, even if she forgot her lines, she knew how to improvise, and somehow the improvisations worked out better sometimes. Here, everything had to be precise, and each take had to be reshot until it was perfect.

Outside, in a huge truck more coffee was brewing, and a gigantic buffet breakfast was laid out for everyone. But Jane hadn't been able to touch any of it. She was too nervous to eat, although she had seen Gabby and Mel go into the trailer along with some of the crew. The food was being done by the best location caterers in New York. Mel spared nothing for his crew and cast. That much was obvious from the suite she had at the Carlyle, and the exquisite wardrobe by François Brac. Jane slipped into the white coat that matched her dress and lit a cigarette, which she stubbed out almost immediately.

'Ready, beautiful?' Zack returned in a business suit and a raincoat, with a briefcase in his hand. They made a handsome pair as she followed him out of the trailer.

There were at least eighty people outside, milling around, everything from paramedics to light men to gaffers and grips. Directors' chairs had been set up, including five new ones with the stars' names stencilled on them. And as Jane saw them, she felt a thrill, and she grinned at Zack like a little girl. It was really happening, and suddenly she was so excited she could hardly stand still.

'I feel like a kid on her first day of school.' She giggled nervously, convinced she had forgotten her lines and feeling faintly nauseous. They walked through the revolving door, and stood in the lobby watching their stand-ins taking their places for the light men to set up for the scene. It seemed to take forever to get the lights set, and it was seven thirty when the director told them they were ready to get started. He was an Englishman Mel had worked with before, and he was extremely polite as he stood to one side, talking quietly with Zack and Jane.

'You've rehearsed the scene before . . . are you both comfortable with the lines?' Now was the time to make any changes, not after five takes. Jane had heard that, with him, sometimes there were as many as twenty. They both nodded, and Zack smiled. 'Ready to go?'

'Yes.' Jane spoke up hesitantly and Zack concurred.

'Good.' The director looked pleased. 'Let's try it. We'll rehearse it once and tape your marks.' There were already strips of tape on the ground marking where the stand-ins had been, but he knew that once they ran through the scene, there would be subtle variations. The scene called for Zack to meet Jane outside the lifts, stop her, grab her arm, and ask her what she was doing there. 'I'm here to see my sister,' Jane would say, 'it's about her daughter.' Zack would try to convince her not to go upstairs, and she would slip through his fingers, into the lift. The lift doors would close, and the scene would end. They would have to shoot the next scene upstairs, where Jane was to be confronted by Bill, but that wasn't on the call sheet for today.

They ran through it once to the director's satisfaction, only two of the tapes were changed, and everyone was told to make room and be quiet. It was crowded in the lobby. It was cold outside, and many of the crew members had moved inside. Besides, everyone wanted to watch the action now. They were all wearing blue jeans and cowboy boots, or sneakers, and heavy jackets, and some wore knit watch caps, or baseball caps, and Zack and Jane stood out in their expensive clothes. It was easy to spot them as the stars.

A voice somewhere near the camera shouted, 'Quiet ... settle down! ...' And then suddenly, 'Action!' as Jane moved across the lobby gracefully, stopped at the lifts, saw Zack, and then turned away as he moved towards her and grabbed her arm. 'Jessica?' he asked, on cue. 'What are you doing here?'

Jane looked at him, as though uncertain what to say, and then defiantly, but not too much, 'I'm here to see my sister, Adrian.'

The scene moved on, the lift doors closed perfectly, and the same voice shouted 'Cut ... good! ... very good ...' The director looked pleased, the lift doors opened, Jane stepped out with an excited smile, she was having fun. The director spoke to them again, and they shot the scene again. Four more times, and then finally, mercifully, 'Print it.'

They took a break, while the stand-ins took their places again for a different scene, and Jane was surprised to notice that it was after eight o'clock. They had already been on the set for over an hour. The time seemed to fly. She wasn't in the next scene, but she wanted to see Bill and Zack. She had never seen Bill work, and was curious to see his style. She stood on the sidelines chatting with Zack as they lit the scene, which took another half hour. She knew that in the studio it took twice that long sometimes, but on location things moved faster, with luck.

'Coffee, Miss Adams?' someone offered and she shook her head. And then she turned to Zack.

'What do you think?' She was anxious for his reaction.

'It felt good.' But it was impossible to tell. They both knew that in the next weeks it would feel alternately terrific and terrible, and that still didn't guarantee them the ratings. The only thing that did was Mel's track record for hits. They were all counting on that, but they had to do their part too, and everyone was ready to pitch in.

Bill came into the lobby looking startlingly handsome in a grey suit, his blond hair shining golden in the bright lights. He looked handsome and young and very intense as Jane watched him. She hadn't realised just how handsome he was. He was gorgeous.

His eyes met Zack's, and Jane moved away as the two men conferred, and it was another half hour before the lighting men were pleased, then he and Zack rehearsed, the tapes were reset, they ran through it again, and a voice called out, 'Let's get quiet please . . . very quiet . . . next one is picture! . . . Very quiet now . . . stay very quiet please . . . and . . . roll camera . . . light it up! . . . Action!' Jane felt the same thrill again. It was amazing what it did to her, just being there. She felt eighteen years old and incredibly happy. It was actually worth the price she had paid for it. She hadn't realised how unhappy she'd been before. The only thing that had kept her going was her part on the soap opera, but now her whole life had come alive. She missed the kids, but she was having such a good time, she missed Jack not at all, and she finally realised how miserable she had been with him. She hadn't let herself think about it until then, but she marvelled at it now. Here she was treated as a person. She was an important part of *Manhattan*, and Mel's confidence in the show's eventual success was contagious. They were all sure of it. Almost.

They wanted it to be just as he said, the biggest show in the country the following season.

The scene between Bill and Zack was more complicated than Jane's had been, and the director had them do it eight times before he finally said the magic word, 'Print', and everyone heaved a sigh. It had been interesting watching Bill. He was so handsome and alive and intense, he was totally different than he was in real life, when he was so subdued and withdrawn, keeping his distance from everyone. She could see now why Mel had hired him, and why every woman was going to be drooling over him soon. He was terrific. But so was Zack, in a quiet, mature way. There was something for everyone. Jane walked back to her trailer with a smile, to dress for her next scene, her opening scene with Sabina. It was going to be shot upstairs in the office they were paying a thousand dollars a day to rent. It was a fabulous place, hanging like a glass box on the corner, with a view of most of New York. But Jane wasn't thinking of the view as she was dressing. She was thinking of Sabina and Gabby, and her counterpoint to them. It was frightening thinking of working with a beautiful young girl, and a big, sexy star like Sabina. She felt like a nobody in their midst, and almost as though he had guessed she would be thinking that, Zack appeared, just as her assistant zipped her dress. It was navy blue and subdued and set off her red hair. It also showed her full bust and tiny waist, and the smooth hips that led to her spectacular legs. François Brac had done well by her after all.

'You look fabulous, Jane.' He had poked his head in the door and he whistled at her, which made her laugh. He didn't look the type to whistle in his elegant clothes.

'I'm scared.' And her eyes said she meant it.

'You'll do great. Number one.' He pointed his thumb upward and Jane smiled gratefully. She needed the encouragement desperately, and he knew it.

'At moments like this I wonder why Mel gave me the job.'

'Don't. The man knows what he's doing. The women

will love you, and the men will go weak at the knees just watching you. Sabina is something else. She's a power trip, but you' – his eyes looked wistful as he looked at her, and his voice was soft when he went on – 'you're all woman, Jane.'

'Thank you, Zack. Will you come upstairs and watch?'

'I think I'll leave you alone. It'll be crowded enough. And I have to change for my next scene with Sabina anyway.' It was supposed to be on a different day, and he'd be wearing another suit. The wardrobes Mel had paid for were enormous. But he knew it was a good investment. No other show had had wardrobes like this, and it gave the series a look that no other had, of quality and class, and expensive, important people. There was nothing cheap about Mel Wechsler, or his shows.

And Zack was right. When Jane got upstairs the office they were using was jammed with people and cameras and equipment. Her makeup woman and hairdresser were waiting for her and they freshened her up as the stand-ins took their marks, and the camera angles were changed several times. Jane saw Gabby quietly standing in a corner in a beautiful grey wool dress François Brac had designed for her. It looked young, and at the same time chic and expensive. Sabina was nowhere in sight, and it was almost another hour before she appeared. A man on a walkie-talkie told them downstairs when they were ready and she shot upstairs, looking incredible in a bright red wool dress with a jacket. There was no question who was the star, as she emerged from the lift with a style and a punch and a panache that was reminiscent of being shot from a cannon. And from the moment she arrived, everything was action everywhere.

'Quiet! . . .' The voice shouted more loudly this time. 'Quiet! . . . stay very still please . . . markers . . .' Jane pressed forward through the crowd to take her place. There had been no rehearsal this time. Sabina felt she didn't need it. And the director respected that. Gabby moved to her mark and stood quietly, waiting, her face expectant and young, and Jane smiled at her briefly. She felt like a horse in a stall, waiting for the race, wondering who would win, or if in fact all of them. Sabina had never looked more lovely. The heavy makeup seemed to strip years from her face, and her hair looked remarkable. She wore large gold earrings and a heavy strand of pearls, and on her right hand was a huge diamond ring. All of it had been borrowed for the shoot from Harry Winston. Mel didn't even want to use fake jewellery. 'Quiet please . . . light it up! . . . Action!' And as though she had been born to the role, Sabina took her place behind the desk and then stood up regally, and stared at Jane, as Gabby came in slowly behind her.

'What are you doing here? And I mean both of you . . .' Her eyes were green diamonds, her voice was a snarl, and as though the lines had become part of her, Jane found herself responding, with the impassioned speech she had rehearsed and rehearsed again, and Gabby spoke her lines as though she were truly Tamara Martin and not Gabby Smith. It was incredible what had happened to them, they were suddenly suffused with the life of *Manhattan*, and Sabina's eyes blazed as she told them to get out and walked around the desk, pressing a button as she went. It was a button that was to call Zack, but that was in the next scene. And Jane was stunned as she heard the voice of the director.

'Terrific! . . . Terrific, all of you! . . . one more time please. . . .' They shot the scene three times, and on the last one he beamed. 'My God, you're good. That's a print.' There was a cheer, and it was impossible to tell which of them they were cheering. Jane wanted to jump up and down and scream with excitement and in the distance she saw Zack, and she felt tears in her eyes. She wondered if she would ever get used to the excitement of the show. Even Sabina was pleased, and Gabby was beaming. It was good. It was better than good. It was great. And they all knew it instinctively.

It took another hour to light the next scene, and people

from the office they had rented were crowded in at the edges, to watch the stars and try to see a little of the action too. But there was nothing to see now except lighting men and gaffers and grips, and lunch was called at exactly twelve thirty. They had to satisfy the unions and there was no point running into overtime that early. They all went back to their trailers for lunch. They only had an hour. And the afternoon flew by as they went through the next scene, and the call sheets were distributed for the following day. Mel appeared on the set in the afternoon, and he looked as pleased as they all felt. He left before they finished shooting, and Sabina went back to the Pierre alone in her limousine, and Zack left in another. He wanted to stop and see a friend before going back to the hotel, and Jane piled into the third one with Bill and Gabby.

'Wow, I'm pooped.' She was amazed at how exhausted she was, but at the same time she felt great. 'What did you guys think?'

'I think I need a lot more work,' Gabrielle said humbly, and Bill looked at her, warming for the first time.

'You were good. Very good. That scene with the three of you is a killer.' Jane thought so too, and she smiled at him.

'Thanks. You looked fantastic in that scene with Zack.' They chatted about the day's takes, and glanced at the call sheets together. They were shooting six scenes the next day, three of them big ones, and they had the scripts to take back to their hotel rooms.

'Want to work on it together tonight?' Gabby looked at Bill hopefully, but he shook his head.

'I work better alone.' He sounded curt, and Gabby looked disappointed again.

'I'll work with you, if you want.' Jane offered to fill the gap, but they only had one scene together, and it was a small one.

'Thanks. I always need help.' Gabby seemed so anxious to do well, and Jane was keen to help her. She seemed only slightly older than her own girls, although she knew that Gabby was ten years older than Alyssa, Jane's youngest child. But it was hard to believe. She looked like a little girl once she was back in her jeans and sneakers, with her shining black hair hanging in two pigtails. Bill didn't seem impressed with her, and he avoided her gaze on the drive back to the hotel, speaking mostly to Jane. And once back at the Carlyle, he seemed in a hurry to leave them and go upstairs. And Jane invited Gabby to her room later on to order room service and rehearse.

'I want to jump into a tub of hot water first, and just lie there.'

'Me too.' Gabby smiled. Bill had disappeared with a handful of message slips, and the two women rode up in the lift together, and it was only as they walked down the hall that Gabby turned to Jane with a discouraged sigh. 'Bill's so goddam unfriendly. He makes it really hard to work with him.'

'I know. He's probably just nervous.'

'So who isn't?' Gabby shrugged. 'We all are. It's a big show, a big break for all of us, except Zachary and Sabina, who're probably used to it. But Christ, he doesn't have to snarl all the time. He acts like he has a burr up him.' Jane laughed, and was reminded again of her daughters.

'Give him time. We haven't got used to each other yet. Eventually we'll be one big family. That's how it was on my old show.'

Gabrielle looked intrigued. 'Which one were you on again?'

'*Our Secret Sorrows*.'

Gabrielle laughed. 'My grandmother was addicted to it.'

Jane looked at her with a rueful smile. 'That was the trouble. They wanted a new look, and younger viewers. So they canned me.'

'Are you sorry now?' Gabrielle was smiling at her. She liked her.

'Hell, no.' Jane threw out both hands philosophically. 'After all, all I lost was a part on a soap, and my marriage.'

Gabby's eyes grew wide. 'Are you serious? Over this?'

'It's a long story. I'll tell you about it sometime. When we have about ten hours to spare and a bottle of brandy in hand.' The two women laughed and Gabrielle let herself into her room with a promise to rejoin Jane in an hour. It was a little like going to boarding school and staying up at night to work together on an assignment.

The two women met again later on, and chatted until midnight, although they knew they had to get up at four thirty. They completely forgot about the rest of the cast and concentrated on their lines. And as they were intent on their work, Bill was getting hysterical, calling his agent. He had tried to get through for hours and it was as though the better the show went, the guiltier he felt about Sandy. He finally got through to Harry, as he held a cigarette in trembling fingers.

'How's it going?'

'Fine.'

'That's all? Fine? You're in the biggest show of your life, on location in New York with Sabina Quarles and Zachary Taylor, working for Mel Wechsler, and all you say is fine?'

'Wonderful then. Look, Harry can you do me a favour?' He was lying on his bed with a worried look, his leather jacket still on. Thinking about her was driving him crazy. What if she died now and Wechsler found out they were married? He had realised since getting to New York that he had to get her to clean up now. He *had* to. He had even called her parents and they didn't know where she was, nor did her friends when he called them. 'Will you check around for me and see if you can find anything out about Sandy?'

Harry was beginning to think Bill was obsessed with her, but he didn't understand the fear or the sense of obligation that drove him. 'Look, why don't you just forget her?'

'I can't. She's got to clean up.' It wasn't even that he loved her any more, but he couldn't just forget her.

'Why don't you call the police? They probably know more

than anyone else.' He was being sarcastic and Bill looked angry, his blond good looks marred by his look of fear.

'That's not funny.'

'It wasn't meant to be. You're a fool if you drag her back into your life now. And Mel isn't going to take kindly to it if he finds out you're married to a junkie.' That was the whole point, at least if she cleaned up, he could quietly divorce her.

'I didn't ask you to call my press agent, I just asked you to find her.'

'How? Go out with a dime bag and see if she wants it?'

'God damn it!' Bill exploded, as he jumped to his feet with the phone in his hand. 'Don't push me, Harry.'

'All right . . . all right . . . I'll try. But for chrissake, Bill, settle down. You have a job to do there. A big one. How did today go, seriously?'

'It's all right, but to tell you the truth, Harry . . .' He had to tell someone, he could hardly stand it any more. 'I'm worried sick about Sandy.' It distracted him constantly. The fear of scandal for himself, and just worrying about someone he had once loved that much.

'I'll do what I can. But do me a favour. Just keep your mind on what you're doing.' Harry had been hoping that he might develop an interest in the young actress he knew had been hired to be in the show opposite him, but there was no sign of that, and Harry was sorry to hear it. 'I'll call you if I hear anything.' But Bill heard it first. Her mother called him, and it was on the news the same day. She had overdosed in a fleabag hotel on Sunset.

17

The paramedics arrived just in time, and there was some question of there being brain damage this time. But when Bill called the hospital, they wouldn't let him talk to Sandy. And two days later, after calling her a hundred times, he was told that she had checked out of the hospital. Her mother said she had disappeared, and no one knew where she was again. All they knew was that she was living with a dope dealer, somewhere in Inglewood, they thought, but no one was sure, and her parents had all but given up on her. She had failed to appear in court on the charges that had been brought against her in late August, and there were warrants out for her arrest. It was a nightmarish situation, and Bill didn't know what to do. There was damn little he could do from New York, and he was struggling to keep his mind on his work. The day after she'd been found, they had had to shoot his only scene eighteen times, and he thought he'd go crazy trying not to think of her.

'Is there anything I can do to help?' Jane asked gently as they rode uptown after work, but he only shook his head and averted his eyes so she wouldn't see all that he was feeling. But it was clear that something was wrong, and when he finally looked at her it was with the eyes of a tired old man.

'No, but thanks.' She was a decent woman, even though he didn't have much in common with her. She talked about her kids all the time. But it was Gabrielle who really drove him crazy. She was so friendly and cheerful all the time, she was like a puppy dog. She wanted him to rehearse with her during every free minute they had and he didn't want to see her. She reminded him too much of Sandy, and that just made things harder for him.

Even Mel noticed that he was gloomier than he had been

when they arrived, but when they watched the dailies every night, his performances were flawless in spite of it.

'He's good,' the director admitted. 'And he'll be better when he calms down. He's wound up so tight he looks like he's going to explode most of the time. But he knows his stuff. The kid is a pro.' It was what saved him, and made the others put up with his dark moods. The only one he really snapped at was Gabby. But she had her own problems, not that she told anyone. Her mother was calling her five times a day, and begging her to spend Christmas with them.

'Darling, give me one good reason.' The voice that was pure Paris and Palm Beach and Newport was more insistent each day, and Gabrielle fought to stay calm. She was tired to explaining it to her.

'I'm working eighteen hours a day, Mother, and I have to get up at four thirty every day.'

'You have to eat. Why not eat here?' In black tie, with two hundred of her parents' closest friends. It made perfect sense to Charlotte, but not to Gabrielle.

'I eat in my room, and usually I rehearse with the cast.' So far it was only Jane, but she was still hoping to rehearse with Bill in their spare time. She was convinced it would improve their performances.

'That's not healthy, darling. You need to get out.'

'I told you. I'll come to Christmas dinner.'

'You've been here for three weeks, and we still haven't seen you. Now I'll expect you tomorrow night. They're all your old friends, and everyone's dying to see you.' It was all rubbish, none of them gave a damn, and she knew it. They were all her parents' friends, and people that she hated. The biggest names in New York, the names one read in *WWD* and *Town & Country*, where the photographs showed their beautiful china and lovely crystal and tables set for 'casserole' dinners of twenty in black tie and evening clothes. It was a life she had abhorred since she was a child, and she felt no differently now. If anything, she hated it more, and it was no longer her life. It was theirs. And these people had never been her friends. All she had ever been to them was 'Charlotte and Everett's daughter'.

'Mother, I really can't. And I don't have anything to wear. I left everything in California.' It wasn't entirely true, there were evening dresses made for her by François Brac that she could have borrowed. No one would have said anything. She knew that Sabina had already worn two or three of the evening gowns when she went out with Mel, and no one cared as long as they were still in good shape for the shoot.

'I'll have them send you something from Bendel's.'

'I don't want something from Bendel's.' She spoke through clenched teeth. 'I don't want to come.'

'We'll expect you at seven thirty.' Her mother hung up, and Gabrielle sat staring at the receiver in her hand.

'Shit.' She never changed. And now she expected Gabby to come to their rotten Christmas party. It was just her luck that she had to be on location in New York. It was like being a child again and being ordered around, just as she had been when she went to Saint Paul's, and even Yale. They just never accepted her growing up. Even now. Even now that she lived on the West Coast and had a career. It didn't mean anything to them. They just pretended it wasn't there, and that she wasn't an actress.

She was in a foul mood the next morning when she got up, which was perfect for the scene she had to shoot with Bill. The script called for a massive argument between them, and it looked truly genuine as she shouted at him, and threw something at him. It couldn't possibly have been any better if they'd rehearsed it for weeks, and they were both pleased when they left the set, although he said nothing to her. She went back to her dressing room, and reluctantly selected a dress. It was a demure black velvet evening gown. She signed a slip and put it in a plastic bag, and she carried it home that night when she rode uptown with Jane in the limousine.

'Going somewhere?' Jane looked pleased with her. She was so damn nice to everyone, sometimes Gabby felt sorry for her. She seemed lonely in a way, and she looked as though she had a crush on Zack. And it was obvious he liked her, but not with any consuming passion.

'I'm just going out with some friends. I used to live here.' She almost apologised, and Jane was happy for her.

'My daughters are arriving tomorrow from Los Angeles. I thought I'd bring them on the set, just to have a look around before we break for Christmas.'

'That'll be fun for them.' But Gabrielle didn't sound enthusiastic. As they drove uptown past assorted overdecorated shops on Madison Avenue, she'd never felt less festive than she did at that moment. And she knew that her parents' apartment would be as overdone as usual, with trees done by their florist that cost thousands of dollars. She had even hated them as a child. Everything was so artificial and so perfect. There was nothing warm and cosy about any of it, the way Christmas was supposed to be, with funny decorations and popcorn strung on the tree, like other kids had. It just looked like another spread in *Town & Country*, and had been several times.

The two women parted company outside their rooms, and Gabrielle went to dress, wondering how she'd got pushed into going to her parents' after all. She had called for a limousine at seven fifteen, and with her hair piled high on her head and the beautiful dress by François Brac, she looked like a tiny princess as she went downstairs again, and ran into Bill, carrying an armful of magazines in the lobby. He looked momentarily intrigued as he saw her, as though he actually cared about what she might be doing. She smiled at him and mentioned the scene they'd done that afternoon.

'I thought it was super.'

'So did everyone else.' He sounded noncommittal.

'Didn't you?'

'There's always room for improvement.' He was always criticising everything and everyone. Jane said it was because he was an unhappy man, but it sounded like a poor excuse to Gabby, for his constantly surly behaviour. It was hard to understand why he would behave like that.

'Don't be so hard on yourself.'

'I'm not. I just know when I could do better. Going to a party tonight?' She was surprised he even cared, he barely said hello to her most of the time, and he was always curt when she spoke to him.

'Just to visit some friends.'

'Nice dress. Borrow it from the show?' There was something derisive about the way he said it, and her cheeks burned with a hot flush she hated herself for.

'Yes, but I signed a chit for it, in case you're worried.'

'Not at all. I hear Sabina wears her wardrobe all the time. It's even in her contract she can keep it, maybe you can make the same deal.' But everything he said had an edge to it, and she wanted to slap his face.

'I'll keep it in mind.' She turned away, flinging the matching velvet cape over her shoulders, and he watched her for a moment and then muttered goodnight before hurrying to the lift to catch it before it went up. She tried to shrug off his remarks, but they had put her in a bad mood for an evening she dreaded anyway. And she knew she was right, when she rode up in the lift on Fifth Avenue and Seventy-fourth, and her parents' butler was waiting on the landing. He was telling people where to leave their coats, and greeting everyone, and he gave Gabrielle a warm hug, as a photographer from *Women's Wear Daily* took her picture. And suddenly she realised what she had done. She had unwittingly exposed herself to the press, and her anonymity as Gabrielle Smith was suddenly in danger. She avoided the cameras all evening, but to no avail, there were four society reporters there, each with a photographer, and the photographers from both *Women's Wear* and *Town & Country*.

'Darling . . . you look lovely . . . welcome home! . . .' Her mother gave her a kiss, careful not to smear her own makeup, and their perfectly matched dark beauty was recorded for posterity and the readers of the Sunday papers. Her mother looked as beautiful as she always did, in a navy satin gown by Galanos, with a matching stole, and an astounding sapphire necklace with matching earrings. 'Your father is waiting for you in the library.' She waved her gently in the direction of her father's favourite room, as hordes of new arrivals pressed her in that direction anyway, while silver trays of caviar and champagne were circulated everywhere among the guests. She recognised roughly half of the help and two-thirds of the guests, and she could barely find her father in the crush that surrounded him near the bar. He was drinking his usual iced Stolichnaya on the rocks, and his eyes lit up when he saw Gabby.

'There she is . . . my little girl . . . oh, my, and how pretty you look. Your mother will be very jealous.' His eyes always danced when he saw her. Everett Thornton-Smith adored his only child, in his wife's opinion, too much so. She had more reasonable feelings towards Gabrielle, although she loved her very much, but it had been a great disappointment to her when Gabby had insisted on her ridiculous career in Hollywood. And she was none too anxious to hear about the show. But Everett told everyone that Gabby was 'starring' in a series by Mel Wechsler. He ticked off the names of the stars, and he grew more effusive about it with each vodka.

'She puts Sabina Quarles in the shade, I assure you!' He smiled benignly at her, with an arm around her shoulders, his dinner jacket cut to perfection by his tailor in London, and the photographers recording his fatherly pride, as the reporters wrote down every word he said.

'Who is producing the show, Miss Thornton-Smith . . . what was the name of the show again? . . .' In Hollywood, everyone knew, but in the social columns in New York, they didn't read a great deal about Melvin Wechsler. 'A starring role, you said . . .' She insisted that she had a small part, and hated herself for coming. She had known it would end in disaster. Two years in Hollywood with absolutely no one knowing who she was, and now it would be all over.

It was worse than she thought. The photographs were not only printed in *W* and *Town & Country* in the next month, they appeared in the local papers the next morning. Large, clear photographs, showing her with her father's arm around her, toasting her with a glass of champagne, and one of her and the butler. 'Everett Thornton-Smith, proud father of Gabrielle, who is starring in a new series by Mel.' They had even had the gall to spell his name wrong, but the picture of Gabby was unusually clear, and all the information she had hated for a lifetime was repeated for all to see, who both of her grandfathers were, Benton Thornton-Smith on her father's side, founder of six banks, the largest pharmaceutical company in the East, and several railroads. Not to mention Harrington Hawkes IV, her maternal grandfather, who made Thornton-Smith look like a pauper. And that morning, she hated them all, as she put down the paper, particularly her mother, for talking her into going. They didn't understand anything, least of all her passion for being just plain Gabby Smith, or how important it was to her career. She had dropped the Thornton at Yale, unable to take the heat she'd taken there with a hall and a library named after her grandfather.

There was a knock on her door just before six, and with a feeling of trepidation, she opened it. It was Jane. She was smiling as though she'd just been given a gift, and Gabby braced herself for the flak she would take that day, maybe even from Jane. She'd taken plenty of it before, but she could have lived without it. No one ever took her seriously once they knew who she was. It seemed inconceivable to anyone that she could be who she was and still work too, and maybe even be good at it.

'Hi.' Gabby waited, but Jane only pranced into the room in jeans and sneakers and a warm parka. The weather had been bitter the day before, and they had three outdoor scenes to do in the park, and four more in the office at IBM. But Jane seemed to be in high spirits. 'What's up?'

'I'm just happy about seeing my girls again. It seems like

ages since I've seen them.' She had bought a small tree the night before, and decorated it especially for them with decorations from the five-and-ten.

'Oh.' Gabby was afraid to say anything more, terrified that Jane and the rest of the world had seen the paper, or just the cast and crew, that was the worst of it.

'You okay?' Jane glanced over her shoulder as Gabby put on her heavy coat.

'Yeah. Fine.' But it was unlike her to be so taciturn, and they knew it.

'Did you have a good time last night?'

'No.' The answer was brief and blunt and Jane didn't pursue it. Gabby had the dress over her arm in the plastic bag, and they took the limo waiting for them downstairs. Zack and Bill usually drove down in the other one, and Sabina was staying at the Pierre, so they didn't have to wait for anyone.

'Gabby, is anything wrong?' Jane was worried about her as they rode to the location in the park, but Gabby insisted that there wasn't. It was freezing when they got out of the car, and there was a chill wind blowing that brought tears to their eyes. It was going to be a real bitch working in that weather. The trailers were waiting for them in the dark, and the gallons of hot coffee and hot chocolate and tea the assistants poured barely kept them going.

As usual, only Zack and Jane seemed in high spirits as everyone else groaned and complained. The wind even managed to whistle through the trailers, and it was Bill who cast the first stone, as he smiled at her sardonically over his cup of coffee.

'Slumming today, Gabrielle?'

She glared at him with eyes filled with fear and hatred. 'What's that supposed to mean?' But she knew. She knew only too well. Damn . . . he must have read it . . .

'I enjoyed my morning paper today. I had no idea we had such a celebrity among us.'

'Oh?' Zack raised an eyebrow in total innocence, and

Gabrielle wanted to kill herself. By lunchtime, everyone would know, and they would make her life a living hell after that. It was the story of her life, and she was so tired of it.

'Too bad you're impressed with garbage like that, Mr Warwick.' She fired the words directly at Bill and walked back to her trailer and slammed the door.

'What was all that about? Private joke?' Zack asked and Bill couldn't resist filling him in. It was certainly an interesting piece of gossip about Miss 'Thornton-Smith.'

'Do you know who she is?'

'I thought I did. Is she the Boston Strangler in drag, or anyone I should know?'

'Ever hear of Thornton-Smith?' Bill looked smug.

'The pharmaceutical company?'

'Among other things.'

'I think I have stock in them.'

'In that case, you own a little piece of Miss Gabby.'

Zack whistled in the bitter cold air. '*That* Thornton-Smith? Are you sure of it?'

'Take a look at the back page of your morning paper. Before the obits.'

'I should hope so.' Zack couldn't resist borrowing somebody's paper, and he handed it to Jane when she came out for her first scene. She read the article with wide-open eyes and a look of amazement.

'And she's such a nice girl, you'd never know . . .'

'Just think,' Bill added with a chuckle, 'beneath our simple little Miss Gabby Smith lies a Rich Bitch.'

'I wouldn't call her that,' Zack defended.

'I should say not!' Jane was blunt, and she was annoyed at Bill's attitude, but suddenly she understood why Gabby had been so uptight that morning. She must have seen the paper. And it was obviously not something she bragged about, which was admirable of her. In fact, Jane thought even more of her than she had done before, and she told her so later that morning. 'Honey, I think you're terrific.'

Gabby smiled bleakly. 'But everyone else won't. The crew

will hate me if they ever hear about it. And I've been so careful in Hollywood, and now because of that stupid party, everyone will know. I tried to tell my mother that' – she had tears in her eyes as she remembered the futile exchanges – 'she just doesn't understand. She thinks it's something to be proud of. But I'm not. It's been a pain all my life, and now it's going to ruin my career after two years of killing myself to make it on my own.'

'And you have, so what's the big deal?' Jane was both motherly and philosophical as she put an arm around her.

'Did you hear what Warwick said this morning? He asked me if I was slumming. And that's just the begining.'

'He's just being a kid, Gabby. He's impressed and he's probably jealous. He doesn't know how to react to it. And neither will anyone else, unless you show them. Just let them know that this is what's important to you and forget the rest. But I still think it's nice to have all that behind you.' She thought of how dependent she had been on Jack Adams for twenty years, how frightened and browbeaten by the sadistic bastard. That would never happen to Gabby. 'Be grateful for it, and don't hide it. There's no shame in coming from a family like that.' She laughed. 'Everyone's embarrassed about something, most people that their family isn't fancy enough. You, you think yours is too fancy. You can't win, can you?' Gabrielle laughed and Jane gave her a squeeze, but it was no shield from the barbs that began to rain on her by lunchtime. By the time they came back from their break and moved to the offices at IBM, everyone had seen the photograph of Gabrielle with her father, and read the piece, and some of the remarks were funny, but most were unkind and Sabina's was the worst as they set up for a scene in the lobby.

'No wonder you got the job, Gabby,' she beamed evilly. 'Talk about typecasting ... does Mel know your father?' She moved away then to have the makeup people freshen her makeup and Gabby had to turn away to hide tears. She could have killed Bill Warwick for starting it by telling

Zack, though they probably would have seen it anyway. And Sabina would have told them. She even mentioned it to Mel with a vicious little laugh that afternoon, and he felt sorry for the girl. He called her that night, when she got back to her hotel. And it was a long time before she answered the phone, and when she did, her voice was husky.

'Yes?'

'Hi, Gabby, it's Mel. I'm sorry about what happened today. It was just rotten.'

She sighed as her lip trembled. 'Yeah . . . no big deal. . .' But she could hardly talk through her tears. She had been through it so often before, but it hurt anyway. They spoiled all her fun. And now she knew she would be cast as Miss Rich Bitch forever. 'I'm used to it.'

'It hurts anyway. And I'm sorry about Sabina. The trouble is, sweetheart, they're all jealous. They'd all love to come from a family like that and have that kind of money and background behind them. They can't even imagine it, and to them this is the only living they've got.'

'I know. But I work just as hard as they do.' She sniffed and he wished he could put his arms around her. She was just a little younger than his daughters would have been, had they lived. And she was a nice girl. It wasn't fair for all of them to torment her. By the end of the day, a hundred and thirty people had been talking about it, and probably a third of them, if not half, had made inappropriate comments. It was like a nightmare. And all because she'd gone to a party at her parents' house, and it had wound up in the papers.

'You probably work harder, Gabby. And that irks them even more. You don't have to, but you do. They fantasise that if they had parents like yours, they'd sit on their backsides and eat chocolates, and hell, who knows, maybe they resent you because you don't. Maybe it annoys them that you don't fit their image of the fairy princess. Instead you want to work in the coal mines with the rest of them. And they want you up there on the throne in a pink tutu.' The image made her laugh in spite of herself, and she felt better. 'In any case, they're like kids. In two weeks they'll forget about it and they'll be talking about somebody's new contract, or somebody else's affairs, and they won't give a damn what your last name is. Believe me, they have the memory span of very small insects. Kind of like roaches.' She laughed again and was grateful to him. She had been so down. Jane had gone to the airport to pick up her daughters, so she had no one to cheer her up. And that son of a bitch Bill . . . she would have liked to kill him. . . 'Can I interest you in some dinner by the way? We could go to Gino's for some pasta.'

'That's okay. I just thought I'd go to bed early. It's been kind of a rough day.'

'Have you eaten?'

'No, but I'm not really hungry.'

'Nonsense. You have to eat, otherwise you'll get sick in this miserable weather. I'll pick you up in half an hour.'

'No, Mel, really . . .'

'This is your producer speaking. Be downstairs. I'll be there at eight fifteen.' He hung up the phone, and turned as Sabina came into the room in a green velvet dressing gown the colour of her eyes, and gold high-heeled slippers trimmed with feathers.

'Who was that?' She glanced at the diamond watch he had bought her the week before, and began wondering what they were going to do for dinner.

'It was Gabby.' Mel sighed, and sat back on the couch, admiring the exquisite woman walking towards him. She was a pleasure to look at, night and day. Even at four in the morning, she was both beautiful and sexy. 'Poor kid. They gave her a rough time today.' He didn't accuse Sabina, but they both knew she had been the worst offender.

Sabina shrugged. 'She deserved it.'

'How can you say a thing like that?' Mel looked unhappy. 'She's a sweet girl, she's actually damn good at what she does, and she never gives anyone a bad time.'

'She's taking work away from people who need it.' He was surprised at how bitter Sabina sounded.

'Maybe she needs it too. For her soul, for her sense of self-worth. It isn't just a matter of money. You know that. She loves what she does, and she's good at it.'

'Then let her do it for the Junior League. She doesn't belong in the business.'

'You mean that, don't you?' He was stunned, and wondered how many others felt like her. Probably too many.

She nodded, without embarrassment. 'I do mean it. There are those of us who have fought long and hard to get where we are, we've hung on by our fingernails, we've starved, we've survived, we've done everything we have to. And we deserve to make it. She's been playing at it for two years, and two years from now, she'll marry some playboy with a name like Courtney or Funston and she'll get married and move to Park Avenue or Palm Beach and have babies. Meanwhile, she's taken a slice of our share, and I don't see why she should.' Sabina walked to the bar and expertly mixed herself a martini, eyeing him over her drink, as he looked at her with disappointment and displeasure.

'That's not a very generous attitude, Sabina.'

'I'm not always a very generous person.' And she wasn't afraid to admit it to him or anyone. 'I don't like frauds and she's one. She's masquerading as a church mouse, and the fact is she's a dizzy debutante gone to Hollywood. I told you she was hiding something. She's a fraud.'

'I wouldn't call her that.' He stood up as Sabina watched. 'And she's a damn fine actress.'

'Where are you going?' She wondered if she had really offended him, but if she had, it was too bad. She was who she was, and she never made excuses for it.

'I'm taking the dizzy debutante to dinner, because when I called her she was crying in her hotel room.'

'Send her a box of tissues, she'll get over it.'

'Stop pretending to be so heartless. She's no threat to you. She's a kid. You're a star. And a great one.' He knew how to handle them both and Sabina smiled at him.

'Thank you. And what am I supposed to do while you play Red Cross to little Miss Boo-Hoo?'

'Whatever you like, my love.' He kissed her neck, and looked into the green eyes that entranced him. 'You said you didn't want to go out anyway, that you were too tired. That's why I asked her.' Sabina shrugged. He was right. But she wasn't crazy about his having dinner with Gabby. She was twenty years younger after all, and not entirely bad-looking. Not only that, apparently she had a handsome fortune. But so did Mel, although it was of his own making and that was never quite the same.

'Just see that you behave,' she teased, but she wasn't worried. They had something pretty fantastic going between them.

'By the way.' He glanced over his shoulder at her, as he went to get his coat. 'I forgot to tell you I chartered a boat for us in the Bahamas over Christmas.' He was startled by the look in her eyes. She didn't look pleased, and he couldn't understand it. 'Something wrong?'

She hesitated, and carefully set down her martini. 'I have to go back to California.'

'For four days?'

'I've already made plans.'

'I see.' He couldn't resist turning to her as he stood in the doorway. 'I would have thought that the last few weeks would have superseded that, Sabina. I seem to be mistaken.'

'I'm sorry, Mel.' There was something sad in her eyes, but she offered no explanation.

'So am I.' He was quiet as he rode uptown in the limousine, to pick Gabby up for dinner.

18

Jane's daughters rode downtown with her in the limousine
the next morning with Gabrielle, complaining about the
hour. For them it was even earlier, as they hadn't adjusted
to New York time yet. Gabby was shocked by how unpleasant
they were to their mother. After all her delight at seeing
them again, they were barely civil to her. And they talked
constantly about their father, as though he were some kind
of god.

They appeared to be both rude and spoiled, and they
had obviously been heavily programmed by their father.
It began to annoy Gabrielle seriously by the time they got
downtown. She had never seen two girls be so unpleasant
to their mother, but she had very little contact with teenage
girls in her daily life. She herself was an only child, most of
her friends had no children at all, and the only one who did
had a two-year-old boy.

But Alexandra and Alyssa were something else. The only
thing that shut them up finally was when Zack Taylor gave
them his autograph, and then they spent the rest of the
morning staring at Bill, and whispering to each other and
giggling. Even that didn't endear them to Gabrielle. She
thought they were brats, and was almost tempted to say so,
but she didn't want to hurt Jane's feelings.

But Bill annoyed Gabby even more than the girls when
he made another crack at her when they broke for lunch.
He asked her if she was going to La Grenouille or La Côte
Basque, or perhaps it was going to be the Colony Club or
Quo Vadis. And for some reason, she decided she had had
it. She turned to him with blazing eyes and grabbed his arm
so hard it surprised him as he stepped back.

'Listen, you weak son of a bitch, I'm surprised you've
stopped feeling sorry for yourself long enough to even

notice anyone else, let alone worry about where I eat. And when I need advice from you, about my acting, or my social life, I'll ask for it. In the meantime, just shove it, mister, or I'm going to let you have it.' She stood barely more than five feet two inches tall, and he was so startled he grinned, and so did Zack and Mel standing nearby. Mel was pleased. His pep talk had obviously worked the night before. She stalked off to her trailer, but he could see by her walk that she was feeling better. He had stayed with her until almost midnight, and taken her to hear Bobby Short after their pasta dinner. And when he got back to his own hotel, Sabina had been sound asleep. They had made no mention of their respective Christmas plans that morning. He had decided to keep the chartered boat anyway, and to hell with her. If she wanted to see someone else, let her. They had made no promises to each other, but somehow he had expected her to be more loyal to him than that. It was as though she was trying to prove a point, that he didn't own her. He still wanted her to go with him, but he wasn't going to beg, and she hadn't offered to change her plans.

The rest of the shooting went smoothly, and two days later they all disbanded for Christmas. Mel flew to Nassau to meet the boat he had chartered for the week, and Zack and Sabina took separate limousines to the airport. They met at the gate to the flight to Los Angeles, and they chatted for a moment, but they took separate seats in first class, and neither seemed anxious for the companionship of the other. They each had plenty to think about, and Sabina noticed with interest that he was met in Los Angeles by a man of approximately Zack's own age, and they drove away in Zack's Rolls-Royce, which the other man had brought to meet him. Sabina stood wondering what their relationship was. She still had her suspicious about Zack Taylor.

She herself went home for the night. The next morning she took a plane to San Francisco.

* * *

The crew stayed in New York for Christmas. It would have been too expensive and complicated to fly them all home, and they had made plenty of plans. Before he left, Mel had organised a party for them at Maxwell's Plum, and Gabby ran into Bill there, despite all her efforts to avoid him.

'Slumming again?' He was slightly drunk, and he looked pale. Gabrielle had no idea what was really bothering him and she was sick to death of him. Their eyes met and hers blazed into his.

'Why don't you get off my back?' she muttered as she disappeared into the crowd. He had tried to track Sandy down by phone all afternoon, but to no avail. Nobody knew where she was and he had given up.

'Merry Christmas to you too, princess.' She was beginning to dread working with him. And if the show was a success, that would be even worse. She'd have to put up with him for another season. But her evening with Mel had done her good. She had decided not to take any guff from Bill or anyone, and she had a feisty look about her as she made her way through the crowd at the bar to Jane standing with the girls. Alexandra was clearly impressed by the decor, although she wouldn't admit it to Jane, and Alyssa was finally warming up. Gabby found herself wondering how Jane put up with them at all. They talked constantly about their dad, as though he were perfect. He was skiing with their brother in Sun Valley, they said, and Alex actually had the gall to say she was sorry she hadn't gone with him.

'Really?' Gabby opened her eyes wide. 'I'm surprised you think so. Sun Valley is so dull. Kind of tacky too.' She smiled. To hell with them, she thought to herself. Jane was too good for them. 'Do you come to New York a lot?' She was turning the knife a little bit, and Alex squirmed, admitting it was the first time with embarrassment. 'I guess your mom will be coming here a lot, now that she's such a big star. We'll probably be shooting on location in Europe next year.' There had been talk about it for a while, but it was just talk, and Alyssa's eyes grew wide with excitement.

'Really? Mom, can we come?' She sounded like a little girl, and Jane smiled at her. It was obvious that she adored them.

'We'll see, sweetheart. It depends if it's when you're in school or not.'

And then suddenly, Gabby had an idea. She looked at Jane, past the girls. 'Would you like to come to my family's for Christmas Eve?' She had just given in to her mother that afternoon. There was no point fighting them now, and she knew it would please her dad if she was there, and she had nothing else to do. She hadn't been home for Christmas for three years. And her mother had been thrilled. They were just having a few friends, as they always did. And this time Gabby knew 'a few' meant no more than ten. There was plenty of room for three more. If they wanted her, they had to accept her friends. She would have invited Bill too, if he hadn't been such a jerk. But he was, so she didn't.

Jane looked touched that she asked. 'Are you sure we wouldn't be imposing on a family affair?'

'Not at all. And I could use a few people on my team.' She lowered her voice. 'I hate going home. It's always such a strain.' Jane envied her as she thought of it, her own parents had been dead for years, and this year she didn't even have Jack . . . or their son . . . but at least she had the girls.

'We'd love to come, if you're sure your parents wouldn't mind.'

'They'd be thrilled.' It was bending the truth a little bit, but Gabby felt better going home on Christmas Eve with Jane and the girls. They went to the apartment on Fifth Avenue in a limousine, and a light snow had just begun to fall. Jane started singing. 'White Christmas' on the way, and the spirit was contagious so Gabby and the girls started to sing with her.

One of the maids was stationed at the door, taking coats, and Gabby cringed a little inside, as she saw Jane's eyes widen at the opulent decor. It was one thing reading about the Thornton-Smiths, and another visiting them. There was the usual overdecorated tree, perfectly done in silver and green, with antique German angels hanging on it and little knots of fruit, stretching up to the second floor, and the enormous living room filled with Louis XV furniture looked sumptuous and elegant as Gabrielle's mother walked quickly toward her and gave her a kiss, shook Jane's hand, and introduced her to everyone as 'one of the actresses in Gabby's show'. Gabby blushed, but she was pleased when her father made a fuss over them, and there were even little gifts for them. They went into the dining room. The table was set for fourteen, and their closest friends were there; the Armstrongs, the Marshalls, old Mrs Hampton, the Proctors, and William Squire Hunt. They were people Jane had read about and it was all a little bit like a dream, being there with them. Charlotte was wearing a heavily beaded red satin evening gown, and Gabby had worn dark green, a dress her mother had sent her from Bendel's after all, and not one of her evening gowns from the show. Jane had worn an exquisite taupe chiffon Brac, and she looked magnificent, and the girls looked innocent and sweet. It was a storybook night, and they sang carols afterwards and sat by the fire, and Gabby was actually glad she had come. Her father read from *A Christmas Carol*, as he did every year, and there was brandy and buttered rum and eggnog. The entire evening was a feast, and Jane was actually sad to leave when they finally did. She and Charlotte had got along extremely well. They chatted about Hollywood, and Charlotte was fascinated, as were the other guests.

'You'll have to come and see us on the set while we're here,' Jane urged, and for once, Gabrielle didn't even cringe.

'I'd love to.' Charlotte was thrilled, and promised to come down the following week. The two women kissed, and Gabrielle kissed her parents goodnight, and yawned as they got into the car waiting downstairs. She sat back against the seat next to Jane, and looked like one of the girls.

'You know that wasn't half bad for once.' She grinned mischievously and Jane laughed.

'Shame on you. They're wonderful. You're a very lucky girl.'

Gabby groaned and smiled at the girls. They thought she was lucky too. In fact, they were enormously impressed with her, and with Jane as well. They had finally realised that their mother wasn't so bad after all. If she knew people like that . . . 'Wait till we tell Dad . . .' Alyssa said, and Jane laughed. They were funny kids, but wasn't everyone, and as Jane went to bed that night, and she kissed the girls good-night, she found herself thinking of Zack and wondering where he was, and with whom, at Christmas. He hadn't called her since he left, and she couldn't get him out of her head, as she drifted off to sleep, thinking of the party she'd gone to with Gabby.

19

There was a definite chill between Mel and Sabina when he returned. He got back two days after they all went back to work, and for the first few days he slept in his own suite of rooms, for the first time since they'd left California. But Sabina didn't say anything. She offered no explanation as to why she had gone home, and it was Mel who finally cleared the air, when he took her back to the hotel after the shooting one night.

'I'm sorry if I've been upset.' His eyes were gentle but still hurt.

'You've had a right to be.' Her voice was kind as she looked at him. 'But I couldn't change my plans, Mel. No matter how much I wanted to.' He didn't ask her why, or who meant that much to her. He couldn't imagine that anyone did. She was self-centered and spoiled, and she thought of herself most of the time, yet she was nice to him. They got along well. Maybe wanting more than that was asking too much of her. Maybe they just had to accept what they had, for as long as they had it. What right did he have to expect more of her?

'Are you seriously involved with someone?' It was all he wanted to know. He didn't want to make a fool of himself, even for her. He was too old for that.

'Not the way you think. This was an obligation I have every year.' And it was obvious she didn't want to explain it to him. 'Sort of a family thing.' He wasn't sure he believed what she said, but it was a comfortable lie, for both of them.

'I didn't know you had any family.' She didn't answer him, and he took her out to dinner after that, and they got back on the right track again. He moved into her room again that night, and she teased him as she lay in his arms, sipping a glass of champagne after they made love.

'I was afraid you weren't going to speak to me again.' She eyed him with her extraordinary green eyes, and he felt his heart melt again. He was surprised at how much he had come to care about her. More than he would have liked, but she had got under his skin somehow when he wasn't looking.

'Why would I be foolish enough to do that?'

'Because I'm so independent sometimes.' The feline look came into her eyes and he laughed. She was right.

'You are, aren't you? . . . have you ever wanted to be otherwise? To be tied down to anyone?'

She was honest with him as she shook her head and offered him a sip of her champagne as they lay naked in her bed. 'No. Oh . . . maybe once . . . when I was very young . . . but not in a long time. Maybe never since then. I don't think I'd do well tied down.' She was tied down in other ways, but not to a man. 'I was madly in love with someone several years ago, but we never thought of getting married. Actually, he was married to someone else. And that suited me very well.' It sounded awful to Mel, because he still remembered how wonderful it had been, being married to Liz.

He looked sad as he looked at his friend. 'I used to like being married very much . . .'

There was compassion in her eyes. 'I know . . . that must have been terrible for you . . . I mean when . . .' She hated to say the words, for fear of bringing him pain.

'It was. I thought I wouldn't survive it. But I did. And I never wanted to do that again . . . to care so much . . . and to lose it all . . .' It was unbearable, just thinking about it . . . his children . . . his wife . . . everything. . . . 'I'm content now. I'm used to being alone.' And he enjoyed being with her. He was willing to give her plenty of room, and she appreciated it. She was grateful for his lack of questions about her Christmas plans, more than he knew. Another man might not have tolerated it. And she was well aware of it.

'Would you marry again?' She was curious, in some ways she thought he would.

'I'm not sure. I've never wanted to. And I wouldn't want to have children again. I'm too old now.'

'Nonsense.'

He smiled. 'I don't mean physically. I mean in other ways. I wouldn't want to do that again. It takes a lot of energy and time and love to bring up kids, and I put that into my work now.' He rolled over and kissed the inside of her arm. He was a strong, vital man, youthful in many ways, and he was content with his life. 'And I have enough energy left over for you, I hope . . . and enough love . . .' His voice was soft. 'I do love you, you know.'

'Thank you, Mel.' She kissed him in response, without directly answering him, and then after a long time, she whispered the words that frightened her so much. She avoided saying them whenever possible. But this time she said them. 'I love you too . . .' There were tears in his eyes when he kissed her then, and he gently took her in his arms and made love to her.

20

Mel gave a beautiful party for the cast and crew on New Year's Eve. He took over the entire discotheque Le Club, and everyone had a marvellous time, drinking champagne and dancing all night long, and singing 'Auld Lang Syne' at midnight. He held Sabina in his arms, and kissed her, as a small group near them cheered, and she laughed and threw her arms around Zack after that. He had been dancing with Jane, and he kissed her gently on the cheek before Sabina interrupted.

'Happy New Year, sweet friend . . . I hope it's a wonderful year for you . . . for all of us . . .' He looked at Jane with a bittersweet look she didn't understand as Sabina swept him away. And Jane found herself kissing one of the cameramen, and then embracing Gabrielle, as the director came over and kissed them both. The only one missing was Bill, and most of them had no official dates. They were just together, as Mel had hoped long before, like one big happy family. Gabby was relieved not to have to deal with Bill. Jane had even brought her girls, who were awed by it all. It had been an unforgettable holiday for them, and they were leaving the next day to go back to Los Angeles while the entire cast returned to the West Coast in two weeks.

Zack danced with Jane again afterwards, and he held her close in a way that he never had before, and it stirred her very soul. They hadn't had much time alone since he'd been back, but she'd been busy with the girls, and there were a lot of last-minute changes in the scripts. The evening ended for most of them at four a.m. and double-decker buses Mel had rented took them back to their hotels. Zack sat next to Jane and held her hand, and Sabina and Mel sat side by side in the backseat. Members of the cast had begun noticing them together recently, but no one said anything.

They seemed right for each other somehow, and when Zack dropped Jane and the girls off at their room, Alyssa turned to Jane with a curious look.

'Are you in love with him, Mom?'

'With whom?' For a moment she was taken off guard, and she blushed. 'With Zack? Of course not, we're just friends.' But Alexandra wasn't so sure. She had seen the way he looked at her, and she was suspicious of him, but at the same time she liked him. They both did, but they still thought Bill was the better-looking of the two.

Meanwhile, he was passed out in his room, having drunk an entire bottle of Scotch alone. But loneliness and his preoccupation with Sandy had finally got to him. The girls were disappointed not to have seen him again, Alex had had fantasies that at midnight he might be standing nearby, and might kiss her too. Mel was right, all the young girls in the world would be panting at his feet soon.

Jane took them to the airport the next day, and she was sad once they'd gone. She'd be seeing them again in two weeks, but by then, Jack would have done a number on them again. Although she hoped that there would be some lasting effect from their trip. She knew they'd been enormously impressed by Zack and Bill, Gabby's family, the shooting itself, the parties on Christmas and New Year's Eve. But she longed for the solid life they had once shared, even with its lies. Everything had seemed so normal and secure then. It wasn't, of course, but she had lied to herself . . . for so many years . . . she was thinking of that when Zack called her.

'Want to go for a walk?' It was snowing again, and she loved the idea. She bundled into her heavy coat, and they headed down Madison Avenue, glancing at the shops, and talking about the girls.

'I think the trip was good for them.'

'They're good kids.'

'Thank you. You don't have any children, do you, Zack?'

He smiled and shook his head. 'No.' She had never asked

him that before, and he could have, by someone somewhere. 'I've always been a little sorry about that. I guess I never found the right girl.'

'It's not too late.' She smiled, and he looked at her wistfully.

'Maybe not.' And then they walked in silence for a while, lost in their own thoughts. The turning point into a new year was a thoughtful time, when one weighed the past against what lay ahead. And they both had good things in store in the coming year. The show was looking good to all of them, and they talked about it, as they often did, as they walked toward Fifth Avenue on Fifty-ninth. 'Want to go to the Plaza for a drink?'

'Sure.' They ordered toddies and then went back outside, and he hired a hansom cab to drive them through the park as she snuggled next to him, amazed at how comfortable it was just being with him. Suddenly he looked down at her and she thought his eyes were damp, from the cold she thought, but she wasn't quite sure.

'I wish I'd met you twenty years ago ... maybe even twenty-five ...' And then he laughed, and held her gloved hand tightly in his own, and the hansom cab took them right to the door of the Carlyle. They had dinner in her room that night, and rehearsed the next day's scenes. But she was thinking about what he had said, and she wished she had met him earlier too. 'What were you thinking just then, Jane?' They were relaxing on the couch, like old friends. She felt as though she had known him for years, and she liked that about him. She liked a lot of things about Zack. His looks, his elegance, his charm, his thoughtfulness, his intelligence, his kindness ...

'I was thinking how nice you are ... what a good actor, and what a nice man, and that I like you a lot.'

His eyes met hers. 'I like you too ... you've become very special to me.' She had the feeling he wanted to say more, but he never did. They started talking about the others instead. Gabby, and Sabina and Mel, and Bill who was still so difficult.

162

'I wish he'd ease up on Gabby. He's so hard on her.'

'Sometimes I think he's half in love with her.' It was very perceptive of him, but Jane looked shocked.

'With Gabby? He's so awful to her.'

'Just like a little kid. Have you ever watched a nine-year-old taken with a girl? He'll go right up and punch her in the gut, and then go away pleased with himself, as though he's said something really important to her, and he has.'

Jane laughed at the imagery. 'It certainly sounds like Bill. Think he'll grow up?'

'He might.'

'She's such a nice girl.'

'So are you.' He stood up then with a yawn and gave her a warm hug, and a few minutes later he was gone, leaving Jane wondering if he was ever going to start anything with her. Alyssa had been right. She liked him very much . . . maybe even more than that . . . not just his striking good looks . . . but what was inside. That was the real beauty of Zack, the man he was inside. He was a very, very special man. And Jane suddenly realised she was falling in love with him.

21

The last two weeks of shooting seemed to fly. Everyone got along well, and the scripts flowed easily. Each scene seemed better than the last, and the words 'cut and print' were heavy in the air. On the last day of their location shoot, everyone gave a cheer, and Mel invited Sabina, Zack, Jane, Gabby and Bill to 21 that night to celebrate. They had a week's break ahead of them when they got back to Los Angeles before they started shooting again, this time in the studio. Jane said she had to look for a new house, her time was up at the one she had shared with Jack and she was going to look in Beverly Hills. Bill thought he might go skiing with friends, Gabby said she just wanted to get warm again and Sabina said she had to go to San Francisco for a few days. They had a wonderful time, and the next day everyone was quiet on the flight home as they all thought of what was waiting for them. Zack sat next to Jane, and Sabina and Mel, and Gabby and Bill carefully chose seats at opposite ends of the plane. They no longer spoke to each other, except during scenes, the rest of the time they avoided each other like the plague.

Back in Los Angeles it was business as usual. There was a lot of editing to do, Mel had a dozen meetings lined up, Sabina quietly disappeared, Bill left to ski, promising not to let his face get tanned and screw up the continuity when he came back to work. And Jane found a new house in Bel Air she was crazy about. It was small, but large enough for her and the kids. It had a pretty little pool and a tall gate for privacy. It barely hurt to move out of her old house, and this time she stayed clear of Jack, and Gabby kept her company while she packed. But Jack never showed up anyway. The girls said he had a girlfriend who worked for him, they weren't too fond of her and she was very young, twenty-one or twenty-two, and according to them she had big boobs and no brains. Jane thought to herself that that would suit him perfectly, and for a minute, she felt sorry for the girl, and then she decided to hell with it.

She moved into the new house as soon as the papers were signed, and they were already back to work by then. Everyone looked happy and relaxed, even Bill, although he had looked high and low for Sandy when he got back, and no one had any idea where she was. But he was anxious to find her now. He wanted to see her into safe port and then get divorced quietly somehow. He just prayed he'd get away with it, without anyone finding out. But there was no sign of her anyway, although he had left messages for her everywhere. And he had gone to Mike's Bar as soon as he got back. It was fun seeing the old faces, especially now that he was doing well.

They started back to work on February 4th, and on 1st March Jane's divorce papers came. She was on the set, quietly reading some lines that had just been changed, when someone dropped an envelope in her lap that had come that afternoon. She opened it. And that was it. It was over. She was divorced. Twenty years down the tubes. And in spite of herself, she started to cry, and everyone walked quietly away, except Zack, who came over to see what was wrong. She blew her nose and handed the papers to him.

'I know . . . it's stupid of me to cry . . . and he was such a jerk . . . it's just that . . . I don't know . . . it's like saying that half of your life has been wasted.' She was almost forty years old and suddenly she felt it.

'Come on,' he held out a hand. 'Are you in any more scenes today?' She shook her head and blew her nose again. 'Let's go get something to eat. I know a terrible bar where they make great hamburgers.' She hesitated and then stood up.

'I'll take my makeup off and be right out.' He was waiting for her in clean jeans and a starched white shirt, Docksides and no socks, when she emerged in a pink jogging suit and her hair pulled back in a rubber band. They looked like two ordinary folk, as they got in his car and left the lot. She had left the papers in her dressing room. They looked so ugly to her and it all reminded her of Jack. She was grateful to be with Zachary. She didn't want to be alone. And she laughed when she saw Mike's bar. It was terrible, and dark, and smelled of beer, but the people inside all looked young and healthy and clean and she realised that most of them were probably actors. Zack was right, the hamburgers were as good as he had promised.

They had just finished eating, and Zack was sipping his beer when he noticed Bill Warwick sitting in the far corner with a girl. He hadn't been in any of the scenes that day and he hadn't been on the set, and Jane suddenly looked over at him too, and they both saw the look of pain in his eyes. He was with a girl who looked as though she were desperately sick. She was rail thin and had dark, matted hair. She was dressed in what seemed to be almost rags, and they saw him shaking his head, near tears, and then finally hand some money to her. Jane turned away, feeling as though she had seen something she shouldn't have. He looked so griefstricken and so distraught, and he hurried out as soon as she left, without noticing Zack and Jane where they were sitting.

'My God, who do you suppose that was?' Jane looked sad for him. It was obvious that he cared about the girl.

'I don't know, but no wonder he's depressed most of the time.' They sat in silence after that and then went back to Jane's new house in Bel Air, but she was thinking about Bill and the girl. There was something so haunting about her. And she looked a little bit like Gabrielle. But Gabby was so healthy and radiant and strong. This girl looked as though she were half dead. 'She looks as though she's on drugs,' Zack said quietly, and Jane suspected he was right, and she was sorry for both of them.

'Want to go for a swim?' she asked him.

'I didn't bring a suit and I'd look pretty funny in one of yours.' He grinned.

'I won't look if you want to skinny-dip.' She was so comfortable with him she didn't mind.

'I can't promise the same.' But he had always been a perfect gentleman with her. Recently, she'd been almost sorry about it. 'But I'll do my best.' She poured them both a glass of wine, and she handed him a white terry cloth robe, and they both went to change, and she felt both exhilarated and depressed at the same time. Depressed over what she'd seen of Bill's personal life, and she hoped it wasn't serious between him and that girl . . . and depressed about her divorce papers coming in . . . and exhilarated to be with Zack. She was always so happy when she was with him. There was something very special about their relationship.

They both came back to the pool in a few minutes, dressed in identical terry cloth robes, and she turned her back discreetly as he got in, and he swam away as she climbed down the steps, her resplendent body more beautiful than ever in the evening light, and a moment later she was in the pool, and swimming to his side. The water felt wonderful on her skin, and he dove underwater and swam away, and soon they were playing tag, and laughing like kids, forgetting their nakedness, until they stepped out of the pool, and Jane suddenly decided what the hell. She reached for the robe unselfconsciously and put it on and saw that he was watching her soberly.

'You're beautiful, Jane.'

'Thank you.' She turned away and he got out and put the other robe on, and they went back inside and finished their wine, sitting in her partially furnished living room with its beautiful view. It was a magical night, and Jane drank more than she normally would have. She was so comfortable with him and it had been a difficult day, and it seemed perfectly natural when he leaned over and kissed her softly on the lips, but he did nothing more than that. And then he kissed her again, and she felt her whole body long for his touch, and she moved closer to him, and gently touched his chest, not sure what to say to him. She felt totally free and at ease, and the girls were spending the week with Jack, so she didn't have to worry about them coming home and walking in on them. She hadn't slept with anyone in seven months, and she was suddenly desperately hungry for Zack, sitting beside her.

'You're so beautiful.' He gently parted her robe, as though to appreciate her, and she closed her eyes with a look of desire, and then opened them again.

'I want you so much . . .' It was almost easy to say the words to him, and then suddenly he turned away. He put down his glass and stood up and walked toward the view, he stood there for a long time as she watched, knowing something was wrong, but not sure what. 'What is it, Zack?' She wondered if it was something she had said, or done, or if she had been too forward with him. 'I didn't mean to . . .'

He was quick to turn around at the pain in her voice. But the pain in his eyes was far greater. 'It's nothing you did . . . don't ever think that . . . on the contrary . . . you've almost changed my life . . . almost . . . but not quite.'

'Why would you want to change anything?' She was confused, and he knew he had to be honest with her.

'Because I haven't slept with a woman in more than twenty years . . . twenty-five to be exact . . . that's a long time, Jane . . . .'

'Yes, it is.' She looked very gently at him, and he came back to sit next to her, with a sigh, his whole body seeming to sag, with regret and relief, and the need to unburden himself to her. 'I went to boarding school when I was very young . . . fourteen to be exact . . . one of the very best schools . . . and it was kind of a joke then . . . a lot of the boys played around with each other, "everyone did it". I never did. It never appealed to me . . . until the new English teacher came. He was tall and beautiful and blond . . . kind of like Bill, and about the same age. And he wanted me to be "his special friend". He took me fishing with him, shared books with me, took me on camping trips. I admired him . . . too much . . . and on the second camping trip, he climbed into my sleeping bag, and told me how much he cared about me, how special I was to him, and he made love to me . . . I was fourteen years old. And I didn't know what to do. Who to tell. I didn't think anyone would believe me anyway. Everyone was crazy about him. And he was related to the headmaster somehow. When my parents came, I didn't say anything. I didn't say anything for two years until he left, and I swore to myself I'd never do anything like it again. I knew it was wrong, no matter how much I admired him'. Jane watched him with wide eyes, but there was no condemnation there, only sorrow for the boy he had been thirty years before.

'When I went to college, I fell in love with a beautiful girl, we even got engaged when I was twenty-two. She was wonderful, and she was going to be an actress too. We were going to have the perfect life, and four kids . . . until she met someone else. And I was devastated. We were both too young. And there was no one else after that . . . until my first goddam film. I wanted it desperately, and the director was a real son of a bitch. I was twenty-three years old, and he got me roaring drunk. And the next morning I woke up in his bed. He had even had one of his little pals take pictures of it, me passed out cold and he . . . you can imagine the rest. He threatened to blackmail me if I didn't go on sleeping with him. I did . . . and I guess I felt the die was cast after that. He hung on to me for almost a year, and by then it was too late. I was terrified someone would find out. I didn't sleep with anyone for two years after that, and then I met a nice man who was twice my age. I got involved with him, and he was extremely discreet. No one ever knew. And there was only one other man after that . . . it ended a number of years ago, and we're still friends. I've always been terrified someone would find out. That would do a lot for my image, wouldn't it?' There were tears rolling down his cheeks when he looked at her again and she gently wiped them away. 'The crazy thing is that I never wanted another woman after Kimberly . . . until I met you . . . and then I thought everything might change . . . but I can't . . . I can't go back . . . and I don't want the gay scene any more either. But I don't want to drag you into all that. What if I fell in love with another man . . . next year? In ten years? Then what? You're devastated all over again? You've had enough pain in your life without me.'

She was crying too. 'I love you, Zack.' She loved his pain and his honesty, along with the rest of him. 'I don't care about all that. I'm sorry it happened to you . . . I'm so sorry . . .' Her voice broke on a sob and he held her close, and kissed her again.

'I care though. I care for both of us.'

'Shhh . . .' She kissed him and he held her close for a long time, and when she looked up at him again, it was dark outside, 'Stay here tonight.' It was a whisper in the darkened living room.

'I can't.'

'Why not?'

'It wouldn't be fair. I don't want to make love with you.'

'Just hold me then . . . don't leave me alone . . . I need you too much . . .' The funny thing was that he needed her too, more than he knew how to say, more than he wanted to admit. They lay side by side on the couch, until she fell asleep, exhausted by the emotions of the day. And he lay in the dark, looking at her, holding her close, and he felt a stirring he hadn't felt in more than twenty years reach up from deep in his soul. But he didn't do anything. He just lay there next to her, crying for the past, and the boy he had been, and desperately wanting her.

22

'Very quiet now . . . and . . . roll camera! . . . light it up! . . . Action! . . . Take five . . .' Sabina stood in the centre of an elaborately decorated living room, with a chandelier overhead, staring at Zack with rage, and she slapped his face with eyes that flashed, and he grabbed her hand.

'I told you . . . don't ever do that again!'

'Stay away from my sister! You work for me, Adrian!'

'You don't own me, Eloise.'

'I own all of you . . . *all of you* . . . do you hear me?' Her eyes blazed and the camera moved in close to them, as the director waved an arm.

'Cut . . . the best so far . . . but let's try it again anyway.'

Everyone relaxed, and Sabina smiled, as the makeup man rushed forward to powder Zack's face. There were hushed murmurs in the crowd, and Sabina rehearsed the words again silently.

'Ready to go again?' The director was standing close to them and turned to someone on his right. 'Let's go to the zoom this time.' He turned back to Sabina and Zack. 'That was very good. Let's just try one more.' And then to his assistant again. 'Put us on a bell, please.' The bell rang a moment later, warning everyone that they were about to roll.

'Scene twenty-five, take six,' a voice rang out. 'Roll camera . . . Action, please!' Sabina moved forward with flashing eyes and slapped Zack again. He caught her hand and repeated the same lines. This time was even better than the one before and a moment later the words rang out. 'Cut! . . . very good . . . and it's a print!' Everyone walked off the set with a smile, including Zack, who had been slapped six times. It didn't bother him, but he was glad they were through for the day. He glanced at his watch, said something to Gabrielle in an undertone and hurried off to his dressing room, as Gabby went to find Jane.

She was taking her makeup off. She had been in five scenes that day, and one of them had required sixteen takes. It was a long day for everyone. They worked two six-hour shifts every day, with a one-hour break for lunch. And they stopped at exactly twelve hours, so there were no penalties for overtime. Everything worked by the clock. And it was seven o'clock when they stopped that night.

'Want to go out somewhere for a hamburger?' Gabrielle looked casual. She had grown up a lot in the past six months, working with all of them, and her acting had improved. She was still working with her coach, but the experience she was getting was invaluable. And people were being kinder to her again. There had been a lot of talk for a while, but eventually as Mel had said, they lost interest in it. There were other scandals to talk about, and plenty of gossip on the set. Who she was became less exciting to everyone, and she worked like a pro. The crew respected her for that, and Jane had grown immensely fond of her.

'I was going to have dinner with the girls tonight.' She smiled at her, but she looked sad. She felt a thousand years old. She hadn't told anyone on the set but it was her fortieth birthday, and she had had happier ones. 'Do you want to come along? We thought we'd go out for hamburgers.'

'Sure. Do I have to change?' She was wearing ragged jeans with holes in the knees and she looked worse than usual. But Jane didn't care. She got into her old pink jogging suit and her sneakers. There was no reason to dress. They weren't going anywhere in particular, and Alex was giving her a hard time again. She still held her mother responsible for the divorce, although she was impressed with her role on the show. At least Alyssa had come around. They had turned fifteen and seventeen in the past month, and Jack had just given Alex her own car, a Rabbit convertible, and she liked to drive everyone everywhere.

Gabrielle and Jane walked off the set as they were moving

the wild walls of the Martin home. The elaborate living room had already disappeared. 'How was the last scene?' Jane smiled. 'Did you watch?'

'They did it in six takes. It looked pretty good.'

'Is Zack black and blue?'

Gabby laughed. Privately, Jane referred to Sabina as the Dragon Queen. 'He'll live. He had a date, he said, he left right afterwards, but he looked okay.' Everyone had left quickly that night, and Gabby followed Jane home to her new house in Bel-Air, where the girls were waiting for her. It was almost eight o'clock by then, and the two women had a glass of wine, and then Alex offered to drive them to the Hard Rock Cafe for their hamburger. The girls were nicely dressed for once, in clean slacks and nice tops. Jane felt guilty going out in her pink jogging suit but she was too tired to change, and Gabby looked even worse, as they chatted in the backseat. Jane admonished Alex not to drive too fast, and then suddenly Gabby looked annoyed.

'Damn . . . Zack has my script for tomorrow, and I need it tonight.'

'I can give you mine when we get back to the house. I'm only in the last two scenes.' They were all working hard, but Gabby shook her head.

'I've got notes on mine. Do you mind if we stop at his place?' She turned to Alex and told her where it was. 'I'll just run in, and get it . . . you don't mind, do you, Jane?' She did, but she didn't want to say so. She was tired and depressed, and she wanted to eat and go home to bed. The girls hadn't said anything about her birthday, and she was sure they'd forgotten it.

It took them another fifteen minutes to get to Zack's house and when they got there, Gabby asked Jane if she wanted to come in.

'I thought he said he was going out at nine.'

'That's okay . . . I'll wait here.' She sat with the girls while Gabby went inside, and Alexandra turned to her.

'Can't we go in and see his house, Mom?'

173

'He's busy, sweetheart. And it's not fair for all of us to drop in on him.'

'Come on . . . everyone says it's fabulous. . .'

'Alex, please . . .' But the exuberant teenager had already jumped out of the car, and Alyssa followed suit. 'Alex! . . . girls! . . . please! . . .' They were impossible, they were already halfway to the front door, as Jane got out to bring them back. They rang the bell just as she reached the front step, and she was about to tell them to get back in the car, when the door opened and she was suddenly propelled up the front steps and inside by the two girls, as a roar of voices greeted her ears, and all she could see was a room filled with faces and balloons.

'Surprise!' two hundred voices said.

'Happy birthday, Mom!' She could barely see the girls through her tears, and Gabby was standing next to Zack. He had done everything, and he had invited everyone she'd ever known, the cast and crew of *Manhattan*, some old friends the girls had called for him, the entire cast of *Sorrows*, whom she hadn't seen in almost a year, her agent . . . everyone!

'Oh my God!' All she could do was cry and laugh as she was passed from arm to arm, being kissed and hugged, and then suddenly she was looking up at Zack, beaming down at her. 'What did you do! . . . oh my God!' She looked down at her pink jogging suit and laughed through her tears. She hadn't even combed her hair. 'Look how I look.'

'You look beautiful, and not a day over fourteen!'

'Oh, Zack . . .' Their eyes met and held, and she kissed him on the cheek that had been slapped six times that afternoon. Even Sabina was there, smiling benevolently at her, in a fabulous white jersey jumpsuit, with the pearls she had gotten from Mel.

'Happy birthday, kid.' Sabina grinned and kissed her lightly on the cheek. The two women weren't close friends, but they weren't enemies. And everyone had kept the surprise well. Mel gave her a big hug, and even Bill was there, smiling at the look on her face. No one deserved it more than she. She was nice to everyone in the cast, even the actors no one else knew, and the crew was crazy about her. There was a huge cake in the dining room, and a band playing outside. It was the most beautiful party she had ever seen.

'Happy fortieth, Jane.' Zack had an arm around her as he walked her around the enormous living room, so she could see everyone. There was even a dance floor outside, and a huge buffet piled high with two-dozen varieties of Mexican food, which the girls had insisted was her favourite.

'How did you do all this? I didn't suspect anything.' She was amazed, and the tears flowed again, as she looked up at him, deeply touched by all he'd done. No one had ever been as good to her as he was. She reached up silently then and put her arms around his neck, and the crowd cheered as she kissed him lightly on the lips, as Sabina approached with a scowl.

'I told you to stay away from my sister, Adrian.' The crowd roared as he pretended to cower.

'Don't hit me again, please . . .' He pretended to rub the oft-offended cheek, and everyone laughed as Sabina grinned and went back to Mel. Everyone had a good time, and no one saw Bill slip away quietly before the cake was served. Jane sent the girls home at twelve o'clock. They had to go home to their father that night. It was actually his day with them, but he had let them go out because of Jane's birthday. They would be back to Jane the next day. And the rest of the guests stayed until almost three.

She was exhausted when they finally left, and she stayed to talk to Zack, to thank him again. Someone else had taken Gabby home around two, and Zack had promised to drive the birthday girl home himself. But they were in no hurry now, as they sat drinking champagne by the pool.

'I don't know what to say.' She had never been so touched. 'It was just beautiful . . . the most beautiful night of my life . . .' She knew she would cherish the memory for the rest of her life.

'You're a special girl.' He gave her a warm hug, and looked into her eyes. He had planned it for two months, ever since she had mentioned she was having her fortieth birthday soon, and Gabby had helped, and the girls. Everyone had pitched in willingly for Jane. There was no one more liked on the whole show, except perhaps him. Jane and Zack were nice people, and they cared about their fellow crew members, they were thoughtful, decent, respected by all. 'I wanted to do something special for you.'

'Well, you sure did.' She sipped her champagne and looked at him. His confessions to her had changed nothing between them, if anything they had grown closer in the last month. He had taken her out to dinner a few times, and they didn't talk about it. But he was enormously relieved when he didn't sense a change in her.

'You've done a lot for me too, you know. . .'

'Are you kidding? I haven't done anything.'

'Yes, you have.' But he didn't know how to put it into words. 'You've made me think about a lot of things.'

'You've helped me over the worse time in my life. The divorce would have been even worse without you, Zack.'

'I don't see how I helped, but I'm glad if I did.'

The nightmare had dimmed, thanks to him, and she felt like a whole new person now. Each of them was more because of what the other gave.

She looked up at him with damp eyes then. 'No one's ever been as kind to me as you are. . .'

He leaned forward and kissed her lips. 'Then they were fools.' But he had been a fool too, for the past twenty years, he had allowed fear and regret to rule his life. By his own guilt, he had forced himself into a life in which he had never quite fit. But suddenly he didn't care about it as much any more. She didn't, so why should he. He had even explained it to his friend, a few weeks before. And Bob hadn't been surprised. He had always sensed that Zack would go the other way again, and now he was almost sure he would.

'I can't do that to her,' Zack had said.

'Do what? Be honest? You already were, and she didn't give a damn, did she?' Bob was pleased. He cared a great deal about Zack, and he had had another lover himself for several years, a man who meant everything to him. But Zack troubled Bob. He deserved so much more than that. And he had so much to give. He only hoped Jane was worthy of him.

'Happy birthday, Jane,' Zack whispered and she smiled happily. 'Want to go for a swim?' The night was warm, and neither one of them was tired. They had long since passed that point, and they were happy and comfortable lying by the pool, drinking champagne in the star-filled night.

'I didn't bring my suit.'

He laughed softly. 'Where have I heard that before? Seems to me we managed without one somewhere else. . .' At her house, when she'd moved in. 'We could try again.'

This time he stripped off his clothes easily in front of her, his powerful body rippling with energy almost like a boy's, and she quickly took off the pink jogging suit, and folded her underwear carefully. She felt only slightly self-conscious with him, and she saw that he was admiring her as he waited for her to get in. They swam quietly side by side, and then without a word, he took her in his arms when they reached the shallow end, and she stood, encircled by his warmth, feeling his desire mount as he held her close and they kissed. She was breathless when they stopped and he kissed her again, gently feeling her breasts this time, and then exploring more with gentle hands, and caressing lips. He led her to the steps, and as though they had waited a lifetime for that, he gently made love to her, with the warm water lapping over them, and their murmurs soft in the night air, as they rose in ecstasy and then lay as one, on the steps of his pool as he smiled down at her.

23

Bill left the party at exactly ten fifteen. He liked Jane, and he thought it was nice of Zack to give a party for her, but he just wasn't in the mood. He had seen Sandy for the first time in months a few weeks before, at Mike's. She had called him and asked if she could meet him there, and when she had, all she had wanted from him was five hundred dollars. She begged him, saying that she needed a place to live, and she didn't have a dime. He'd been afraid it would go right into her arm. She looked terrible, and it had broken his heart to see her like that, but he knew there was nothing he could do for her and she was in such bad shape he hadn't even mentioned a divorce to her.

He finally gave her what cash he had, a little more than three hundred dollars, and she had almost run out of the door. She had called him again that day, and had sounded frightened this time. She asked if she could see him that night at eleven o'clock, and just to be sure he didn't miss her, he had left Zack's place quietly forty-five minutes before that. But she hadn't showed. And at midnight, he had gone to Mike's for a beer, and then gone to Malibu and just driven around. He had to get her out of his head, she was going down the tubes fast, and he knew that one of these days, she'd OD again. Maybe for the last time.

It was after two o'clock when he got home, and when he did, the police were there. Four cars with flashing lights and an ambulance, and he had a terrible sense of impending doom, as he hurried breathlessly up the narrow walk and opened the door. They were waiting for him, and the bedroom door was closed. The policemen looked grim. There were other men in suits, and a man with a camera, and two of the cops drew guns as he walked in. He felt himself grow pale as he stopped where he was, and put up his hands, as he stared at them.

'What's wrong . . . where's . . .' He knew she was there. She had to be.

'She's still in the other room.' He didn't like the way they said 'still'. As though someone had left her there. 'Where've you been?'

He still had his hands in the air and he didn't dare move. He wondered if the paramedics were working on her, if she was all right, but he was too shocked to ask. 'I was out driving . . . in Malibu.'

'What time did you leave?'

'Around twelve o'clock. I was waiting for . . . for someone . . . and they didn't show up, so I went out for a beer.'

'Who were you waiting for?'

'My . . . a friend.' He had almost said his wife.

One of the policemen walked to the bedroom door, and signalled to him to come along. 'Is this your friend in here?' He indicated for Bill to follow him, and there were more policemen in the other room. The dog had been pushed into the bathroom, and Bill could hear him whining in there. But nothing had prepared him for what he saw when he walked into the other room. Sandy was lying on the bed, her clothes torn off, such as they had been, her tiny, frail body no bigger than a child's, and she had been shot in the chest and the head. Her eyes were open and her blood was everywhere. She was dead and he gave a terrible moan as he took a step toward her and then fell back, feeling faint and ill. Two arms caught him before he fell and he staggered back into the living room.

'Oh my God . . . oh my God . . .' He was whimpering like a child. She was dead . . . dead. He stared glassy-eyed at them. 'Who did . . . what . . .' He couldn't find the words and they shoved him roughly into a chair.

'You tell us. Your neighbours heard the shots. Do you keep a gun?'

'No.' He shook his head.

'Who is she?'

'She's my wife . . . we've been separated for the last six months.'

'Let's see your arms, bud.' They had seen the tracks on hers, but his were clean.

'Anyone see you after you left here?'

'The bartender at Mike's Bar.' He thought he was going to throw up and he closed his eyes.

'How long were you there?'

'About half an hour.'

'And after one o'clock?'

'I was just driving around.'

'She was killed within the last hour. Any idea who would want to kill her?'

He shook his head miserably, the tears spilling from his eyes. She'd been shot. Like an animal. And then he looked at them. 'She called me tonight. And she sounded scared.'

'Of what?' They had no sympathy for him. They had seen it all before. And heard weak stories like his.

'I don't know. Her connection maybe . . . maybe a pimp . . . she was picked up last summer on prostitution charges, to get money for drugs . . . she was a decent girl.' He turned to them as though it mattered what they thought. 'She was just all messed up with the drugs.'

'Apparently.' The cop in charge signalled to one of his men, and the men from the ambulance came in with a stretcher and a tarp.

'Where are you taking her?' Bill stood up as though to keep her there, and they shoved him back into the chair.

'To the morgue. And we're taking you downtown.'

'Why?'

'Can you think of any reason why not?'

'I didn't murder her.'

'Then you can tell the lieutenants that. Homicide gets this one now. We're holding you on suspicion of homicide.'

'But you can't do that . . . I . . .' Before he had said another word, one cop snapped on the cuffs, and another read him his rights, and the men from the ambulance emerged with the stretcher covered by the tarp, with only a tiny form under it. There was nothing left of her. He stared at her as she left, remembering the blood in the other room, and he prayed there had been no pain, that it had been fast . . . the son of a bitch had killed her in their bed, where they'd been so happy once. . . He felt as though in a dream as he stumbled to the car, surrounded by the men, and a few minutes later he was on his way downtown, in the backseat of the car, handcuffed and shocked. This couldn't be happening to him. But it was. . .

He was told he was being held for forty-eight hours while the investigation went on, and they interrogated him for two hours. But he had nothing else to say. He felt exhausted and sick, when they took off the cuffs, made him strip, searched him thoroughly, handed him back his clothes, and shoved him into a cell with three other men. Two of them were drunk out of their minds – one of them asleep – and the third threatened to kill him if he came within an inch of him, and he sat on the narrow cot, with the mattress that smelled of piss, wondering what was going to happen to him.

'Can I make a phone call?' he asked the guard.

'Tomorrow morning at nine o'clock.' But it was ten forty-five before they led him from the cell to be interrogated again, and they let him make the call then. By then, he was four hours late for work, and he had been in every scene. He didn't know who else to call, so he called his agent, and the secretary left him on hold while the inspectors champed at the bit, anxious to talk to him again.

'Tell them to hurry up.'

'I can't. I'm on hold.' He was panicked that they wouldn't let him complete the call. This was serious. This was his life they were talking about now. And then Harry finally came on the line.

'What's up? How's it going, kid?' His voice was cheerful. He was in a good mood. But not for long. Bill told him where he was and why, and Harry sat at his desk, stunned. 'You're *what*? Are they out of their minds? ... Holy shit ...'

'Can you get me a lawyer, Harry? And for chrissake don't tell anyone.'

'Are you kidding? By tonight, the whole world will know. Jesus Christ.'

'For chrissake!' Bill's voice roared into the small room and the inspectors stared at him, interested. 'Just find me a lawyer and get me out of here. And call the set and tell them I won't be in for a few days.' They both had the same thought at the same time, but Harry said the words.

'Just wait till Wechsler hears about this.'

'I'll talk to him when I get out. I'll explain everything.'

'That's the understatement of the year.' This violated his contract to the nth degree. The morals clause was taken care of, if nothing else. Not to mention how pissed off Mel was going to be because Bill had lied to him. 'I'll call my lawyer. And don't talk to anyone.'

'Great.' He glanced at the men waiting for him. 'And Harry ... thanks.'

'I'll do what I can. And, kid ... I'm sorry. ... I know how you felt about her.'

'Yeah.' Tears filled his eyes again. 'I did.' He hung up the phone and stared at the inspectors who wanted to talk to him but he refused until his lawyer came.

When he wouldn't talk, the detectives sent him back to his cell. The two drunks had been released, and the man who had threatened to kill him sat staring at him all day. It seemed hours before the attorney showed up, and he wasn't too encouraging. They were considering charging him with murder one.

'But why, for chrissake?'

'Because she was killed in your house, she was your wife, you were separated, and you have no alibi. For all they know, you were furious with her, you hated her, you were pissed off about the drugs. There are a thousand reasons why you could have wanted to knock her off.' The attorney was brutally honest with him.

'Don't they have to prove I did it?'

'Not necessarily. If you can't prove otherwise. They can hold you over for a preliminary hearing, if the DA files a complaint against you.'

'Do you think he will?'

'Did anyone see you that night, after twelve o'clock?'

Bill shook his head miserably. 'Not after I left Mike's. I just drove around.'

'Have you ever talked about this girl? Told anyone you were angry about the drugs?'

He shook his head, and then eyed the man Harry had sent. He was about forty-five, and seemed devoid of personality. Bill just hoped he knew his stuff. 'We never told anyone we were married, as a matter of fact.'

'Why not?'

'Her agent didn't want us to. She had a big part in a series then, and he thought it would hurt her image as an ingenue.'

'What about you? Anyone know?'

Bill shook his head again, and told him about the lie he'd told Mel when he got the job. 'They'll probably dump me anyway after this.'

'Maybe not.' It was the first encouraging thing the attorney had said. His name was Ed Fried. And Harry had sworn he was good. 'He may feel sorry for you. It's a hell of an experience for anyone to go through. Who do you think might have done it?'

Bill thought about it for a little bit, and shrugged unhappily. 'I don't know. Her connection probably. Someone must have followed her to the house . . . maybe a pimp . . .'

'She was into that too?' Ed asked.

'Yeah . . . once anyway . . .' It was ghastly, having one's life spread out like that. Then he looked at Ed again. 'Can you bail me out?'

The lawyer shook his head. 'You're being held on

suspicion. They haven't even set bail yet.' He decided to tell him the rest. 'And if they charge you with murder one, they won't.' What he was hoping was that they would drop it to a lesser charge, if nothing else. At least he could get him out then.

'Great.' Bill looked glum. But he looked worse than that when he saw the evening paper. It wasn't the headline. But it was on the first page. 'Actor accused of slaying wife.' It mentioned both their names, listed the old charges Sandy had been convicted of, her drug habit, getting kicked off the show, and it said that Bill was currently filming Mel Wechsler's new series and was slated to be television's new heart-throb in the coming year. 'Not likely,' he said to himself, as he lay down on the stinking cot and closed his eyes. They didn't interrogate him again that night. He just lay there, and thought about her . . . with a bullet hole in her heart and three in her head, and the life they had once shared that had faded like a distant dream.

24

'Oh my God . . . oh Jesus . . .' Jane saw it first, as they sat waiting for the lights to be set for the next scene. One of the cameramen had picked the paper up at lunch, and left it lying on a bench. She handed the paper to Zack wordlessly and he stared at her.

'Is that Bill?' He looked stunned.

'It has to be.' And he hadn't come to work that day. His agent had called at eleven o'clock, and they had been shooting around him all day, which had caused a certain amount of confusion for all of them, because they were all doing scenes they hadn't rehearsed before, and nothing had been done in less than fourteen takes that day. Everyone was testy as a result, and neither Zack nor Jane had slept that night, but they looked happy anyway. Or they had until Zack read the article, and Jane was staring at him. It explained why Bill had seemed so unhappy much of the time.

'It says he was married to her. He never said anything . . . did you know?' She looked at Zack in surprise as Gabby walked over to them. It was an unusually hot day on top of everything, and everyone was hung over from Jane's party the night before.

'If it takes me another sixteen takes to shoot the next scene I'm going to kill myself.' She sat down on the bench and looked at both of them. 'What's up? You look as sick as I feel. Too much Mexican food last night or too much wine, or both?' She smiled. It had been a beautiful night, and it really had been a surprise, which was gratifying, but Jane handed her the paper without a word. Gabby read the article and looked up. 'Holy shit. But that can't be . . .' It couldn't be. It wasn't possible. How could he have killed her like that? . . .

The word spread like wildfire, in whispers, between takes. And the police arrived before they left the set for the day. They announced that they wanted to talk to everyone, and they asked everyone to stick around for a while. It was already seven o'clock by then, but no one said a word, as they poured themselves coffee in styrofoam cups, and the inspectors spoke to the director before anyone, and then asked Zack to step into his dressing room. It was half an hour before he returned. It looked like they were going to be there all night, as Jane whispered to him when he came back.

'What did they say?'

'Not much. They wanted to know if he ever talked about his wife . . . if we'd ever seen her . . . if he said anything . . . if he looked upset yesterday. I told them no one knew he was married. And the only time I'd seen him with a girl was a few weeks ago at Mike's.' They both remembered the bedraggled girl they'd seen him with, and Jane wondered if that was the girl who'd been shot. And then Zack looked at her unhappily. 'They asked me what time he left the party last night, and I said I thought it was around ten. I probably shouldn't have told them that.' He looked as though he felt bad that he had. None of them had grown close to Bill since shooting had begun, yet he was one of them, part of the family, and Zack didn't want to cause more trouble for him. Jane looked at him sympathetically.

'I was so excited about everything, I didn't even see him go.'

'Neither did I,' Gabby said.

They talked to Sabina after that, and then Jane, and then some of the other members of the cast. It was ten fifteen before they called in Gabrielle, and by then they had let most of the crew go. Jane stuck around waiting for her, and Zack had promised to take them both home, so he was there too. Everyone was talking openly now, about how depressed Bill was sometimes, how morose he had been in New York, how surly much of the time. It made Jane sick as she listened to them, and her heart went out to him. She said something to Zack and he looked dubious.

'I don't think you should.'

'How would you feel?'

He glanced at his watch. He was still wearing the clothes he had worn in his last scene, and his makeup had started to run. 'They probably won't let you anyway.'

'We can try. There's no harm in that.'

He smiled at her, and whispered the words. He still felt the glow of the night before. He bent low next to her so only she would hear. 'I love you, Jane.'

'I love you too.' They exchanged a look meant only for them, and it seemed a very long time as they waited for Gabrielle.

She was in the main makeup room, with the police. They had started interviewing people there.

'Did you know him before the show, Miss Smith?'

She shook her head. 'No, I did not.'

'Did he ever mention his wife?'

'No.' She shook her head again, looking extremely calm, and watching them. She had been thinking about it ever since she'd heard, and she was certain he hadn't killed his wife. But she wondered if he had still been in love with her. That would have explained the way he had behaved for all these months. Things were coming into clearer focus now.

'Did you ever see her on the set?' They handed her a photograph of Sandy in better days.

She looked at it and shook her head. 'No.'

'Would you say Mr Warwick was angry yesterday? . . . say, last night?'

She smiled at them. 'Not at all. We all went to a surprise party for Jane . . . Jane Adams . . . and Bill was there.'

'What time would you say he left?'

'A little after ten o'clock.' She knew Zack had said the same.

'Do you know where he went? Did he say?'

She smiled, and then looked away from them. 'I met him

at my apartment later on.' She looked into their eyes again, demure, faintly embarrassed, but anxious to be honest with them, it seemed.

'Did you leave the party with him, Miss Smith?'

She shook her head. 'I left later on. About twelve.' She had left at two, but by then everyone was too drunk to care.

'And you met him . . . where?'

'At my place. Didn't he tell you that?' She looked young and innocent and surprised and embarrassed again, and the inspector questioning her shifted his weight in his chair. She was a very pretty girl and she was wearing a robe that kept opening and revealing one small breast as she leaned anxiously towards him. She even looked a little like the photo of the girl. And then he thought of something else.

'Did you two have a fight?' Maybe he had taken it out on the other one, if they looked so much alike. He had to think of everything.

She laughed like a child and played with her long black hair. 'Not at all. On the contrary . . .' She actually managed to blush.

'What time did he arrive?' The cop narrowed his eyes and she looked at him pensively.

'It must have been a little after twelve.'

That certainly changed everything. But why hadn't he told them that? He asked Gabby as much and she shrugged.

'I don't know. I guess he thought it would embarrass me.' She lowered her voice as though the walls could hear. 'No one knows about us. I . . . it would complicate everything and, you know, the morals clause . . .' If the morals clause were invoked every time two actors went to bed with each other, Hollywood would have had no one left to work, but they didn't know that and the chief inspector nodded his head solemnly.

'I understand.' He stood up then. 'We may have to talk to you again, Miss . . . uh . . . Smith. Thank you very much.' They dismissed her to rejoin Zack and Jane and they let everyone go for the night. It was a sombre group as they left the set, no one spoke, and everyone appeared to be lost in thought, as Jane shared her idea with them.

'I thought maybe we could drop by and see Bill.'

'You think they'd let us in?' Gabby looked dubious, but she would have liked to see him too. She had stuck her neck out for him, but she was sure she had done the right thing. She just knew instinctively he wasn't guilty of the crime, no matter what the cops said. He wasn't that kind of man. If he had wanted to kill her, he would have done it a long time ago. And when they talked about it, Zack agreed.

'He had a look in his eyes as he followed her out that day at Mike's . . . as though he still cared about her very much.' Gabby seemed to flinch as Jane watched, but she spoke in a normal voice.

'I think he must have been. I think that's what has been eating at him. Probably being secretly married to her didn't help.'

'The police said they'd been separated for months,' Jane said as they climbed into Zack's car, 'but I think Zack's right. When I saw him that day, I thought the same thing. He looked devastated by the way she looked. She looked so terrible, poor thing. . .' Jane looked pained as she remembered her.

'What do you suppose really did happen?' Gabby asked.

'It probably had to do with drugs.' Zack glanced at them both as he started the car. 'Apparently Bill claims she had called him on the set. I didn't know anything about it, but she could have, and she asked to meet him at his place. She never showed up, he went out for a drive, and when he came back, there she was . . . dead.' It sounded gruesome to all three of them, as Zack drove towards the jail where they had been told he was. It was well after ten o'clock by then and he was sure they wouldn't let them in. But when they asked, they were surprised. The inspectors had just got back from where they'd interrogated them, and they agreed to make an exception for them, 'because of who they were'. Their tone annoyed Jane, who felt desperately sorry for Bill, but they were all grateful to be allowed to see him. They were locked in a room alone with him, with a guard outside, and a window that allowed him to see everything that went on. Jane and Gabrielle had been told to leave their handbags outside, and Zack had been frisked. The door was locked behind them as soon as they stepped in. It was actually an interrogation room and far more civilised than visiting would have been in the jail. Bill himself was led in through another door, cuffs had been put on and taken off again as he was allowed to enter the room with his friends, and he stood staring at them with tears in his eyes, not knowing what to say, as Jane threw her arms around him and hugged him tight, crying herself.

'Everything's going to be all right . . . I know it will.' But he couldn't speak for a long time. He shook hands with Zack, and stared at Gabrielle. He looked filthy by then, and he hadn't shaved in almost two days. He looked ravaged by what he had seen, and what he had felt, and where he was, and as though he thought life would never be the same again. And in some ways it would not. It remained to be seen if Mel would keep him on the show, but more importantly if he was going to be charged with killing the girl.

'We couldn't believe it, Bill. It sounds like a very poor script.' Zack sat down in a chair and Bill followed suit, looking at them gratefully.

'Neither could I. It's been like a nightmare. They can hold me for another twenty-four hours with no further evidence. And after that, they can extend it for another twenty-four.' It meant two more days of terror and hell, and they stared at him in disbelief.

'But why?' Zack didn't understand how it was possible, without conclusive evidence.

'Because I have no alibi. I was out driving around by myself. No one saw me after twelve o'clock and it happened between one and two. She was found at my place, and apparently that's enough. They think I was upset about her life, and I was. I've been sick over it. She was killing herself.'

They all knew that now. 'But I would never . . .' He was too choked to speak, and Gabby gently touched his hand, and waited until he raised his eyes to look at her. And when he did, she was calm, and she spoke to him quietly.

'I told them you were with me that night.'

For a moment he just stared at her, as though he didn't understand what she'd said, and then he shook his head, as she kept looking at him. They were both aware that there might be listening devices in the room, and she wanted to be careful what she said.

'What did you say?'

'I told them you met me at my place after I left Zack's.'

He continued to stare at her. 'Why?' Why had she done that for him, after all the shit he had given her for months? Why would she do anything for him? He was stunned.

But she continued to look him in the eye, as Zack and Jane looked on. 'I told them that because it's the truth. You don't have to lie to protect me any more, Bill. It's all right.'

He wanted to shout, 'But I wasn't there, and I still didn't kill my wife,' but he didn't dare say anything because of the likelihood of hidden microphones in the room. And Zack and Jane stared at them, confused. They were both sure nothing was going on between them.

But Bill looked at her intensely, for the first time seeing only her. 'I didn't kill her, Gab . . . I swear I didn't . . . she called me that day, and she was scared. She said someone was after her, and I don't know who. Three weeks before that, she said she owed everyone money, including her connection, and she was worried about that. She said she had nowhere to live. But I only gave her three hundred dollars because I was afraid that if I gave her more, she'd go crazy with it and overdose again.' There were suddenly tears in his eyes again, and he hung his head, feeling relief and some kind of warmth around him for the first time in twenty-four hours. 'We were so much in love . . . I wanted her to clean up so bad . . . but she never would. I think she'd just gone too far and she didn't care any more.' She wasn't

191

the first to go that route, and all three of them felt sorry for him. There was no doubt in anyone's mind. Except unfortunately, the cops'.

Jane gently rubbed his neck as he cried and hid his face in his hands, and Zack shook his head unhappily. 'Can't your attorney do something, Bill?'

'He's trying. But it looks terrible, she was just lying there.' He gulped down a sob, remembering how she had looked with the bullet wounds in her head.

'Did they find the gun?'

Bill shook his head. 'No. And I've never had a gun in my life. I've never even held one, except on some kids' cereal commercial I did once, when I played a cowboy riding a rocking horse in a giant bowl filled with fake cereal, and I don't even think that was real.' They all smiled, but there was precious little to smile about.

Gaby looked at him intently again. 'Just tell them that you were with me. It's all right . . . I told them myself we were on Galey Avenue.' She realised that he might not even know where she lived. He had no reason to, and he continued to stare at her in disbelief, as the guard outside the room unlocked the door and gestured at all of them.

'That's it for tonight, folks. You can come back tomorrow during visiting hours. Two to four, on the seventh floor.' Great. Perhaps they would consider suspending shooting so everyone could visit him. He looked at them like a child being deserted in a terrible place and their hearts went out to him as Jane held him tight, and then Gabby hugged him cautiously. He squeezed her hand for an instant as he let her go, thanking her silently for what she had done for him. She might just have saved his life. And then Zack hugged him too, and there were tears in his eyes, and they snapped the handcuffs on Bill again, and the three of them left him there.

They were all three silent on the way downstairs, and they were back in Zack's car, hungry and tired and drained, before anyone spoke again. Jane turned around to look at Gabby in the backseat of the Rolls, which they had left parked outside the jail.

'I didn't know that . . . you and Bill . . .' She wasn't quite sure what to say and Gabby shrugged, obviously not anxious to say more. But as Zack glanced at her in the driving mirror, he knew exactly what she'd done, and why. Perhaps better than she knew herself. She was in love with him.

25

They didn't interrogate Bill again that night, but they asked him about Gabby first thing the next day with his lawyer there. They had spoken to several people on the set, and had found out about the animosity between Gabby and Bill. They knew she was lying for him about being together that night.

'It was a dumb thing to do,' the detective said. 'Did you put her up to it?'

Bill shook his head miserably, hoping she wouldn't get in trouble now. Suddenly, this was a nightmare for everyone. 'She didn't mean any harm. She just thought—'

'Yeah, I know.' Women did that all the time, though usually for men they liked better than people said Gabby liked Bill. It was no crime, but it was dumb, and it never worked. 'But you still don't have an alibi, pal.' His eyes were cold.

'I didn't kill my wife.' Bill looked grim, repeating the same words he'd said over and over again.

'Do you think she was still in love with you?' They were just fishing now.

'I don't know ... we cared about each other a great deal ... a long time ago.' His voice was soft and they were recording everything he said. 'She's been in no condition to care about anyone for a long time.'

'Do you know who her lovers were?'

'No.'

'Were you jealous of anyone in her life?'

They were watching his reactions carefully. 'No. I don't even know who was in her life.'

'We've been told she was turning tricks.'

Bill said nothing at all. 'How does that make you feel?'

He looked the interrogator in the eye. 'Sad for her.'

'And mad? . . . does it piss you off, Bill?'

He controlled himself. 'Not any more. It was all part of her sickness.' They were getting nowhere with him, and eventually they sent him back to his cell.

And after that they went to see Mel. He was tight-lipped and displeased and said he knew nothing of Bill's personal life. He also told them that he was unable to tell them whether or not Bill would be continuing with the show. They were shooting around him that week, but they would have to stop shooting completely within the next few days, unless he was released. They reported it to Bill, when they told him they were extending their hold on him.

'How does it look?' he asked his attorney desperately that night.

'Not good, I'm afraid. Nothing else has turned up. They can't find anything on her, and none of the neighbours saw anyone go into the house that night.'

'Jesus H. Christ, Ed, this is incredible. How can they do this to me? For lack of anything else, they're going to charge me with killing her? Just because they don't know who really did?' He wondered too if it had hurt him that Gabby had lied for him.

'That's possible.' He was inured to the injustices of the criminal code. He dealt with it every day. Although he felt vaguely sorry for Bill. He suspected he probably hadn't killed the girl, but he was going to have a hell of a time proving it. 'You have a damn good shot at a trial.' It was the only encouragement he could give. 'Because they would have to convict you beyond a reasonable doubt, and there's plenty of doubt in this.'

'Do you think it'll go that far?' He looked shocked. And the man in his cell had threatened to kill him again the night before. He was beginning to wonder if he would survive the ordeal. Maybe he'd never even get to trial. Maybe they would kill him right here, in jail. It had happened before, to other unsuspecting souls.

'It could go that far, Bill,' the lawyer said. 'We'll know

tomorrow sometime.' And they did. The district attorney filed charges against him, and the only compromise they made for lack of concrete evidence or a definite motive on his part was that they reduced the charges to felonious manslaughter, assuming that maybe an argument had broken out, and they had fought, and maybe he'd killed her without intending to, although they would have liked to charge him with murder one, but they were afraid it wouldn't stick. And the manslaughter charges were much more believable, and would be harder to fight.

He stood dumbstruck as they read the charges off to him and announced that he was being held on fifty thousand dollars bail. He called Harry as soon as he could, and Harry promised to get him out. It would take five thousand dollars cash, and he had to put up a bond for the rest. He was only grateful that he could. A preliminary hearing had been set for two weeks hence, and he was released at eleven o'clock that night. Bill cried as he walked outside, and Harry put his arms around him, unable to believe what had happened to him.

26

Bill was reminded of the first day he had gone to see Mel as he waited in the reception area, and it seemed an eternity while he was waiting. But there wasn't the same joyous anticipation this time. Instead, there was a leaden feeling in his stomach. Wechsler's office had told Bill's agent that he was not to report to work on Friday, he was to go and see Mel instead. At nine o'clock in the morning.

And it was nine fifteen when the secretary finally called him. Her face was blank, despite the fact that he had been on the news and in the papers every day that week. She acted as though she had never seen him before. And he was certain that Mel was going to can him on the spot. He had every reason to, and worse yet, he had grounds for suit. Bill had lied to him about his marital status when he signed the contract.

'Hello, Bill.' Mel's eyes were polite, but there was no warmth there this time. And Bill suspected that he was livid.

'Hello, Mel.' Bill sat down quietly across the desk from him. He looked neat and well shaven, although pale. It had been a grisly week and he hadn't slept in days. It seemed incredible how much had happened. And there had been photographers waiting outside his house that morning.

Mel looked into the younger man's eyes for a long time, and got to the point right from the beginning. 'I'd like to know why you lied to me, I mean about being married.'

'I feel very bad about that. I knew it at the time. I was scared, I guess. Sandy was in such bad shape. And our marriage had always been a secret from the first.'

'Why? Was she into drugs when you married her?' He had been wondering if Bill was too, or had been then. A lot of questions had crossed his mind in the last three days, since Bill had been arrested.

'No, she wasn't. But she was on *Sunday Supper.*' Mel had read that in the papers the day before, and he thought he remembered her. A pretty young girl, who looked a little like Gabby. He wondered if that had anything to do with Bill's constant animosity to her. It might have been a transference of his anger at Sandy. 'Her agent felt it would blow her image if she was married. She was supposed to be fifteen years old on the show. And she looked it. I wasn't too crazy about the idea, but I went along with it. She wanted me to, and . . .' He shrugged. 'I don't know . . . then she got into drugs and got kicked off the show. One thing led to another and we kept the marriage a secret. And then she was in and out of trouble with drugs. She went in the hospital, but she kept going back to the drugs when she got out. It was awful.' He felt like crying but he controlled himself. He didn't expect Mel to feel sorry for him.

'What about you? Were you involved in drugs with her?' He felt he had a right to know, and he was furious with Bill.

'No, sir.' He appeared deadly honest as he looked into Mel's eyes. 'I swear to you that I wasn't. I tried to get her to clean up but it was hopeless. The day before you called me last summer, she got busted for drugs, and prostitution, and she had spent the very last dime I had. I was desperate. And when you asked if I was married, I lied to you. I didn't want you to find out what kind of shape she was in, and we were just breaking up.'

'Did you get divorced?'

He shook his head miserably. 'No. By then, I was afraid of the publicity for me if I did. I didn't want you to find out I'd been married, so I didn't. And I lost track of her. She just kind of disappeared while we were in New York, and I never saw her again, until a few weeks ago. I wanted to ask her for a divorce then, but she was in such bad shape I never brought it up. She hit me up for some money, and then she called me the other day . . . I guess you know the rest. I came home and found the cops, and . . .' His eyes filled with tears and for a moment he couldn't continue.

Mel's voice was very quiet in the room. 'My lawyers have advised me to sue you, Bill.' And nothing in his demeanour said that he wouldn't.

Bill looked at him with anguished eyes. 'I understand.' He couldn't argue with the man. He was guilty of fraud. But not murder.

'But I'm not going to. For now.' Bill stared at him in disbelief. Mel didn't tell him that it was Sabina who had turned him around, and had begged for mercy on Bill's behalf. 'I think you have enough trouble on your hands without that.' He was mouthing Sabina's words to him. 'But you could hurt the show. Very badly. *Very* badly. If you're convicted of killing her, it's going to hurt our ratings. In fact, it could destroy us.' Bill was agonised with guilt as he listened.

'I didn't do it, Mel. . . Honest to God . . .' His eyes filled with tears and they spilled over on his cheeks as he looked at the older man. 'I didn't kill her.'

'I hope not.' Mel was sincere. He honestly liked him.

'I offered to take a lie detector test for the police, and I'd be happy to take one for you.' They had refused him, but Ed was going to have him take one anyway, to show to the district attorney, whether it was admissible or not. He had nothing to hide from them.

'That's up to your attorneys, Bill. Where do you stand legally?' Mel looked tired. This had been a strain on him too. It had been hard on all of them. But hardest on Bill, who looked ravaged.

'I go to a preliminary hearing in two weeks, and we're still hoping they'll drop the charges then.'

'And if they don't?' He was realistic, and he had a show to produce. A big one.

'I go to trial ninety days after that.'

'When's that?' Mel frowned as he picked up his glasses and read the calendar on his desk. 'Sometime in June?'

'I think so.'

Mel nodded. He was thinking of the show. Of all of them.

He had been thinking about it all night, all week, and all that morning. 'I think what we'll do is continue shooting. You can have time off for the hearing, of course. And the hiatus begins on June 1st.' He paused, gnawing on the end of his glasses. 'We're going to shoot two final scenes, one according to the schedule we have now. And another one in which you get killed. If we need to, we can run that next year, and explain your disappearance.' It was still a poor second choice for him. A wife killer was hardly going to become America's hero. 'If you're acquitted, we may ask you back after the hiatus, as planned, at the end of August. If you're not, we'll have the final show we need. But I want some time to think this out. If you're acquitted, you and I are going to have to talk. About honesty, your goals. You can't just expect to drop a bomb like this on us and have us welcome you home with open arms.' He still wanted to fire him, but Sabina said it would be bad for the show, and she felt sorry for him. He was just a kid in her eyes and this was such a terrible thing for him.

'I understand that.' He did, but he was griefstricken anyway, and he was sure they wouldn't have him back after the hiatus. Why should they?

'This has been hard on everyone. And you most of all. Who is your attorney?'

'Ed Fried. He's a friend of my agent.'

'I want you to speak to Harrison and Goode. Tomorrow. And we expect you back on the set on Monday.'

'I . . . uh . . . I'll see the attorneys in the afternoon, if they're willing to meet me on a Saturday.' Mel raised an eyebrow, and Bill fought back tears again. 'Sandy's funeral is in the morning.'

Mel looked away. The pain in the man's eyes was almost more than he could bear. Maybe Sabina was right . . . the poor kid . . . 'I'm sorry, Bill.'

Bill nodded and wiped his eyes. His whole life had come apart in a matter of days. It was truly a nightmare.

'I also want to make clear to you that if we don't ask you

back after the hiatus, there will be no severance. We want you to sign a release to that effect now.'

'Yes, sir.' He would have crawled, done anything, to mollify Mel now. He would have given his right arm and left foot if he wanted them. But he didn't.

'But I also want you to speak to our attorneys to see if they can help you. Criminal law isn't their thing, but I'm sure they can refer you to the right people.' Mel cleared his throat and put on his reading glasses again. They were little half-moons that made him look older than he was, and somehow like the principal in a boys' school. They seemed strangely appropriate for this meeting, and Mel always frowned when he wore them. 'We'll cover your attorney's fees.' Sabina had pressed him to do that too.

And Bill looked stunned. 'I couldn't . . . Mel . . .'

'We want to. For two reasons. For the good of the show, it's important that you get acquitted, but also' – his voice softened a little as he looked at the frightened man sitting across from him – 'because we give a damn about you. Everyone is sick that this happened.'

This time the tears spilled over and he stood up to shake Mel's hand. 'I don't know how to thank you.'

'Be back on the set on Monday, and get yourself acquitted at the trial.'

'Yes, sir.' He waited, but the meeting was over. He shook Mel's hand again, and closed the door softly as he left the office. As he walked downstairs, he felt as though one load had been lifted from his shoulders and another one had been added. He hadn't been canned effective immediately, but he realised that it was likely he would be during the hiatus. That final scene they were planning for him, where he would be killed, was a powerful thing for them to have, and he knew it was likely they would use it. But he was also deeply touched that Mel was supplying him with attorneys. He knew they would be the best, and he prayed that they could help him.

He got in his car outside Mel's office, and drove to the

set. He felt awkward when he got out, and a little afraid to see them again. But he had to eventually, and he knew he had to talk to Gabby. He hadn't seen her since the night she had come to the jail with Zack and Jane, and he had to ask her why she had lied for him. If nothing else, he wanted to thank her for the effort she had made, however misguidedly.

They were shooting a scene between Sabina and Jane when he arrived, and the bell rang just as he walked onto the set. He froze where he stood and stayed out of Sabina's line of vision. He knew how she hated to be distracted during a big scene, and that was one of her major requests, and everyone did their best to respect it. It was one of the reasons why they rarely had visitors on the set, because they unnerved her.

When the director shouted, 'Cut', Bill moved away from where he stood, and a few members of the crew spotted him. Some of them said hello quietly, others ignored him. It was awkward for them too. They didn't know what to say, and it was the first time he realised that some of them probably thought he had killed her. It was frightening to think of it, and he wanted to shout onto the quiet set, 'I'm innocent,' but instead he walked straight to Gabby's dressing room and prayed she was there. He found her reading a script and drinking a cup of coffee. She looked up in surprise as he walked in, and then smiled hesitantly. She knew he had got out, but she hadn't called him.

'Is this a bad time?'

She shook her head, and smiled at him. 'No, it's okay. How're you doing?'

'All right. I guess. I just saw Mel.'

She frowned. 'What did he say?' They had all wondered about that.

'He's a decent man. He'll let me stay till the hiatus.'

'And then?'

'I guess that's it. They're going to shoot a final scene with me getting killed, just so they have it in the can, if they need it. I go to trial in June, and there's no way of knowing how that will work out.'

'That's a nice optimistic point of view,' she chided him, and poured him a cup of coffee. He took it with still trembling hands and sat down across from her.

'I'm not at my most optimistic just now.' And with good reason, but his eyes softened as he looked at her. 'I owe you an apology and my thanks. I've been awful to you all year. And I don't understand why you did what you did, trying to give me an alibi. I didn't deserve that from you.'

She was straightforward with him. 'I don't think you killed her.'

'But you don't know that. No one does.' He had felt the vibes as he came on the set. No one was sure of him any more. He had become a stranger in a few short days. And yet some of them had stood by him, but no one as staunchly as Gabby. 'They knew you were lying anyway, but it was a noble try. And you could have got into trouble for lying to them.'

'I thought it was worth a shot.' Their eyes met and held.

And then he closed his eyes and then looked at Gabby again. 'I don't know why you even talk to me, after the way I've treated you.'

'Dumb, I guess.' She smiled and set down her cup of coffee. 'I won't deny you've been a complete prick sometimes, and I would have liked to kill you in New York when you told everyone who I was and showed them the paper, but no matter how big a pain in the neck you were I knew it was a rotten thing happening to you.' She hesitated. 'Is this why you've been so uptight so much of the time?'

'I guess . . . I was so worried about her, especially while we were in New York. I kept thinking she'd OD and it seemed so unfair that my life was going so well, and hers was going down the tube. And I was scared stiff about having lied to Mel about being single when he hired me. I wasn't even sure if I should push her for a divorce because I was afraid he'd find out then, if there was some publicity.' He looked up at Gabrielle oddly then. 'You look a little like her, you know. I think that bothered me too. You were so fresh and alive and normal and healthy. Maybe I resented that.' Gabrielle watched his eyes. He looked desperately sad. 'I just kept thinking that she could have been like you . . . if she wanted to . . . she had a terrific career going for herself when we got married.'

'Why'd you keep it a secret?'

'It's a long story, but her agent wanted us to, and the show she was on . . . and then I lied to Mel . . . it's been a real mess.' He sighed. 'But it's not much better now. I go to trial when we go on hiatus.' He told her about Mel's offering him their attorneys, and she was impressed.

'He's a hell of a nice man. He took me out to dinner in New York when I was so depressed.' Thanks to him, but she didn't say that.

'He's a real mensch.' Bill used the favourite Los Angeles term. But he was. A real man. A father figure. A hero.

And then Gabby looked at him with a mischievous grin. 'You think Sabina's sleeping with him?'

Bill laughed. It was the first levity he'd heard in days. They were like two kids, gossiping about their parents. 'Probably. She knows where the good stuff is. That jewellery of hers doesn't all come from Santa Claus.'

'I think he's in love with her.'

'I think he's a hell of a decent man, and even if he fires me, which I'm sure he will, he deserves a lot of good things in his life.' Bill sighed, thinking of the show again. 'Have I missed much this week?'

'Nothing too hot. We're shooting around you. You coming back on Monday?' It was funny, they were suddenly like old friends, though they had hated each other before, but what she had done for him had won his friendship forever. She was a terrific girl, and he was mortally embarrassed about the way he had treated her until then.

'Yeah.' And then, as though he needed to tell her, he spoke in a sad, quiet voice. 'Sandy's funeral is tomorrow.'

She winced. 'I'm sorry. Is there anything I can do?' He shook his head. There was nothing anyone could do now. For him, or for Sandy . . . His apartment had been cleaned up by a service Harry had hired. He couldn't have faced her blood on his bedroom walls. And the dog had been taken to the vet to board until Bill came home and caught his breath again. He had already decided to move, he wanted to get the hell out of there. Besides, whoever had got her might come back for him, though he doubted it. He was taking the fall for that other guy, and he would have been crazy to kill Bill, and thus prove that he hadn't killed Sandy.

Bill looked at Gabrielle, as though seeing her for the first time. She was a pretty girl. Even prettier than Sandy. 'Thank you for everything.' He stood up, not sure what else to say. He remembered her warm hug in the jail but that seemed awkward now, and someone knocked on the door just then.

'You're the next one up, Gabby.' It was one of the assistants and Gabby called out in answer.

'Thanks. I'll be right out.' She looked into Bill's eyes then. 'Everything's going to be all right, Bill. It may be rough, but it'll be okay in the end. It has to be. You're innocent. You'll win. Just hang in there.'

'Thanks.' He decided to hug her after all, and he left the set quietly again a few minutes later.

27

Sandy's funeral was the bleakest moment of his life. Her parents were there, sobbing painfully, her younger brother, and older sister. Her sister kept squeezing her husband's hand. Her little brother sobbed, and all of them looked sadly at Bill. At least they believed he hadn't killed her. A few of her friends from her old show had come too, but it was one of those terrible events that one expects to be difficult, and turns out to be much more so. Because of the bullet wounds, the casket had been closed, which was a relief for him. He didn't want to see her again, even without that, she was so tiny and frail and shrunken, her body ravaged by the excesses over which she'd lost control long before, her face only the shadow of what it had once been, her laughter all but forgotten.

'She was so sweet when she was a little girl,' her mother sobbed in Bill's arms as he fought back tears. 'She was all eyes ... and she used to help me make cakes ...' She couldn't go on, and even her father hugged him. The minister shook hands with all of them, and they went to the cemetery in rented grey limousines. Bill rode with Sandy's older sister and her husband. They were quiet, devastated by it all, and Bill had the feeling that they weren't as sure of his innocence as her parents.

'She told me she owed a lot of people money for drugs,' her sister said, still unable to believe that her baby sister was dead. They were only two years apart, but her sister wasn't nearly as pretty. 'I guess ...' She looked at Bill questioningly, as though expecting him to confess on the way to the cemetery. They ran out of conversation long before they arrived, and they all stood dumbly staring at the coffin, as her mother sobbed even more hysterically and the minister read the Twenty-third Psalm. Bill felt as though he were living a bad dream. And he kept thinking of the day they had got married. Now it was all over. It was odd to realise that he was a widower. Sandy had still been his wife when whoever it was had killed her.

The ride back to the city seemed interminable, and he found himself wandering aimlessly. He couldn't remember where he'd left his car, and when he found it again, he had forgotten where he was going. And then he remembered. Harrison and Goode. Mel's attorneys. He had time to stop for a cup of coffee on the way, and he sat staring into space, the coffee growing cold, as he thought about her again, and then forced himself not to. And as he paid the check, he saw the waitresses staring at him, not as they had before, wondering if he was the star of some show, but this time because they had seen him on TV and in the papers. He hurried out to his car, and drove to Santa Monica Boulevard to see the attorneys.

They were on the thirty-fourth floor of the ABC Entertainment Centre, and Stan Harrison had already called in two criminal lawyers to consult with them. It was a long, arduous afternoon, and like Ed Fried, who had sent over his file, they thought he had a good chance of being acquitted at the trial, if no further evidence turned up, but they thought it unlikely that the case would be dismissed before that. And as it turned out, they were right. Two weeks later, he appeared in superior court for a preliminary hearing, and he was bound over for trial. The judge felt that there was enough doubt in the authorities' minds to warrant a trial, and there was no talking him out of it. The trial date was set for June ninth. And Bill felt as though he were watching a very bad movie.

He had to hurry back to the set that afternoon, because he was in three scenes. He was working harder than he ever had before, and putting more into his role. He felt as though he owed it to Mel, and to everyone. And he wanted to infuse something more into the character before he left him.

They finished shooting that night at eight o'clock, running an hour into overtime, which they seldom did, but Sabina had trouble with a big scene with Zack. She kept blowing her lines and she had finally stalked off the set in a rage. They eventually got it right, but it took twenty-two takes and everyone was exhausted. Even Zack, who never complained. But Bill could see he'd had it when he left with Jane. He had noticed them together a lot recently and wondered if the subtle rumours he'd heard were true, or just the usual Hollywood talk. Someone he'd met at Mike's said he thought Zack was gay, but he certainly didn't look it. And they said that about everyone sooner or later. But maybe he and Jane were just friends. It was hard to tell, they were very discreet, even more discreet than Mel and Sabina.

'You look beat,' Gabby said to him as they left the set together. It had been a long day for all of them, but longer for him, with his appearance in court.

'Thanks.'

'How'd it go?' Gabby had offered to go with him, but he had declined. He wanted to deal with the ugliness in his life alone. There was no reason for her to go, and it still embarrassed him that she was being so nice to him after the shabby way he had treated her all winter.

'They held me over.' He knew all the terminology now, and wished he didn't.

'For trial?'

He nodded. He had resigned himself to it. He just hoped his lawyers were right and he'd get acquitted. 'Yes. June 9th.' It seemed a lifetime away, yet he knew it would come much too quickly. 'We'll have just started our hiatus. Mine will be permanent by then.'

'Stop saying that. You've been doing great things with your scenes lately. I've been watching you.'

'I figure if I'm gonna go, I'll go in style. At least maybe this way everyone will miss me.' He smiled ruefully at her and she shook her head at him. She was wearing her dark hair in a long silky braid down her back, and she flung it easily over her shoulder.

'Stop talking like that. No final decision has been made.'

'What do you think? No matter what happens at the trial, do you really think they'll keep me, Gab? No show can afford that kind of scandal, particularly a brand-new one, hungry for the ratings. They'll have to get rid of me, just to satisfy public opinion.'

'What difference does it make? Even if they get rid of you in real life, you'll be on the show all year. By then everyone will have forgotten. They might as well keep you on.'

'Tell Mel.' But he was only teasing. He respected Mel's decision, whatever it would be in the end.

'I might,' she teased, but they both knew she wouldn't.

'Hungry?' He was beginning to treat her like a little sister as he looked down at her.

'So-so.'

'Want to go for a hamburger somewhere?'

She thought about it. 'I don't know . . . I've heard so much noise and talk today. You want to come to my place for some pasta?'

'Can you cook?' He looked amused. Gabrielle Thornton-Smith cooking? But he didn't say a word of it, or even breathe the word *slumming*.

'Actually, no.' She smiled up at him. 'But I can fake it.'

'How do you fake pasta? That can't be easy.'

'I pretend the sauce doesn't come out of a can, and you pretend you love it.'

'Sounds fair enough. Do I have to call my agent for the part?'

She laughed, pleased that he was in such good humour. He had been really depressed the first week back, and for once she didn't blame him. The crew gave him a hard time, and even the cast was cautious about him. There was somehow the sense on the set that he might have done it, and her heart ached for him. She knew what it was like to be shunned by all of them, and it made her want to protect him.

'Do you want to leave your car here? I can always pick you up in the morning. You're on my way.'

He was surprised that her apartment was as simple as it was. Despite the income he suspected she must have, and her salary, which he knew more about, she lived very modestly in a garden apartment with no view, and a small cosy bedroom. She had put posters up everywhere, of places she had been to and places she wanted to go to. And there were a million pots in her kitchen, which she seemed seldom to use, except tonight in his honour. It was obvious she wasn't overly familiar with the stove, and the pasta was not the best he had eaten by far. But neither of them seemed to notice as they chatted about the show, and for once steered clear of any talk about his troubles.

'What's your family like, Gab?'

'Rich.' She grinned. 'That's what you wanted to hear, isn't it?'

He laughed. 'Other than that. Do you like them?'

'Occasionally. All my mother thinks about is clothes, and my father thinks she's terrific.' It was a simple summary, but not entirely without cause.

'Brothers and sisters?'

'Only me.' He was an only child too and he often found it a burden. He had wanted to have children with Sandy eventually, but it was never even a possibility in the condition she was in so soon after they were married. 'When I was a little kid, they spoiled me rotten. And they went crazy when I decided to become an actress.'

'My parents weren't overly thrilled either. My father wanted me to sell insurance like him. They never really understood me, as the saying goes. They live back east and I haven't seen them in three years. I sent them a Christmas card telling them I'd got married, and my mother wrote back to tell me how hurt they were not to have been told, or introduced to Sandy before. Then they sent us a salad bowl, and I've hardly heard from them since. I'm not very good about staying in touch. I have nothing to say to them.'

'My father wanted me to become an attorney. I guess we both blew it.' She didn't seem upset and he smiled at her.

'They won't think so next year. You'll be the hottest young star in Hollywood.' They both wondered if he'd still be on the show, but neither of them said anything.

'Maybe not. Maybe the show will bomb and get cancelled.'

Bill laughed. 'Not likely. Not one of Mel Wechsler's shows. He has the Midas touch.' He reeled off his successes on both hands, and Gabby smiled.

'Amazing, isn't it? I still wonder how come he picked me.'

'Because you're good.' Bill said it with a warm smile, and he meant it.

'So are you.' It was honest praise from both of them, and they *were* good. They both worked hard and had great skill. Mel had chosen his cast well, and they both knew it, at least about each other. 'Sabina still scares the shit out of me sometimes. Jane makes everything so easy, and Sabina just oozes tension.' Gabby looked very young as she said it, leaning her head on her hand, as they sat in the midst of their dishes on the kitchen table.

'She loves playing star.'

'Sometimes I wonder what's inside her.'

'Not much. Diamonds and mink and Mel's bank account. The usual stuff.'

Gabby laughed and then looked serious for a moment. 'I think there's a lot more to her than we know. She's just very private.'

'Like you?' He was intrigued by her, he had been ever since he found out who she was, but jealous too. It seemed unfair to him sometimes that some people had so much while others had nothing. But at least she didn't show it. He had fantasised that she had a butler and a maid and mink carpets, and she wasn't that way at all. She was extremely simple and direct and honest . . . and warm . . . he felt a lot of things about her that he hadn't before, and he didn't know quite how they tallied up. She was a strange girl, intelligent and proud, with powerful loyalties, and a strong sense

211

of friendship. She would have killed for Jane and Zack, and to outsiders, she even defended Sabina. To her, *Manhattan* was like a family, even more so than her own. And Bill was part of it, no matter how ornery he was, and they both knew he had been very much so.

'I'm exactly who I appear to be. Gabby Smith, actress. I work hard, I cook lousy, and who my grandfather was is not my fault. I've almost stopped feeling guilty.' The show had been good for her. And even Bill's tormenting her had made her grow up, although it hadn't been easy. 'Somehow that just isn't important.'

'I guess you're right.'

'I hated it when I was a kid. Someone has always tortured me about it.'

He looked instantly guilty. 'Don't say that. You make me feel like a shit again.'

'You were.' But she didn't seem to hold it against him. 'But I lived through it. You'll live through what you're going through now, and you'll be better for it.' She was a strong girl, and he liked that about her. As he listened to her, he realised that she was nothing like Sandy. Sandy had been weak and self-indulgent. There was nothing of that about Gabby.

He looked at his watch then and realised it was after midnight. 'I should go.' They both had to get up at the crack of dawn the next morning. 'Do you want to rehearse this weekend?'

She nodded pensively. She had given up on that with him a long time ago, but she looked up at him and smiled. 'Okay . . . I think I could use it.'

'Thank you for dinner.'

'Any time. I do canned corned beef hash too. And . . . instant ravioli?' He laughed and she followed him to the door.

'Do you want me to help clean up?'

'Of course not. The maid will be in in the morning.'

'Really?' At least some of his fantasies were correct, but she only laughed and shoved him out the door.

'Of course not, you dummy. I'm the cook and the maid . . . and the chauffeur. Hey,' she called out to him as he got into his car, 'don't forget to pick me up tomorrow. Six forty-five?'

'I'll be here. Good night.'

She waved as he drove away, and walked slowly back inside and closed the door to her apartment.

28

He picked her up five minutes late the next morning, looking sleepy, and Gabby got into the car with a yawn and a smile. She had stayed up too late cleaning up after their dinner and reading the next day's lines. She was always well prepared, which was something he admired her for. In ten years in the business he had worked with a lot of actresses who didn't do their homework. He commented on it as they drove to the studio, and she smiled at the praise. It was incredible how different he'd been ever since his arrest, and sadly enough, ever since Sandy's murder. As devastated as he was about her, and as hideous an experience as it had been, in a strange way he seemed free now. But she didn't mention it to him, and when they got to the studio, they went their separate ways. They both had to get changed and have their makeup done, and Gabby had to get her hair done. She was to wear it in a French twist, and she had to report to the hairdressers by seven thirty.

She looked like a different person when she met him later on the set, wearing a red suit and high heels, and diamond earrings.

'Miss Thornton-Smith?' He swept her a bow and she made a face at him.

'Go to hell. The name is Tamara Martin.'

'Sorry, you look just like . . .' But the teasing was friendly now, and they ran through their lines twice while the stand-ins took their marks. The scene was lit half an hour later, and the day began for them as the bell rang, the assistant asked for 'Quiet please . . . very quiet now . . . roll cameras . . . light it up . . . action!' It was a familiar refrain to them, and the scenes went smoothly for them, and for the other actors working that morning.

He had a meeting with his attorneys in his dressing room

during lunch, and Gabby had lunch with Zack and Jane. They were warm and affectionate with each other, and she looked at them with a wistful smile.

'You two make me lonely.'

'Now, now.' Zack gave her a hug as he helped himself to another Coke. 'By the time you're as old as we are, you'll be married with ten children.'

'Not likely.'

'What isn't . . . mind if I join you?' It was Bill, looking tired and a little depressed, but he'd been looking for her, and someone had said she was probably in Jane's dressing room, where he finally found her.

'How did it go?' Her eyes were worried as she glanced up at him, still holding her sandwich.

'Okay, I guess. They make me feel like Jesse James.' But it wasn't funny to him, or to any of them. The stakes were too high, and it was tragic to think of what had happened. 'I hope they know what they're doing.'

'So do I,' Gabby said in a whisper, as Jane watched her. She had also noticed the change in Bill and mentioned it to Zack, who figured the scare had made him reach out to all of them. He only hoped that some good would come of it in the end, and not more disaster.

'Who's up next?' Bill asked.

'Sabina, Zack, and seven extras,' Jane answered. 'I'm through for the day, but I thought I'd hang around.' She was waiting for Zack, Gabby knew, but she didn't say it.

'What about us?'

'You and Gabby are after, with Sabina's "lawyers".'

'That should be a familiar scene.' They all laughed. The last moments of freedom went too quickly. Zack had to go back to the wardrobe mistress for his next suit, and Gabby sat for a few minutes with Jane, while Bill ate an extra sandwich. He was ravenous after the tension of dealing with the attorneys. And then he walked Gabby back to her dressing room, while Jane wondered what was going on between them.

'Want to go out for a pizza tonight, Gab?' He looked down at her in the doorway, and she smiled up at him.

'You're not going to get awfully tired of me, seeing me all day on the set, and for dinner too?'

'Don't be a jerk. I'll take you to my favourite bar.'

'Do I have to dress?'

He laughed. 'Not exactly. Do you play pool?'

She made a face. 'Billiards. Sorry. But don't tell anyone.'

'Don't worry. I'll teach you.'

He took her to Mike's Bar when they finished work, and they ate hamburgers and played pool and he introduced her to Adam. 'My co-star, Gabby Smith.' There was no talk of the 'Thornton', and no teasing this time, and Adam looked at her with open admiration. Several of the men did, and it made Bill realise how pretty she was. He glanced at her as they drove home and he asked her the question that had been bothering him all day.

'Am I cutting into anyone's time?'

'Hmm?' She looked confused. 'Sorry?'

'I mean, are you seeing anyone?'

'Oh.' She shook her head. 'Not at the moment.' The truth was that she hadn't had a serious date since she'd started working on *Manhattan*. She never had time, and no one she cared about had crossed her path in a long time.

'I was wondering about that. What's a pretty girl like you doing unattached?' It sounded like a corny line but he was curious.

'I don't know ... maybe I work too hard. Maybe I'm hung up about people knowing who I am. I haven't thought about it much, I just haven't had time.'

'That's a poor excuse. How old are you, Gabby?'

'Twenty-five.' She had had her birthday while they were in New York, and she had celebrated quietly with her parents. 'You?'

'Thirty-three going on ninety.'

'I thought you were younger.'

He laughed. 'Is that a compliment or an insult?'

'Maybe both.' She laughed too, and relaxed as he drove her home. 'You look younger on screen actually.'

'I won't after the trial.'

'Stop worrying about that.' But she couldn't blame him. 'Wouldn't you?'

'Yes.' She was honest with him. 'But I just know it'll turn out all right.'

'Even if it does' – he looked sad again, thinking of it – 'I won't be coming back to *Manhattan*.'

'You don't know that yet, Bill.'

'I just don't think Wechsler will buy it. I've given him enough headaches for a lifetime, and I can see his point.'

'Mel's a decent man, he won't let you go unless he feels he has to.'

'I would in his shoes.'

She smiled gently at Bill. 'Then it's a good thing you're not.' He smiled at her then, reminded of what a fool he had been, and wondered how he could have been so blind to her for so long, but he had been obsessed with Sandy. He tried explaining it to her over a glass of wine, when they got back to her apartment. It was spotless and there was no sign of the dinner the night before. He wondered if she really did have a maid, and didn't want to admit it. But she seemed amazingly neat as she poured the wine, and took out some snacks, and then put everything away. She was organised and tidy, and intelligent.

'You know, you're amazing, Gabrielle.' He even liked her name.

'Don't be silly. Why?'

'Because you're in control of everything you do, your life, your career, even your apartment. I can barely get my socks to match in the morning and feed my dog on time.'

'What kind of dog do you have?' She was curious about him now. She wanted to know more.

'A Saint Bernard named Bernie. He's a slob, but I love him. I've had a hell of a time finding a place that will take both of us though.' And he was anxious to move as soon as possible, understandably, after all that had happened. 'Want to look with me this weekend? We could rehearse afterwards, or have dinner, or both, or . . .' His voice trailed off and she laughed. He was like a kid who had found a new best friend, and she was it. And she was both touched and flattered.

'I'd love to.' She had nothing else to do and she enjoyed his company, and that night before he left he kissed her, hesitantly, as though he wasn't sure what she would say. But she stood in the doorway, enjoying the sensations he gave her. 'Goodnight,' she whispered.

'I'll see you in the morning. Can I pick you up again?' He gently touched her face with his fingers.

'Sure. But you're going to get tired of me.'

'Stop saying that.' He suddenly had the feeling that he wouldn't, not for a long, long time, and maybe never.

She curled up in her bed that night, thinking of him, and she felt her body grow warm at the thought of him. There was so much about him she liked, and he was so different now, so much warmer and more open. And the next morning when he picked her up, there was a long-stemmed pink rose on her seat, tied with a white ribbon.

'For you, mademoiselle.' He held it out to her, and she took it, pleased. It was a lovely way to start the day.

'You're spoiling me, Bill.' She was almost afraid to let herself believe it. What if he changed again, if he slammed shut as he had before . . . what if . . .

'You deserve it. You deserve a lot more than that. But the florists aren't open yet. It's from my neighbour's garden.'

'Thank you.' They exchanged a warm smile and he kissed her again before they got out of his car. 'Thank you for bringing me to work.'

'Thank you for trying to save me, even if you were crazy to do it.'

She made a face. 'Oh, shut up.'

He was still amazed she had done that. It had been quite a thing to do. For all she knew, he had killed Sandy.

The set was bustling that day. There were visitors, which always made everyone nervous at first, but they were friends of Mel's, and they had to put up with them. The lighting men seemed especially slow and during one of the big scenes a plane flew just overhead, and they had to shoot the whole thing again because the sound man picked it up with his equipment. Gabby was tired at the end of the day, and she yawned when Bill drove her home.

'I'd offer to cook dinner but I don't think I can stay awake that long.'

'It's okay. I should get home to Bernie anyway. There was no dog food this morning, and the poor hound must be starving.'

'You'll have to introduce us sometime.'

Bill smiled as she got out. 'That's a deal. Hey . . . you forgot something.'

'What's that?' She leaned back into the car and he took her face in his hands and kissed her.

'I'll miss you tonight.'

'Me too.' It was funny she had lived twenty-five years without him, and now an evening without him seemed empty. There was a sudden urgency to their lives now, and he called her when he got home and had fed the dog. He hated the cottage now, it seemed haunted to him. And he hoped he'd find something else that weekend.

'I'll pick you up tomorrow,' he promised before he hung up, but she sounded hesitant.

'You don't think people will start to talk?'

'Do you think anyone cares, they have their own lives to think about.'

'I guess you're right.' And she was amazed at how anxious she was to see him the next morning. It was like being four-teen again, and waiting all night to see your favourite boy in school . . . your latest crush . . . but he was more than that. He was interesting and fun, and serious at times, and they shared all the same interests. They loved going to the mountains, and wind surfing and sailing and skiing. She hadn't skiied at all that year because she had been too busy working on the show.

They rehearsed in her dressing room when they got to work, and they were both surprised at how well all their scenes went that day. They did them all in three takes, and even the director was pleased. He praised them both when they went to lunch, and Sabina eyed them with her best feline look.

'And what have you two been doing after hours, children? Rehearsing?' Gabby blushed and Bill returned her stare. Sometimes she annoyed the hell out of him, especially when she picked on Gabby, which she still did often. Gabby was still the ingenue, and she was young enough to be Sabina's daughter, which Bill suspected irked her.

'Matter of fact, we have.'

'My, my . . . sometimes the best love affairs start out with a little touch of hatred. And you two certainly had your share of it this year. Kiss and make up, kiddies?'

'Oh, go fry an egg, Sabina.' He put an arm around Gabby and walked her to her dressing room. 'Sometimes she is such a pain,' he muttered as Gabby took off the coat she'd been wearing on the set.

'She just needs to air her claws from time to time.'

'As long as she doesn't sharpen them on me or you . . .' he grumbled and helped himself to a soda, and then he turned to face Gabby again. She was looking beautiful. The expensive clothes of François Brac suited her to perfection, but she only shrugged when he mentioned it.

'They remind me too much of my mother.'

'That can't be all bad, if she looks anything like you do in them, princess.' But the 'princess' was said with kindness now, and not venom.

Gabby sat down in a comfortable chair with a sigh. She was tired. They had worked hard that week, and she was glad it was Friday.

The next morning he picked her up and they went to see four apartments and a town house. He didn't fall in love with any of them, but at least they were a change of environment. The house was available on a month-to-month basis, and they were willing to take the dog, so he took it.

'It's okay, I guess.' He shrugged as they settled down to hamburgers at Mike's, before they went back to her place to rehearse. 'I just keep wondering if I'm going to be around three months from now. It's a little hard to make plans right now.' He was facing the fact that he was going to trial, and there was always the chance that he could go to prison. It sobered him every time he thought of it. In fact, it terrified him, and it made him question the wisdom of getting involved with Gabby. He had no right to hurt the girl, and he said something to that effect as they finished dinner.

'I'm a big girl, Bill. I can take care of myself. I know what you're facing. But I also know you didn't do it. I always believed that, right from the first minute I heard.' It was a hell of a vote of confidence from a girl he had been so unkind to for six months.

'Your faith in me means a lot.'

She smiled gently. 'I told you . . . you deserve it.' They chatted for a little while, and then went back to her place to rehearse. She went and got the scripts, and they ran through two scenes, but her mind wasn't on it for once, and she kept making mistakes. 'I'm sorry, Bill . . . I must be tired.'

'Come here.' He pulled her down on the couch next to him. 'You're such a brave girl . . .'

'What makes you say that?'

'I don't know, you have this way of taking on the world . . . I admire you a lot, Gabrielle.' And he did. He kissed her, and they both forgot the scripts. He kissed her long and hard, and she caught her breath when she finally pulled away.

'Is that in the next scene?' she teased.

'We'll have them write it in,' he whispered. 'I think it really works.'

'So do I . . .'

He kissed her again, and she found herself lying in his

221

arms, as her hands wandered into his shirt, and he ran his over her skintight jeans. They were soft and old and he could feel her taut young body under them, and he swelled with desire for her.

'I want you . . . I want you so much . . . but I don't want to louse up your life. . . .'

'Don't worry about it.' She had never met a man she liked as much, no matter how short their time together was. But she also refused to worry about the future. It would take care of itself. 'I love you. . . .' She hadn't meant to say the words, but they had slipped out, and he looked startled, as he looked up at her, lying on top of him, her small frame barely pressing down on his large one.

'I love you too, Gabrielle . . . it's crazy . . . I want to love you enough to stay out of your life and spare you a lot of pain, but I can't seem to make myself do it.' She kissed him this time, with a passion so urgent that he forgot his qualms, and he carried her into the other room, and laid her down on her bed. He peeled off her jeans, and gently unbuttoned her shirt, as one would undress a child, and she watched as his clothes came away from his magnificent body. And then they forgot everything in each other's arms, everything except the love they shared, which had grown from the ashes of pain and hurt and disappointment. They had a great deal to give each other, and Bill had never been happier as they lay on her bed afterwards. 'Where have you been all my life, little girl?' he whispered as she nestled into his arms, and fell asleep. He smiled as he looked down at her and stroked the long silky black hair that long ago had reminded him of someone else, but no longer did. She was the only woman he loved now.

29

'Do you think they're having an affair?' Zack asked Jane over breakfast one morning.

'Bill and Gabrielle?' Jane smiled at him. 'I think it's possible. I'm not sure he wants to get involved with anyone right now. He's very nervous about the trial, understandably. But I think it might be stronger than both of them. You know, the funny thing is that even when he was giving her such a hard time, I always thought they'd be perfect for each other.'

Zack leaned over and kissed her. 'That's what I love about you. You're psychic.' They were sitting naked beside his pool, eating breakfast. The girls were with their father for the weekend, and they were going to relax and go antiquing for her new house, but she found she didn't care about it quite so much any more. She seemed to be at his place most of the time, especially when the girls were with their father. It was strange even thinking about him now. He was like a total stranger. She had only seen him once since the divorce and he suddenly looked bitter and hard and a little bit crazy. 'You know, I was thinking the other day. What do you want to do during the hiatus?'

'I hadn't even thought about it. Alyssa is going to camp, and Jason and Alex have summer jobs. Jason's working on a ranch in Montana, and Alex is working at the same camp where Alyssa goes.'

'How about going to camp with me this year?' He smiled at her happily. His life had never been better than it was with her, and the past seemed like a distant dream now. 'What about going to Europe for two months?'

Jane looked thrilled. She had never been. 'Wow!'

'The South of France . . . a few weeks in Italy. Austria . . . Maybe even the music festival in Salzburg. What do you say, my love?' He leaned over her and kissed her neck as she beamed. There was no mention of his earlier trips to Greece with his gay friends. That was part of the distant past, and it was all over.

'That sounds fabulous.'

'I'll start making reservations. What about Ireland? We could rent a car and drive . . . and Switzerland! . . .' He was as excited as she was. 'And Spain!' She laughed with delight, and chatting excitedly, they made a list. It was turning out to be the best year of her life, and of his.

'You know, I like being forty years old,' she mused with a satisfied grin. 'It's turning out to be very glamorous.'

'So that's what it is.' He looked pleased. He had just ordered a mink coat for her, from François Brac, and he was going to give it to her as soon as they got back. But the trip to Europe sounded wonderful to both of them. 'Wait till you get to be my age!'

'Speaking of which . . . Sabina has been in a hell of a mood lately.'

'She's just tired. Everyone's ready for a break.'

They only had another six weeks to go, and he was right. That morning, Sabina was lying next to Mel's pool, and she thought she had never been so tired in her life. And oddly enough, they were discussing the hiatus too. She had to go to Paris for three weeks to work with François Brac on the wardrobe for the following year, but after that she was free, and Mel had just suggested meeting her in Europe.

'Can't you come to Paris with me this time?' She looked like a disappointed child and he kissed her fingertips, and then the tip of her nose, and her lips.

'I wish I could, sweetheart. You know what it's like just before we air. There's a hell of a lot for me to do here. But I'll come over as soon as I can. How about a couple of weeks in Cannes?' He had always liked staying at the Carlton.

'What am I going to do in Paris by myself?' She was pouting unhappily at him.

'Hopefully miss me desperately.' Their affair had gone on all through the show, and they suited each other well. She still did what she wanted most of the time, and he gave her plenty of room. She had gone away on several weekends alone, and he never asked her where she went. It bothered him a little bit, but he knew that was the way she was. And he didn't ask her to be any different for him. He wouldn't have expected that of her. He accepted her as she was, and she suited him perfectly, with the exception of her occasional moods, like now. But Zack had been right, she was just tired. They all were, and so was Mel. It was a tremendous amount of work pulling together a series like that. And now he was working on publicity for the autumn. He was planning a grand gala to watch their first night, with plenty of press and hoopla afterwards. But he was still worried about Warwick going to prison.

'I think he's screwing Gabrielle,' Sabina had said bluntly.

'Maybe it'll do him good.' He smiled at her. 'Maybe they're in love.'

Sabina smiled. She liked Mel's romantic streak. He lavished plenty of it on her, and she was happy these days. They all were. 'So tell me about our trip.'

'What about Cannes? And Venice for a week?'

'It sounds divine.' She tilted her hat over her face, and only one green eye peeked out, and she was smiling at him. 'You're very good to me, Mr Wechsler.'

'Am I?' He reached under his newspaper and pulled out a small box. The wrapping told her it was from Bulgari.

'What's that?' The single green eye looked intrigued, and he handed it to her.

'I guess the paper boy left it for you, Miss Quarles. You'd better check it out.' He handed it to her, and with a single gesture, she flung the hat aside, and began unwrapping the gift. He still thrilled her with his constant gifts. This one was a beautiful emerald ring, and she grinned broadly when she opened it, and slipped it onto an impeccably manicured finger. She kept herself beautifully. She was a star, and that was something she never forgot, especially these days. And neither did he.

'It's beautiful, Mel.'

'It reminded me of your eyes.'

She thanked him with a long kiss, and they walked slowly inside, she in a white bikini, and the splendid emerald ring. And he in his bathrobe. And it was a long time before they came outside again. And when they did, they were both smiling.

30

On the last day of shooting, everyone was tense, watching the final scene. It was a scene no one really wanted to see, yet they found they couldn't help it. It was the additional scene Mel had had written, in which Bill was killed . . . in case he didn't come back to the show. It was a confrontation between him and Gabrielle, in which her boyfriend shot him. And at the very end, Sabina got the news her son was dead. It was a powerful scene, and everyone stood silent as they watched it. And Bill looked grim as they shouted 'Print', and he got up.

Everyone remained silent, awed by the implications of it. And Bill looked around ruefully, as though saying goodbye to them. The tears on Gabby's cheeks were genuine, and even Sabina was quiet for once. Zack touched his arm as he walked away.

'They'll never have to use it, Bill. Don't worry.' His eyes were kind, and Bill wanted to thank him, but he was too choked up to speak. The cast crowded around him and Gabby put her arms around him unselfconsciously and cried. It was a hard day for all of them. The last day of the first season's shows. They were going on hiatus for about two months. Mel had ordered a splendid lunch for all of them, and the cast and crew mingled as everyone started to relax and talk about their plans for the summer.

Gabrielle blew her nose, and Jane put an arm around her. 'Relax, it's all over.' The scene was, but they all realised that Bill's problems weren't. He had to face the trial in nine days time, and he was dreading it, as was Gabby. She had put off her summer plans and decided to stay with him. They were going to Lake Tahoe the next day, and then coming back to spend a week conferring with his attorneys.

Jane and Zack were leaving for Rome the following

week, and going on to Venice after that, and then on to the French Riviera for a month, Paris for a few days after that, and a week in London on the way home. She could hardly wait. And Sabina was leaving for Paris and her appointment with François Brac. The crew all talked excitedly about their plans; Europe, the Grand Canyon, and a number of them were going home, some were going east, and others were just hanging around to relax before they started shooting again in August.

'It feels like the last day of school,' Gabby said, as Bill smiled at her. She was still so young, and so sweet, and she had been so good to him. He was deeply grateful to her, and to everyone. By the time they left the set that day, everyone had said a word to him, touched his arm, shaken his hand, said some word of encouragement wishing him well. They really were a family now. And Mel made a point of saying a word to him too.

'I'll be in town, if your attorneys need me to take the stand on your behalf.' He had already told them as much, but he wanted Bill to know it too. 'We're all rooting for you, Bill.' But he still didn't know if he'd keep the job. Everyone else had been given new contracts to sign before they left. Everyone except Bill. But he couldn't worry about that now. He was worried about his life, and the trial. It was hard to believe that it was almost time to face the music. He had thought about calling his parents once or twice, and he suspected they must have heard the news, but they didn't contact him, and he didn't really want to talk to them either.

'Are you going anywhere?' Zack asked Gabrielle as they ate egg rolls and chow mein on the set. It had been catered by Chinois, and there were also pizzas from Spago.

'Not for a while.' He understood why, and nodded somberly, and then glanced at Jane. They were both excited about the trip. They were spending that weekend with the girls, and then leaving as soon as the girls left for camp on Monday.

'We'll give you our itinerary and you can call us when . . .

228

after it's over.' Bill walked over to them and put an arm around Gabby's shoulders, and answered for them both.

'We'll call you, Zack . . .' And then, 'I hope I see you next year . . . all of you.' It was a difficult day for him, and he took everything out of his dressing room when he left. There was no reason to think he'd be coming back after all. And Gabby helped him carry everything to the car, shopping bags and a suitcase, and two plants she'd given him. It was depressing doing that, but he had insisted that there was no point leaving it for someone else to do later.

'You'll just have to haul it all back here in August,' she encouraged and he smiled.

'I sure as hell hope so.' But he didn't look convinced and they were quiet as they finally drove off the lot, having kissed and hugged everyone, and cried some more. It was more like leaving home than like leaving work for the summer. The show had come to mean a great deal to all of them, and they were all curious about the plot of the scripts for the following season. Mel had made a little speech, wishing them all a good holiday, and hinting at big surprises in store for everyone.

'I just hope they don't surprise me by killing me again,' Jane had whispered. She had gone through it once on *Sorrows* and was terrified of its happening again. She had come to love this show, and the people she worked with.

'There's no chance of that.' He thought she was a much better actress than Sabina.

'Ready for the mountains?' Gabby asked, as Bill drove her home. 'I've got all my stuff packed.'

'Almost.' He smiled over at her, the grief at leaving the show beginning to dim a little bit. He was looking forward to a few quiet days with her, alone in the mountains. They had debated about where to go, Yosemite, or Lake Tahoe, or somewhere else. He had finally decided to rent a condo on the lake. He just wanted to go fishing and lie in the sun and be with her. They both needed the rest, especially given what was in store for them. There was no way of knowing how it would turn out, and although his attorneys were optimistic, they could make no promises. 'Want to stay at my place tonight, Gab?'

'I'd love to.' She picked up the bags and equipment already waiting in her front hall. She had her own fishing pole and hiking boots, a sleeping bag in case they decided to camp out. It was a far cry from the six matched Louis Vuitton suitcases Sabina was taking to Paris. And Bill smiled as he helped her carry her gear to his car.

'You certainly have the right equipment, Miss Smith. Do all debutantes wear hiking boots?'

'Always. Especially at the cotillion.' She grinned at him. She had always loved the outdoors, and she was thrilled to know he did too. She had gone on a three-week pack trip in Wyoming once while she was at Yale, and it had been the high point of her college years, especially when their guide had shot a bear. She told him about it as they drove to his house and he laughed at her.

'Don't expect me to do that, kiddo. I'd run like hell, with you under one arm and my backside under the other.'

She laughed. 'It was fun . . .' She had also shot the rapids on the Colorado River two years before, and she wanted to go to Brazil, to the Amazon, one day.

'You're supposed to want nothing more exciting than lunch at the Polo Lounge and a charge account at Giorgio,' he teased, but he was happy that she didn't. She was someone very real, and if anything, she disliked all the frivolous accoutrements of her career. She was much more excited about going to Lake Tahoe with him than she would have been about going to a Hollywood party.

She helped Bill pack his gear late that night, and the next morning at five o'clock they set out on the twelve-hour drive north to Lake Tahoe. They stopped for a quick lunch on the way, and arrived in the clear mountain air of Lake Tahoe at four thirty. Gabby looked like an excited little girl as she flung her arms wide and grinned at him. The condo was beautiful, and they had plenty of privacy, with a hot tub in a little private garden.

They went for a swim in the lake, and went to a steak restaurant Bill knew and liked in Truckee, and they took a long walk in the mountain air before they went to bed. It was an idyllic life for both of them, and a relief after the strain of leaving the set of *Manhattan*.

'I've never been happier,' she whispered to him as they walked home, feeling peaceful and quiet. But Bill was quiet, deeply troubled about the trial. Nothing seemed real to him any more, everything he touched was tainted by the threat of the trial, and what might happen to his life in a few days . . . in two weeks he could be in jail, possibly for years . . . it was a sobering thought as he took her hand and they went back to the condo. She wanted to make him forget everything, but it was difficult now. They sat in the hot tub before they went to bed, and they made love in front of the fire, but in his eyes she could always see the worry and the terror. There was no getting away from it any more, and she felt a ripple of fear too as she watched him sleep that night. She got up before dawn to make cinnamon rolls they had bought at the store, and a fresh pot of hot coffee.

'Rise and shine.' She kissed his ear and he brushed her away, and then opened one eye to look at her.

'What are you doing up at this hour?' It was dark outside, and his voice was deep and sexy.

'I thought we were going fishing in the lake?' They had rented a small boat the night before, and she had all their gear neatly arranged by the door.

'What time is it?'

'Five fifteen.' She grinned at him. 'I thought you'd want to get an early start.'

He laughed and sat up in bed. 'Oh, sure . . . of course . . . why didn't you wake me up at three, and then we could have caught some poor unsuspecting fish sound asleep in his bed? You really take this stuff seriously, don't you, Gab?'

'Sure. In Wyoming, we got up at four every day to catch fish to eat for breakfast.'

He made a face, as she handed him a piping hot cinnamon roll and a mug of steaming coffee. She was wearing her blue jeans under her nightgown. She had put them on when she got up because her legs were cold.

'I like your outfit . . . a lot. François Brac?'

'No.' She smiled. 'Gabby Smith. How's the coffee?'

'Terrific. I may have to hire you to make me coffee every day back home. As it so happens, the position is open.' He had wanted to ask her to live with him when he moved, but he had restrained himself. It wasn't fair to her to start something that would only be painful for both of them if he got sent away. The trial affected everything he did, and it had for months, no matter how much they tried to pretend it wasn't coming. Even now, they were trying to crowd three weeks of holiday into two days. But she was such a good sport about it. And he was surprised at how relaxed he felt by that night. She had caught three fish and he had caught one, and they'd had a picnic near the lake, and then gone swimming again. She cooked dinner for him in the condo that night, and they avoided everyone. Neither of them had any interest in the gambling and night life on the Nevada side, and the next morning they went fishing again, and then came back to the condo to eat lunch and make love, before driving back to Los Angeles.

'I hate to leave.' She looked around nostalgically, as though she were going to remember it all for a lifetime.

'So do I. Maybe we can come back in a few weeks.'

She was thinking of something else, as they packed the last of their things. 'Want to come east with me instead?' She hadn't mentioned it to him before, he had so much on his mind, but this seemed a good time to ask him. It would give him something to look forward to, and assure him that she was confident about the future.

'To see your folks?' He was touched when she nodded.

'I think we'd better wait before we think about things like that.'

'They want me to come to Newport, and I said I'd try. But I want to go to Maine. I have friends who lend me a house there every summer for a few weeks, if I want it. It's very primitive, it's on a little island. But I really love it.'

'My nature girl.' He had never realised how much she liked the outdoor life. It was a far cry from Sandy and her depressing addictions. 'How'd you ever get this way?'

'An aberration, I guess. My parents think I'm crazy.'

'I don't.' He reached over and pulled her onto the bed, and unzipped her jeans, and they made love again before they left on the long drive. Her hair was flying free in the wind, and he looked more relaxed than he had in months. She had been right. The trip to Tahoe had been just what they needed.

They pulled into his driveway just after midnight that night, and they felt as though they'd been away for weeks. He carried all their gear inside, and she decided to spend the night with him.

'I can drop you off at your place on my way to the attorneys' tomorrow.' He looked suddenly sad and she looked at him questioningly.

'Can I come?'

'To the lawyers?' He seemed surprised.

'I'd like that very much . . . I want to be there with you. . .'

'It's not much fun.' That was the understatement of a lifetime, but she walked over to where he stood and put her arms around his neck.

'I happen to be in love with you, Mr Warwick . . . for better or worse . . . at Lake Tahoe, or at the lawyers'.'

He didn't say a word to her, but when he kissed her, there were tears in his eyes. He hated himself for dragging her into it, but he needed her now . . . more than she knew . . . more than he had ever needed Sandy.

31

The law offices of Harrison and Goode looked serious and well decorated, combining modern decor with English antiques, and some very fine paintings. The senior partner's wives had hired the best decorators in town, and the office looked more like New York than Los Angeles. Gabby was relieved at the knowledge that they were the best in town, as she waited in the reception area with Bill. She had stopped at her place to change and she was wearing a dark blue linen dress that her mother had bought her years before at Bergdorf's.

'You're sure you want to come?' he had queried her again as she dressed, and she told him to shut up and go to make them some coffee. He found everything he needed in her tiny kitchen, and half an hour later she had been dressed and ready, looking very proper with her long hair in a neat bun. All she needed was a pair of white gloves and she would have looked ready for lunch at the Colony Club in New York, where he knew her mother had taken her often.

And as they waited for the attorneys to call them in, he was glad she had come. It gave him a feeling of quiet strength just to have her near him. He introduced her to the attorneys, and it was obvious that they approved, and without thinking, he introduced her as Gabrielle Thornton-Smith, but she didn't object. It was obvious that her name had impressed them. Stan Harrison even mentioned that he had met her father. Then he introduced the criminal attorneys who had been brought in by the firm to work on Bill's case. They were sober and well prepared, and they spent three hours preparing him, explaining the pitfalls of the case, the dangers, and their line of questions. Bill was exhausted when he and Gabby finally left the office at lunchtime, and they were expected to come back the next day.

'God, I feel like my head is swimming after all that legal garbage.' He suddenly looked tired and pale, despite the tan he had got that weekend. It was a tremendous strain for both of them, but Gabby looked composed, and she suggested they stop for groceries on the way home.

'I'll make some lunch and you can lie by the pool and relax.'

He looked down at her tenderly. 'What did I ever do to deserve you, Gab?' Especially after the rough time he had given her for so long, but all of that was forgotten.

'Just bad luck, I guess. You know what a pain in the neck debutantes are.'

'Slumming again, eh?' He gently pinched her behind as they got out of the car at the supermarket and she only laughed.

'I used to want to strangle you when you said that word.'

'In this case it happens to apply perfectly.' But not nearly as aptly as it did the following week, as they got out of the car at the courthouse. The halls were filled with seedy-looking people, and they saw two defendants brought in in chains, as lawyers bustled through the halls. Bill met his at the appointed time outside the courtroom.

Gabby stood very close to him this time, not because she was afraid, but she needed to be close to him, as though to prove to herself he was still there.

They had been assigned a judge, and his lawyers said he was very tough, but that could play for him either way. He might be turned off by the ugly tales of Sandy's addiction . . . or he might have no sympathy for Bill at all. There was no way to tell. And it was going to be in the hands of the jury.

Gabrielle took a seat in the second row, and Bill moved through a little gate with three of his attorneys to take a seat at the defendants' table.

They waited ten minutes as the courtroom began to fill,

with other defendants, the curious, attorneys who needed papers signed by the clerk, and a few reporters who had slipped in quietly to watch the action. And then the bailiff called out.

'All rise. Judge MacNamara is now on the bench. Court is in session.' Everyone sat down again, and Gabby stared at the back of Bill's head, praying for him that all would go well.

The attorneys approached the bench, assorted papers were passed around, and the prospective members of the jury were led in. Bill was astounded at how many there were. There were close to a hundred. His attorneys had estimated two days for the selection of the jury. Groups of twelve would be put on the stand at a time, and each attorney had the right to release twenty without cause or explanation.

Two men were chosen first, one an elderly Mexican who spoke English well, and said that he felt he would have no trouble understanding the trial. No one in his family was involved with drugs and he had never been arrested. The second man was a mailman, he said, and he looked nervous and pale. The defence excused him for just cause. His daughter had died of an overdose of drugs three years before. It was obvious why they had excused him.

Two women came next. One heavily made up, one who said she had been an actress years before, the other a grandmotherly type who announced that she had never been married. After that came a young girl, a gay man, a woman who said she was married to a cop. It went on all day, with a recess for lunch. People came and went and were excused, sometimes for obvious reasons, sometimes not. The policeman's wife had been excused immediately by the defence. And the prosecution excused the actress and the gay. It seemed endless and why they kept them or didn't sometimes seemed to make no sense. Gabby and Bill were both exhausted when they left that night. It was like looking at random samples of the human race all day long, and it was exhausting to realise how many variations they came in.

'I keep looking at them and wondering if they're going to believe me or not. I can't figure any of them out, except the obvious ones. The cop's wife scared the hell out of me.' But she'd been excused.

'I know. Sometimes I don't understand why they excuse them.'

'Neither do I. I just hope they know what they're doing.'

They were too tired to make love that night, and were almost too tired to talk or eat. They went out to the pool afterwards for a last swim before they went to bed. The nightmare had begun, and it couldn't be stopped now. Not until it was all over.

They went back the next day, and the same process began again. The full jury was not selected until the afternoon of the third day. Seven women and five men and an innocuous-looking man as the alternate, all of them sober, plain, ordinary, like the man at the chemist or the guy in the garage or the woman who sold you a pair of stockings at the department store. None of them remarkable. And his life was now in their hands. The judge called the afternoon recess early that afternoon, and Gabby and Bill were relieved to go home again. She looked at him quietly over the salad she'd made for them to eat. Neither of them was hungry and he was getting testy from the tension.

'Want to go to a film tonight?' she tried. He desperately needed some kind of distraction.

'I'm on trial for murdering my wife. I don't need anything more dramatic than that.'

'We could go to something funny.'

'I'm not in the mood.' It was understandable, but she wanted to help him.

'Want to go to Mike's and shoot some pool?'

'Maybe tomorrow night, Gab . . . I'm too tired to move.' They were both amazed at how absolutely exhausting it was, just sitting there, feeling the strain all day, and not being able to do anything about it.

'Want me to go home and give you some space?'

He shook his head miserably, and reached for her hand. 'No . . . unless you need to get away from me, and I'd understand if you did. I know I'm being a real turkey, but I'm so damn nervous.'

'It's okay.' She leaned over and kissed him. 'You're not. I just don't want to make you more uptight.'

'You don't. You're the only thing getting me through it.'

She stayed with him once or twice, but most nights she went home at the suggestion of Bill's attorneys. The next day, the prosecution began their case, describing a senseless murder of a beautiful young girl, her actor husband tied to her with chains of anger and hatred, resenting her for spending all his money on drugs, desperate to get away from her, willing to do anything to unload her. It was difficult to recognise Bill in the portrait they painted, and he was terrified as he listened, sure that the jury would believe all of it. They made him sound like a homicidal monster. And they described a crime of passion at the culmination of it all, with Bill desperate to be free of her as he realised what she would do to his new career, and his role on *Manhattan*. He was sick with fear by the end of the second day of the prosecution's case, and his lawyers' assurances did little to calm him as they told him again and again that they would get their chance to tell their side of the story. There were few witnesses for the prosecution's side, except one or two actors from her old show, testifying about what a wonderful young girl she had been. And Bill was shocked to see her agent take the stand, saying that he had opposed the marriage to Bill. He said that he thought the marriage added pressures to her she couldn't handle, and that's when her drug addiction started in earnest.

'Son of a bitch . . .' Bill muttered under his breath, and the attorney closest to him gently touched his arm, reminding him that members of the jury were watching.

The prosecution had used everything they had by Friday afternoon, and a handful of photographers had begun hanging around outside the courtroom. They snapped photographs of Gabrielle and Bill as they left, questioned him, pushing the cameras in his face, and got no answers.

Bill met with his attorneys at length on Saturday morning while Gabby did some errands for both of them, and she was back in time to cook lunch, feed the dog, and take a call from Mel Wechsler. He wanted to know how it was going, and he didn't seem surprised to find her there. He knew everything that went on, on the show, and they had made no great secret of their romance before the hiatus.

'I don't know, Mel,' she answered honestly. 'Everything is so stilted and one-sided. It's awful to watch. His lawyers say he'll get his chance next week, and he'll take the stand himself, but it's so goddam scary.'

'I'm sure it is.' He was worried for Bill, and he reminded her to tell him that he was anxious to appear in court for him. Bill had already told his attorneys that, and they had every intention of calling Mel to the stand. 'I'll be here all week. Just tell them to call me.'

'I'll tell Bill you called. It'll mean a lot to him, Mel.' He was always there for all of them when they needed him, no longer like the Wizard of Oz, but like a father.

Bill was touched when he came home, exhausted again. He had lost seven pounds that week, and Gabby had lost five. It was one way to lose weight for the show, but not the way either of them would have chosen.

'What did they say?'

'The same old stuff. They want Mel to take the stand on Monday.' He called him himself after lunch, and told him what courtroom they were in, and Mel promised to be there.

The rest of the weekend alternately dragged and went too quickly. He wanted it to last forever so they wouldn't have to go back to court, and then sometimes he just wanted it to be over. They were back outside the courtroom all too soon, and Mel was there, conferring quietly with Bill's attorneys. They put him on the stand first, as Gabby watched. It was a relief to see him there, as though he could help them.

'Would you say that Mr Warwick was angry about anything?'

'No. I would say he was a quiet, hardworking young man.'

'Did he complain about his wife?'

'No.'

'Did he talk about her at all?'

'No.'

'Did you know he was married?'

'No, I did not.' Mel's eyes didn't waver as Bill watched, remembering the lie he had told him and wondering what Mel would say about that. But Mel didn't let him down. He was there to help him.

'Wouldn't you say that was a little unusual?'

'No, I wouldn't. Not in this business. Many of the actors we deal with keep their marriages a private affair, particularly if it will affect their image, if it's important for them to appear to be single.'

'Would you say that was the case with Mr Warwick, or do you think he was ashamed of her, afraid that she would destroy his career with her constant arrests for—'

'Objection, Your Honour! The prosecution is leading the witness!' Bill's attorneys cut him off, and the objection was sustained.

'Let me phrase that differently. Was it important to Mr Warwick's career to appear to be single?'

'It could have been eventually.'

'Why?'

'Because he's going to be a very big star next year, when the show goes on the air.'

'Would you say that it could be a hindrance to him to have a wife in her condition?'

'Objection!'

'Overruled. Please answer the question, Mr Wechsler.'

'It could be, but I don't think—'

'Thank you.' They cut him off and Bill closed his eyes. There was no hope. They were going to send him to prison. They were painting a portrait of a man who wanted to get rid of his wife, who hated her, who hated her addiction, and wanted her out of the way at all costs so he could pursue his career. It sounded more like murder one again rather than manslaughter, although they were resting their whole case on the theory of a crime of passion, that he just couldn't take it any more, and had killed her.

Bill's agent took the stand next, as Mel took a seat next to Gabby and squeezed her hand. She looked up at him with troubled eyes, and leaned close to him as they listened.

'Would you say Mr Warwick loved his wife?' the defence attorneys asked, and the prosecution immediately objected.

'That's conjecture, Your Honour.'

'Sustained. Rephrase your question.' MacNamara looked annoyed. They were all a bunch of spoiled, badly behaved film stars and he had no patience with any of them. But the important thing was how the jury felt, and there was no reading their faces.

'Did Mr Warwick ever tell you he was in love with his wife?'

'Frequently. He was crazy about her, and he said so.'

The prosecution looked annoyed, and Mel glanced at Gabby, but she was staring straight ahead, willing all of her strength to Bill, with no thought of malice or jealousy towards Sandy.

'Was he bothered by her drug addiction?'

'Of course, he was worried about her all the time. He wanted her to go to cure centres but she wouldn't go.'

'Would you say he was angry at her?'

'No. Never.'

'Would you say he felt that his career was threatened by her?'

'No. I kept telling him to get rid of her, that she would destroy him, but he wouldn't hear it. He was always there for her. He hoped she'd clean up. Even when he was in New York on location, he called me all the time, wanting me to find her, to see how she was.'

'And how was she?'

'I don't know. I could never find anyone who knew where she was. She had pretty much disappeared into the drug scene even before he left. They were already separated then.'

'Did he see her when he got back?'

'I don't know. He didn't tell me.'

'Would you say he wanted to get rid of her?'

'No. Not in that sense. I think he may have wanted to divorce her, but it never got to that point. I think she was too messed up for him to pursue it.'

'Have you ever seen Mr Warwick lose his temper?'

'No, sir.'

'Have you ever heard him threaten anyone?'

'No, sir.'

'Thank you very much.'

The prosecution took over, and they couldn't shake Harry's testimony. He was terrific, and Bill smiled at him as he left the stand. He wanted to stand up and kiss him.

It took three more days to call all their witnesses, including Sandy's parents, who appeared for the defence, but they were barely coherent from the shock of what had happened. And it was obvious that they had disapproved of her and given up on her a long time before Bill had. They talked about a difficult childhood, and an uncontrollable girl; who had run away from home several times in her teens, and dabbled in drugs off and on long before she met Bill or began acting. And they felt that the pressures of her work had been the last straw. They had felt she was doomed from the beginning.

Bill's own parents had called him halfway through the trial, but their call was typical of them. His father sounded disappointed and accusing, and his mother cried on the extension. They made no offer to come west, and Bill wasn't even sure afterwards if they believed him innocent of Sandy's murder.

But the worst day of all was the day that Bill took the stand himself. They asked him all the questions he had dreaded, and tried to make the relationship sound ugly and sordid. They tried to enrage him by painting her as promiscuous, and they made it sound as though he had only married her to use her to get work, and then cast her aside when he got himself a big part on *Manhattan*. They made it all sound so seamy and they pushed him and pushed him and pushed him until he couldn't take it any more, and he broke down on the stand and sobbed, holding his face in his hands, unable to stop the tears, as he thought of the girl he had once loved, and all that had happened since then. It wasn't at all what they said, and he had looked dismally at the prosecutor, with tears rolling slowly down his cheeks, when he was finally able to speak again, and his voice was hoarse with the pain that had been inflicted on him.

'Don't you understand?' The reporters were sketching him furiously, and what one saw now was the raw core of the man, the naked soul of the man who had loved Sandy. 'I loved her.'

'People have killed people they love before, Mr Warwick.' The prosecution was relentless, but the defence had objected then, and they had asked for a recess in which Bill could regain control. But he had broken down again that afternoon, and as Gabby glanced at the jury she prayed that they were feeling sorry for him. It was almost impossible not to. But their faces registered nothing.

On Friday morning, the judge instructed the jury. They had to feel, beyond a reasonable doubt, that Bill had killed Sandy. They had to be sure of it, based on the testimony they had heard, and not based on any emotional interpretations. If they convicted him, sentence would be set in thirty days, by the judge, and they were not to be affected by what the sentence might be. They were only to determine his innocence or guilt, based on the presentation of the defence and the prosecution. Bill's own testimony had been deeply moving and he had broken down several times, but even that wasn't supposed to sway them. They were only supposed to deal with the evidence, the bullet wounds, the absence of the gun, their relationship such as it had been re-created for them, and whether or not they felt Bill had killed her.

He called a recess after that, and the jury was led to the jury room, as Bill stood in the hall with his attorneys, and Gabby hovered nearby. There was no one there for her, and she suddenly missed Jane . . . and Zack . . . and Mel . . . she wished that they could be there now. Mel was waiting for news in his office. And all they could do now was wait. They knew it could take several days before they heard. The attorneys had warned them of that. The jury was going to take as long as they had to.

The defence team lingered in the halls, making conversation in which Bill didn't participate. He couldn't keep his mind on anything except the verdict.

He was talking to Gabby quietly when the bailiff came out and asked everyone to come back inside. The jury had reached a verdict, and the defence attorneys looked worried. They had been conferring for less than an hour, and that was usually a bad sign. It almost always meant a guilty verdict, and was usually in cases where the defendant was clearly guilty of the crime. They had hoped to create far more doubt in the minds of the jury.

'Court is in session. All rise.' The judge emerged from his chambers, buttoning his robe, and he sat down, as Bill clutched the arms of his chair unconsciously, and the jury filed in. They still wore no expressions on their faces. They were like masks. No one looked satisfied or pleased, or sad, no one smiled at Bill, or gave him any encouragement at all. Gabby felt tears sting her eyes, suddenly realising the full force of what was happening. If he was found guilty, he would be led away then and there . . . for Bill Warwick, it would be all over . . . for a long time anyway . . . and for her . . . but more importantly, for him. He could spend as long as eleven years in prison.

'Ladies and gentlemen of the jury, have you reached a verdict?' Gabby was coming to hate the formalities, the words that meant nothing to them, but on which Bill's whole life rested.

'We have, Your Honour.'

'And what is it?' She squeezed her eyes shut, afraid to hear, and Bill was white as a sheet as he watched them.

'We find the defendant not guilty, Your Honour.'

The defence attorneys grinned and Bill stared, as the judge looked down at him. 'You have been acquitted, Mr Warwick.' There was a terrible sob from behind him as he leapt from his chair and rushed through the gate to find Gabby. She flew into his arms and he held her there, the two of them crying, as the lawyers smiled, and the jury filed out. The judge rose. And it was over.

They called Mel from downstairs, and Gabby told him the news through her tears. Bill was still too shaken to talk to anyone, and she apologised for him. He congratulated them both, and there were tears in his own eyes as he hung up the phone. He had told Gabby to have Bill call him when he felt ready.

The news item announcing the verdict was much smaller than the item describing his arrest, but he wasn't bitter about it. He was just relieved. They called Zack and Jane that night, and Jane cried at the news. And Mel told Sabina when he called her in Paris.

Little by little the word spread, and Bill felt as though he was slowly returning to the land of the living. He had never been certain of the outcome. It had been the most terrifying experience of his life. And now suddenly, he was left with the mundane pleasures of real life . . . jogging with his dog in Malibu, shopping at Safeway, watering his garden, taking Gabby out for a hamburger at Mike's, he could even think about furnishing his apartment because he wasn't going to prison. And there were more important things to think about too. Like his job, and their future.

'How about coming east with me now? I think we both need it,' she suggested and they agreed that they needed another week or two to catch their breath. It had been a terrible strain. He helped Gabby bring two enormous bags of her things from her apartment. They made no formal arrangements, but he wanted her to move in with him. They had been through so much together, he almost felt as though they were married, but he didn't want her to rush into anything. She had a lot to think about now. She was part of an important show, her career was going to take off, and she had been through a lot with him. There was always the possibility that she would never want to see him again after it was all over. But she showed no sign of it. She brought all her plants from her apartment, groomed Bernie every day, helped Bill set his place to rights, and she always seemed to be fixing things up, and making them homey. She had just finished moving the furniture around for the second time, when she turned to Bill, and gently asked:

'When are you going to face the music?' She didn't want to push him, but he might as well know where he stood with Mel. It had been a week since the verdict came in, and Bill had done everything to avoid calling.

'What music, sweetheart?' He frowned, pretending to ignore her. 'I liked the couch better the way you had it a minute ago. I saw some great lamps downtown yesterday, by the way. I thought we could pick them up tomorrow.'

'Never mind that' – she wagged a finger at him – 'and you know exactly what I mean. You were supposed to call Mel. And don't ask me Mel who. Mel Wechsler.'

He grinned sheepishly. 'I figure I got lucky once, twice may be too much to ask of my karma.'

'Wouldn't it be better to know?'

'No. I'd rather go and buy lamps with you.'

'Don't be so chicken.' She forced him to call Mel that afternoon. But his secretary said that he was meeting with the networks and wouldn't be back in the office again until Monday. Bill reported it to Gabrielle and she laughed. 'Well, you got a reprieve.'

They had a lovely weekend, relaxing and lying by his pool, they had dinner at Mike's once, and he took her to Ma Maison on Saturday night to finally celebrate their victory. Mel returned his call on Monday morning. He didn't say anything much on the phone. He just asked him to come in that afternoon. And Bill thanked him again for appearing at the trial, and promised to be there.

'What did he say?'

'That he's tripling my salary, you're all fired, and I'm the star of my own one-man show starting this season.'

She laughed. Bill was in such a good mood these days. The thousand-pound weight was off his back, and he was happy. It had been a terrible time for him, but it was all over. Poor Sandy was finally laid to rest, and he could go on with his life now.

'I'm serious, what did Mel say?'

'He said to come in around three o'clock. That's the time he likes firing people best.'

'You're impossible. Can I come?'

'No. It's one thing to have you watch me dragged off to prison . . . but losing my job I can do alone. And he didn't invite you.'

'Okay. I have some shopping to do anyway.'

'New hiking boots?' he teased.

'No. Believe it or not, I need some clothes before we go to Newport. I thought I'd drop in at Giorgio.'

'You? The Queen of Army Surplus?'

'Just don't tell anyone.'

'Your secret is safe with me, princess.' He swept her into an embrace worthy of a musical in the 1930s, and dropped her rudely on the couch as she laughed. He was in such good spirits that he wasn't as depressed as he might have been about losing his job. He hadn't lost his freedom, that was much more important. And it had been a good year on the show. He really couldn't blame Mel for letting him go. The scandal was really a violation of all their agreements, and he knew it.

But he felt sad anyway as he walked into Mel's office that afternoon. It was like coming home to visit his father and he felt as though he had let him down. But Mel was as warm and friendly as he always was, as Bill took a seat across from his desk.

'You're looking better again.'

'I feel a whole lot better than I did the last time I saw you.' He smiled. With or without the job, he would be grateful to Mel for a lifetime. He was a decent man, a good friend, and a great producer. 'I want to thank you for everything . . .

248

for being there . . . and . . .' He felt his eyes mist despite his best efforts for them not to, but it was an emotional time for him. It was like having been terminally ill and suddenly recovering. 'You've done so much for me . . . the show has been wonderful . . .' He almost choked on his words. 'I'm going to miss you.'

'Where are you going?' Mel looked puzzled by his speech, and Bill was confused by the question.

'East with Gabby for a few weeks, but I meant . . .'

Suddenly Mel understood. 'Don't be so noble. I asked you here today to give you your new contract for next season.'

'You did?' Bill's eyes grew wide.

'I did. Although I think we'll hold that final scene we shot just to keep you in line if you get in a funk again.'

'I won't. Do you mean it? You mean I'm back for next season?' Bill stared at him in disbelief.

'You are. You should see how it all came out in post-production, Bill. The show looks so good, people will love it and you! America is going to be riveted to *Manhattan*. You don't want to miss that, do you?'

'Hell, no.' Bill grinned. He had been lucky twice in the past week. It was too much to hope for.

Mel handed a thick envelope to him. 'Show that to your agent and your attorneys, and get it back to me next week sometime. I'm going to Europe as soon as I can, and I'd like to know it's signed before I go.'

'I'll sign it right now.' He was all set to go, but Mel held up a hand.

'It'll wait. Run it past your attorneys, you never know if they want to make some changes. The morals clause is the same' – he grinned – 'just please try not to get arrested.' And there was nothing in it that forced him to be single, which was just as well, because he'd been thinking for weeks about asking Gabby to marry him. But he wanted to wait until the end of the summer, to see how she felt after he met her parents and they'd been together for a while without any major drama.

'Mel . . . thank you so much . . . I'm so grateful to you . . .'
His eyes said everything, and Mel walked him to the door
with a fatherly arm around his shoulders.

'There's no need to be grateful. You're a hell of a good
actor. Just wait till you see what the public says in two
months. It's going to be something.' He was totally confident in the show, and Bill felt as though he were walking on
air as he ran to his car, and drove to Rodeo.

He hurried into the shop on the corner with the yellow-
and-white-striped canopy and he looked around but he
didn't see Gabby. He asked one of the salesgirls and she
said she'd ask, and when she came back, she said that Gabby
was in one of the dressing rooms, trying on some clothes.
She pointed to the one, and he tiptoed to the door, and
carefully opened it, as she stood in a red silk dress trying to
decide if she liked it.

'What are you doing here?' She looked thrilled to see
him, as always.

'That would look nice with your hiking boots.' He looked
her over approvingly and she was instantly impatient.

'What did he say?'

'Who?'

'Bill, stop it!'

'He said he can't fire me, because I have to keep you in line
next year.' He grinned at her and she rushed into his arms.

'Are you serious?'

'I am. The contract is in the car. I'm on again, for the
second season.'

'Fantastic!' She took off the dress, and stood in her
underwear, as the salesgirl came in and smiled. They were
used to scenes like that at Giorgio.

'Did you like the dress?' The girl inquired pleasantly.

'We loved it.' Bill grinned. He bought it for her, and five
others, and they went home to make love by the swimming
pool.

'You'd better start behaving yourself if I'm taking you
home to Newport.'

250

'Oh, no,' he groaned, as he lay naked next to her. 'Can't I just meet you in Maine?'

'Nope. I wouldn't deprive my parents of the pleasure.' She grinned at him, and rolled over on her stomach in the hot sun, as the dog yawned, stretched, and leapt into the pool, covering both of them with water.

33

Their days in the East flew by, and Gabby's parents thought Bill was charming. He stayed at their house near Bailey's Beach and he was surprised at how at ease he was with her father. They had lunch at the Beach Club every day, even on the day it rained, and they went to the Clambake Club for dinner. It was notorious, Gabby told him, because it was where Jackie Bouvier had made her debut.

'You know, I really like your mother,' he had told her as they lay side by side in the guest room one night. It was across from her bedroom, and she padded across the hall every night to be with him, and then went back to her room to rumple the sheets every morning. 'She's a lot smarter than you think.'

'She's all right.' Actually, they were getting along better than usual that year, and of course her parents had no idea of the trauma they'd just been through in California. They just thought he was a nice young actor in 'Gabby's show', as they called it. They promised to watch the three-hour special the first night it came on and Everett told him to come to see them in New York when they were back on location in the autumn. They were going in September this year, and Gabby's mother had announced that she was going to give them 'a little dinner'.

'That means a hundred people in black tie, all the people I hate most in the world will be there. You'll love it.'

'Don't be such a spoiled brat. They love you.'

'Okay, okay.' She looked at him disparagingly and he laughed. She was so young, and a real beauty. There were days when he wondered how he had been so lucky. And only a year before he had been picking up Sandy's needles on his bathroom floor and begging her to get help. But he hardly ever thought of that now, and he didn't think of it at all as they took the ferry to her friends' place in Maine. It was simple and quaint and the terrain around them was solemn and rugged. It was just her kind of thing and a far cry from Bailey's Beach, which she had complained about when they were there. But she played the social game well, and pleased her parents.

They went back to California a week before shooting began, and Jane and Zack had just arrived from Europe the night before. She and Jane had lunch at the Polo Lounge and giggled when they saw Warren Beatty and Paul Newman. They were just like two kids, instead of two television stars, and Jane told her they'd seen Sabina with Mel in Saint-Tropez that summer.

'I don't know how she does it. That woman always looks terrific.'

'It's hard work,' Gabby commented over her salad and wine.

'Don't kid yourself. It takes more than that. She just has a kind of presence. Everyone stares at her wherever she goes.'

'Wait till *Manhattan* airs, she'll really be hot stuff then.'

'You know, she went topless on the beach. Everyone does there. She's got boobs like an eighteen-year-old.' Jane sounded envious. And looking at Sabina, she had decided hers were sagging.

'She should look eighteen.' Gabby smiled wickedly. 'I know the doctor who did them.'

Jane laughed. It was fun to be back in Hollywood again. They were all looking forward to going back to work and the four of them played tennis on their last day and had dinner at Spago. It was like a family reunion but it was nothing compared to the scene on the set the next day. Everyone went crazy, hugging and laughing and talking about the summer. And the old sound man even threw an arm around Sabina. But she didn't mind. She was happy to see all of them too. It had been a great summer. The fittings had gone well with François Brac, and she had had a fabulous time with Mel in the south of France. They were all in high spirits, as they talked about the new scripts. There were apparently big surprises in store too. Someone was going to get fatally wounded. Jane was going to fight Sabina for Zack. And someone else was going to get pregnant.

'Not me, I hope,' Bill quipped over a glass of wine. Their first day on the set was to get back in the groove again. Scripts were distributed to everyone, and they were told that they were leaving on location in two weeks. There was a festive atmosphere in the air, and everyone was excited about their first night on the air. Mel was turning it into a gala event, and they could hardly wait. He had rented Grauman's Chinese Theatre, and was having a giant television screen put up on the stage. The press would be there, and hundreds of other people.

'I have nothing to wear,' Jane moaned as they left, and Gabby laughed.

'What about all your new stuff by François Brac?'

'I'm so tired of it. They're my work clothes!' Jane grinned. 'Want to go to Giorgio with me on Saturday?'

'Sure.' They turned it into a major shopping trip, and Gabby bought a new dress for the party too. A shimmering tube of black sequins with no back. 'Wait till Bill sees this!' she said, as she twirled in the dressing room. She kept it hidden in the box until the night of Mel's party, and his jaw dropped when he saw her.

'Wow! Who is that?' There were no hiking boots in sight now. Her hair was piled high on her head, and she was wearing black satin pumps, and she was carrying the white fox jacket her father had sent her.

Her mother called just as they left the house, in tears, to tell her that she'd been watching the show, and they were just wonderful both of them. In New York, they had already seen it, and she told Gabby she'd never been so proud of her, and Gabby felt a warm glow as she took Bill's arm and they walked out to the limousine Mel had sent for them. It was a magical night, and she felt as though her whole life was about to change. She was right, but it already had. In all the ways that really mattered.

34

The photographers looked as though they were ten-deep as Sabina got out of the car on Hollywood Boulevard in front of Grauman's Chinese Theater. The Oriental decor was familiar to everyone, along with the foot- and handprints in the cement outside, and Gabby had always thought it was fun to see who was represented there, but she wasn't thinking of them tonight. None of them were.

Sabina swept inside in a white satin sheath made for her by François Brac and a floor-length mink coat that Mel had bought her at Revillon in Paris. It was an astonishing piece of fur, and she looked dazzling, with her mane of blonde hair, her brilliant green eyes, and diamond earrings that reached almost to her shoulders. There was no question as to who was the star, but Jane acquitted herself well too in a midnight-blue dress made of sari fabric that dove deep enough in the front to reveal her fabulous cleavage, and her red hair stood out in the crowd, as she took Zachary's arm and they made their way through the crowd, with the cameras flashing everywhere around them. And she was wearing a beautiful pair of sapphire earrings Zack had bought her in London. He had wanted to buy her a ring, but neither of them were ready for that yet. They weren't in a hurry. And they looked happy and at ease as they moved inside to the enormous champagne reception Mel had arranged. Everyone important in Hollywood was there, and every newspaper and syndicate was well represented. George Christy was there too, looking dapper and elegant, and covering the event for the *Hollywood Reporter*.

'Can you believe this crowd?' Jane was still in awe of everything as she chatted with Gabby once they arrived, and Gabby smiled as she looked around.

'This is it . . . isn't it?' They had been put on opposite the toughest opposition the other networks had been able to come up with, and it was tough. A new Sidney Shelton novel filmed for TV directly opposite them, and a major sports group later. But Mel still insisted they had nothing to worry about. They had it made. And Gabby hoped he was right, as they took their seats a little while later.

Everyone settled down as the show came on, and there was alternately silence and cheers and roars of approval from the crowd. And during the commercials everyone talked about how good it was. But there was no way to know until the next day, when they would know the ratings.

Jane was exhausted as they walked into the lobby again. She wasn't sure if she'd been good or not, she was sure that the others were. Sabina sailed out looking like a queen, without a doubt in her mind, as far as anyone could see. The photographers went to work again, and they went on all night long, as fleets of limousines took them to Chasen's, where Mel had arranged for a midnight supper and dancing for three hundred in the Oak Room.

It was a magical evening for all of them, and that night, when they got home, Gabby dived into the pool, leaving her sexy black dress draped over a chair, as Bill watched her in the new dinner jacket he had bought at Bijan for the occasion.

'Well, what do you think?' She smiled up at him from the edge of the pool. It was four o'clock in the morning.

'I think you've the most beautiful woman I've ever seen.' He was more than a little drunk and so happy he was flying, and he loosened his tie, and stripped off his clothes, and a moment later, he was in the pool beside her.

'Think it'll be a hit?'

'I think Mel's right.'

Like everyone else, Gabby was secretly worried about the competition, but the next morning they all knew Mel had been right. The ratings soared and they had had the lion's share of the television audience. The country was crazy about *Manhattan*. And all of his predictions came true. Their agents were going nuts with calls for interviews, photographs, offers of parts during their next break, and everyone wanted posters of Sabina, Jane, and Gabby. Even Harry was going nuts. *Playgirl* wanted a centrefold of Bill, and *Cosmo* offered them more money for the same exposure. The five of them were suddenly the biggest stars in the country. Mel had predicted it all, but it had been hard to believe. It was hard to understand just how it would feel, until it actually happened.

Sabina could hardly go anywhere any more without being mobbed by men and women alike, people begged her for autographs, and a man she had never seen before grabbed her outside the Beverly Wilshire and kissed her and then ran off screaming, 'I did it . . . I did it! . . . I did it!'

'Was I right?' Mel gloated over breakfast the day before they left for New York. He had given her a huge, eighteen-carat marquise-cut diamond ring the day the ratings came in, and there was a pressing question he had been wanting to ask her. But he was biding his time. There was still too much excitement about *Manhattan*.

'You were.' She lay catlike on the couch in his living room. She preferred eating there, and she was reading the latest stack of clippings her press agent had sent her. It was all so damn much fun. She loved it all, the excitement, the recognition, and the money. She didn't even have to worry now. If anything ever happened to her, she was all set. She could have retired and lived well for the rest of her days, and left enough behind to quell all her worries. She glanced up at Mel with a warm smile and a look of pleasure. He was so good to her, and she had never dreamed of owning as much jewellery as she did now . . . or the furs . . . he wanted to buy her a sable coat for the trip to New York. 'It won't even be cold when we get there,' she laughed.

'It will be when we leave. And every girl needs a sable.' It was like a dream, a dream she had always had, and it had finally come true, and this was just the beginning.

He had chartered a plane for all of them to go to New

York, and she had to pack that afternoon. They all had lots of last-minute errands to do. Jane was spending the day with the girls, who were awestruck by it all now. Their friends had practically assaulted them in school the day after the first show. Her son had called from college, and they were establishing some kind of rapport again. Jason had finally understood that his father had been grossly unfair to her, and they were all coming to respect her career as important. She had even invited him on the set, and he had come and been enormously impressed. And she had introduced him to Zack, and Jason was surprised by how pleasant and unpretentious he was. Not like a big star at all. Just like a normal person. The three of them had dinner at a small restaurant Zack knew, and they drove him back to Santa Barbara that night. Jane had cried on the way home, she felt as though she had a son again, and she hadn't in over a year, thanks to her ex-husband.

'You're lucky you have such wonderful kids,' Zack had said quietly as they drove back to Los Angeles. It was the one thing he envied her, and it was the price he had paid for the mistakes he had made in his youth. And at times, he regretted it deeply.

She was spending the night in Los Angeles at Zack's and Gabby was busy at Bill's. She had taken the dog to the vet, and she had had to pack up her whole apartment that weekend. She was moving in with Bill. There was no point in paying rent on an empty apartment for two months, and when they came back, she was going to be living with him. He finally asked when they got back from Maine, and she was thrilled.

'Did you pack my socks?' He hurried in with a whole stack of jeans, and she grinned. It was as though they had always lived like this, and she laughed as she told him she had. She had packed for both of them.

Mel was working late that night, and Sabina's new maid had put all her Vuitton bags in the hall. She thought it was Mel calling to say goodnight when the phone rang, but it wasn't. It was the call she had dreaded for years. And she sat terrified. She had to go to San Francisco that night, and she couldn't leave for New York with the cast of *Manhattan*.

She dialled Mel at home, but he wasn't there yet, and the phone in his office was turned off. She packed a bag, and made a reservation on the last flight out of Los Angeles. And she was already dressed to leave when she tried him one last time, and heaved a sigh of relief when he answered.

Her voice was nervous and stiff as she talked to him and he knew instantly something was wrong. 'I can't leave for New York.'

'My God . . . why?' He was stunned. What was she saying to him? 'Are you sick?'

'No, I'm not. I'll come as soon as I can. You'll have to shoot around me this week.'

'But we can't do that. You're in almost every scene. Sabina, what is it? . . .' He had never heard her sound like that before, and it stirred a distant chord of memory for him, but he couldn't remember quite what it was. 'What's wrong?'

'I can't tell you, Mel.' It was the first time she had shut him out since she had refused to go to the Bahamas with him. 'I'm sorry . . . I just can't.'

'What the hell am I supposed to tell the cast?' He was tired and angry at her for not telling him why she couldn't go. 'That we're going to New York for a holiday?'

'I can't do anything about it.' She looked at her watch. 'I have to go. I'll call you in New York.' And with that she hung up, grabbed her overnight case, and hurried out the door, as Mel stared at the phone in his hand in fury and frustration.

35

Mel did something to her he had never done before. He called an investigator to find out where Sabina was. But the only thing the man could find out was that she had left the night before. Her doorman knew she had gone to the airport, but for two days he was unable to discover anything else, and then finally he found a stewardess who remembered seeing her on the plane.

'Where did she go?'

'San Francisco.' She had mentioned it to him before. She went there periodically to see friends. 'But we can't find her in any of the hotels.'

'Damn.' It was unlike Mel to swear or to pursue anyone like that, but she was the star of his biggest show, and he wanted to know where she was. And there was more to it than that. He wanted to marry her, and he wanted to know to just what extent she was making a fool of him, and who with.

They were shooting around her in New York and it was making everything difficult, and he didn't hear a word from her. But the investigator called again after two more days. 'She's in Palo Alto, possibly staying with friends. It's a simple house, near the university.'

He wanted to ask if she was with a man, but he was embarrassed to. But the investigator made it easier for him. 'The only people that go in and out are three women. They seem to come and go in shifts. They all wear coats when they arrive or leave, but they appear to be nurses. Apparently, she's with someone sick. She's only left the house twice, for a walk herself, and she looks very subdued. We have photographs we can express-mail to you, Mr Wechsler. She's wearing dark glasses and a hat, but it's her.' It was a sick lover, then . . . maybe someone she'd been involved with for

261

years. But why hadn't she said anything? She owed him that much. 'We'll stay on it.'

'Thanks.' He hadn't heard a word from her in four days, and he was still furious with her, but she called him the next day. She sounded bone tired, and he didn't even recognise her voice at first.

'I'll be in New York in a couple of days, Mel. I'll start shooting the first of the week.'

'Thank you very much. Where the hell are you anyway?' The anger in his voice rang out, but she was too tired to care. She'd tell him something when she got to New York. It was all she could do. This was a part of her life that belonged to no one else but her.

'I'm staying with a sick friend.' It was exactly what the investigator had told him.

'Why couldn't you tell me that before you left Los Angeles?'

'I didn't have time to explain, I had to catch the last plane.'

'To where?' He wanted her to tell him herself, she owed him that much.

'It's not important where. I told you all you need to know.' Her voice was cold and hard. 'I'll be there in two days.' And then, 'Don't push me, Mel. This has nothing to do with you.'

'Apparently.' He was deeply hurt. 'I thought we were closer than that, but maybe I've been deluding myself.'

She didn't have the energy to deal with his fears and jealousies and she had no intention of telling him the truth when she got to New York. She had never told anyone. 'Please don't take it personally.'

'How do you expect me to take it, Sabina? You disappear in the middle of the night, no one knows where you are . . . who you're with . . . or why . . . what am I supposed to think?' She could imagine what he was thinking then, that she had run off with another man, but it was so much more serious than that. But for a moment, she felt sorry for him.

'I'm sorry, Mel. Maybe we'll talk about it sometime.'

'You're damn right we will.' But his forcefulness only drove her away, and she hung up without telling him anything more. She sat in the small darkened living room in the ugly little house in Palo Alto. She had come here every month for years. Sometimes more often than that when she wasn't working. Sometimes she stayed for weeks, but it depressed her terribly. And now he had almost died. That was what they had told her the night they called her in Los Angeles.

'Can I get you anything, Miss Quarles?' The nurse on the night shift walked into the room with a gentle smile. It was odd seeing this side of her. On television she was so beautiful and glamorous, and here she looked so tired and almost old. She hadn't worn makeup since she arrived, and she looked as though she hadn't combed her hair in days.

'I'm all right. How's Anthony?'

'He's asleep. Poor little thing. He's so tired, but he'll be all right.' She went in to sit beside him then, as she had since she'd arrived. She had slept in the chair in his room, night after night, holding his hand. It was an agony, watching him, and yet she would have been nowhere else.

She took her place at his side again, and watched the exquisitely etched face in the soft light. Sometimes he looked so young, and at other times so old, his whole life had been an agony, a struggle to survive, and there was so little they could do for him. It was a miracle he had lived this long. He had been born with congenital deformities, he was paralysed from the waist down from birth, his lungs were weak, and he had a severely defective heart. And at first transplant techniques hadn't been developed enough to operate on such a young child. They had operated six times before he was a year old, and then all but given up on him. They had tried again when he was two, and by then he had other problems, and the surgeons insisted that transplants were never done on children so young. Now he was old enough, but no one was willing to take the risk. He wasn't strong enough to survive the surgery now. So instead he lived less than a half life in the house she had bought for him years before, a stone's throw from Stanford Hospital, attended by nurses night and day, watched relentlessly, and one day it would come anyway, the end they had prolonged but that no one could defer forever.

He stirred as she watched him breathe, the monitors given to them by the March of Dimes years before ticked quietly. She was used to watching them now, after years of it. The proceeds of every film poured into an account for him. Now she didn't have to worry about that any more. That was a blessing anyway. It was why she had agreed to do *Manhattan* the year before, because she knew what it represented to him, and there was always the terror that something would happen to her, and then he'd be alone with no one to provide for him. His father had been horrified when he was born, married to someone else, and passionately in love with Sabina, he claimed, but not so passionately that he wanted to stand by Anthony with all his problems. He hadn't even given him his name. He had given her a ten-thousand dollar cheque, which hadn't even paid for the first surgery. And now she had everything she needed for him . . . everything . . . except that she couldn't buy what he had never had. She had been thirty-one years old when he was born, and they had never known why he was born that way. She didn't take drugs, she didn't drink, just an 'accident of nature', they said . . . some accident . . . a child born with almost no lungs, a damaged heart, an injured spine, and yet she loved him desperately, perhaps even more than she would have otherwise. She had wept for days as she held him close to her in the intensive care nursery, monitors attached to him everywhere. And then the surgeries . . . she hadn't worked for a year, but she finally had to go back to work to pay the bills that were mounting up. It had been a constant struggle for fifteen years. Until *Manhattan* came along. She owed so much to Mel, but she couldn't tell him about this. She had never told anyone, never trusted anyone that much. She didn't want Anthony's life, what was left of it, turned into a travesty, with reporters worming their way in, and photographers, especially now that everyone was so interested in her. She could just imagine what they'd do to him. She was always terrified that one of the nurses would talk, though they'd been with her for years now.

He stirred again, but she saw that he looked better. The doctor had said that he was out of the woods again, for the time being. They hadn't even moved him to the hospital this time, because there was no point, Dr Waterford said. It was going to happen one day anyway . . . please God . . . let it be peacefully . . . let me be here with him . . . she had prayed that so many times, whenever she was away. It was why she had had to come back to him when she'd been in New York, and not gone to the Bahamas with Mel. She owed him that. She had given him this broken life, it was all her fault, it had to be. She had always blamed herself. He was fifteen years old and he looked like a five-year-old, as he lay dozing in the huge hospital bed in the bedroom that was his prison.

'Mom?' His eyes were open and they were the same green as hers. He was smiling at her, and she had to fight back tears again.

'Hi, sweetheart. Want something to drink?' There was a pitcher of ice water next to his bed. And he loved apple juice and chewing gum and watching ice hockey games. He had lived his whole life in that room. Fifteen years like that. Without complaining. 'Are you comfortable?'

'I'm okay.' He smiled at her with eyes just like hers. 'Tell me about your new show.' He was whispering. It exhausted him to talk for too long, but he loved hearing about it. She sent him letters all the time, and she called every day, always had, from wherever she was, and she sent him funny things, posters, and mobiles, and books for them to read to him. He was too tired to hold the books himself, but she had taught him to read when he was four. He was such a special little boy . . . Anthony . . . she told him about Mel, and

Gabrielle and Bill, and Jane and her two daughters . . . they were just his age, and it hurt thinking about it. It had hurt seeing them, it used to torment her to see normal children running in the park, holding their mothers' hands . . . she had loved his father so much, and they had owed him so much more than this.

'I love you, sweetheart,' she whispered as he went back to sleep. She hated the thought of leaving him in two days, but he was stable again, and she had to go back to work. This was the reality of their lives. And the nurses always reminded her that he was used to it. It was the only life he knew. This torture and her working.

When she got up and stretched again, it was four o'clock, and she had an overwhelming urge to call Mel again in New York . . . just to talk to him . . . it was seven o'clock in the morning there and she knew he would be up, but he was still so angry at her. There were questions she didn't want to answer, and knew she never would. She went into the living room and lay down on the couch for a while. There was a bedroom for her, but she didn't want to sleep. They had so little time . . . so little time . . . she never knew if this would be the last time. She went back to his room, and took his small, frail hand in her own. She kissed his fingertips, and smiled at him as the tears trickled slowly down her cheeks.

'I love you, sweetheart.' She whispered the words almost inaudibly.

He opened an eye. She had thought he was asleep. 'I love you too, Mom.' He smiled happily and closed his eyes. He was always happier when she was there with him.

36

It was always an agony leaving him, and this time it was no better. She felt a hand clutch her heart and the words stuck in her throat and yet she had to put a good face on it for him. She promised to come back in a few weeks and told him she was going to New York. And he told her he'd watch the show. Then the worst moment came, when she held him next to her, feeling his warmth, the little life he had left in him, and wondered if she would ever see him again. Sometimes she hated herself for not giving everything up to be with him, but then she couldn't have supported him. She had often thought of bringing him to Los Angeles, but he needed to be near Stanford Hospital. There was no choice than this, and it was too late now anyway. They had to make the best of it.

'I love you, sweetheart ... soooo much!' She smiled through her tears and he told her not to cry. He was the bravest child in the world, and she forced herself out the door with a wrench that was a physical pain as she got into the cab, pulled her black straw hat down low, adjusted her sunglasses, and blew her nose. She should have been used to the pain by now, but she knew she never would be. And one day, when he was gone ... she would still remember him ... and the love they had shared that no one had ever known ... it was almost unbearable. How could she even begin to explain it to Mel? And she didn't want him feeling sorry for her. It wouldn't change anything. Nothing would. Not for Anthony. Or for her. It was a tragedy she had never imagined in her darkest thoughts, and yet she wouldn't have given up the joy of loving him for anything.

The flight to Los Angeles was uneventful and tiring, and she only stopped at her apartment long enough to change and pick up her bags, and she left that night for New York.

She was exhausted, and she knew that even her careful makeup job hadn't hidden the rigours of the last week. And if she didn't watch out, and start taking care of herself again, she was going to need a new face-lift before the end of the second season.

The stewardesses catered to her every need, as she travelled in first class, and she took a cab from the airport to the Pierre without anyone recognising her. She had worn another large hat, her dark glasses, and she had a way of turning her head, and avoiding eye contact, which she was convinced affected whether people recognised her or not. She went straight to the desk, and registered, and they escorted her to her suite, where she sat down, took a long breath, and called room service for a drink. It was 3:00 a.m. in New York, and only midnight in California.

She slept for two hours, and called Mel when she got up, to tell him she was there, and there was still a marked chill in his voice when he answered.

'What time did you get in?'

'I got to the hotel at three o'clock.'

'You must be dead.'

'More or less. But I'll live. I just need a couple of nights' sleep and I'll be fine again.' He interpreted that she didn't want to see him after work and his voice was like ice when he answered her.

'Fine. I understand.'

But she decided to put a stop to it or it could go on for weeks. 'No, you don't. But that's beside the point. I'm just tired, Mel. That's all. I've had a hard time, it's been a rough week, but I can't wait to see you.'

'How's your friend?' He sounded hesitant, as though he was unsure of her, of their whole relationship now.

'All right.' He still wanted to know who the friend was, but he didn't think this was the time to ask. And the detective had been singularly unable to come up with any further information.

'Do you want to have breakfast up here with me?'

'I'd love it. I'll be right up.' She came upstairs in blue jeans, French boots, and a white silk shirt that revealed just enough to remind him of how beautiful she was beneath her clothes, and it was difficult to stay angry at her. Her eyes were so tired, and there was something profoundly sad about her suddenly. He had never seen that in her before. She was always so strong, so much in control, so much the star, somehow one never thought of her feeling that way. And he couldn't resist reaching out and taking her hand when the waiter left.

'Sabina . . . what happened to you? Are you all right? *You*, not your friend . . . you.'

'I'm okay.' She looked into his eyes with a tired smile. She wanted to tell him, but there was no point to it. Why? So he'd feel sorry for her? What was the point of that? She didn't see herself that way, she never had. She took care of herself, and of Anthony, and she always had, and always would. She relied on Mel for the good times, but not to cry over her tragedies, or the dying son she had left in California.

She looked as though she'd seen a lot in the past week, too much, he guessed, and he wanted to reach out to her and hold her.

'Who was sick?' It seemed important to him that she tell him.

'No one you know.' She buttered a roll and averted her eyes.

'I figured that much.' He smiled. 'A man you love.' She saw his pain then, his doubt, his fear, and she felt sorry for him . . . and for herself . . . and Anthony . . .

'Yes. But not the way you think.' She had never told another living soul. She had disappeared before he was born, and returned alone afterwards. No one knew. Until now. 'My son, Mel, I have a fifteen-year-old son.' She looked him in the eye, not sure why she was trusting him.

'Good Lord.' He looked stunned. 'Somehow I never thought of you that way.'

She smiled, and sat back in her chair. 'No one does.'

'And he was ill?' He was beginning to understand, he thought, but there was a lot more he didn't know yet.

'He was born that way.' She quietly explained his deformities and she didn't even feel the tears rolling down her cheeks. 'I never know when, or if, I'll see him again, Mel. And when they called the other night . . . I had to go . . .' Her voice was gruff, and he gently wiped away her tears, feeling his own, remembering how he had felt when his children had died fifteen years before . . . probably around the time that he was born . . . their tragedies strangely linked in time.

'Why didn't you say something?'

'Why? I've never told anyone. I carry my burdens alone.' She seemed almost proud of it, and he respected her, but he had never loved her more than he did just then. His heart went out to her.

'You don't have to any more, Sabina. I'm here for you.'

'I know you are. But Anthony is mine . . . I love him with all my heart . . . and I never want anyone to torment him about my career, my life . . . Anthony belongs only to me.'

'What about his father? Hasn't he done anything to help?'

She shook her head. 'I don't think he would have anyway. But he couldn't deal with the realities of Anthony's life. I've never seen him since Anthony was born.'

'The bastard.' Mel looked fierce as he looked at her and she smiled and sighed, philosophical after fifteen years.

'Some people are, my love. But not you, you've been so good to me.'

He decided the time was now, the moment he'd been waiting for. 'I want to marry you.'

His words took her breath away. And slowly she shook her head. 'I can't, Mel . . . I can't . . . that's not in me . . . .'

'But why?' As long as there was no one else, as long as she loved him as she said she did. He hadn't wanted to marry anyone since Liz had died, but now . . . he knew Sabina for what she was, and he loved and respected her for it.

'I'm not sure I could ever do that, Mel. I tend to my own responsibilities, my own life . . . and there's Anthony. I can't burden you with that. What if something happened to me? You'd feel responsible.'

'Is that so terrible? Isn't that what love is all about?' Love was all about what she felt for the child, but for the rest? . . . she hadn't wanted to be married in years, and yet she was so at ease with him, so content . . . so grateful for all he did . . . but was that enough? Did that justify marriage?

'Couldn't you be satisfied as things are?' She was curious. What did he want from her? A contract? A guarantee? They were too old for kids, or she was anyway.

He nodded slowly. 'If I had to be, yes . . . I could be. But there's more than this. A kind of security that comes from knowing you belong to each other forever, if there is such a thing.' They both knew better than that.

'I could promise you that, right now, right here, without ever having to get married in a church, or by a judge. I don't know, Mel.' She stood up and walked around the room, thinking of all he had said. 'Maybe one day, Mel. Is that good enough?' What he wanted was a promise from her, some confirmation of her love, and that didn't seem so ridiculous. She liked feeling secure about him too, she just didn't feel a need for marriage anymore. Not now.

'Will you give it some thought, Sabina?' His eyes were filled with hope and she bent to kiss him gently on the lips, surprised at how hungry she was for him after only a week.

'I will.' And then she laughed. 'Why would you want to marry an old bag like me?'

'Because you're a big TV star. I told you it would change your life.' She laughed and he pulled her onto his lap. 'What you're telling me is that you want to live in sin, is that it?'

'For a while. Could you manage that?'

'I think I could. Just don't wait to change your mind till I'm too old to carry you over the threshold.'

'Is that part of the deal?' She smiled, happy to be with him again. He balanced the pain she felt for Anthony.

'It's supposed to be.'

'Hmm,' she mused. 'You know, I've never been married before.' And she still wasn't sure if it was too late for her, but it didn't seem to matter very much just then. She had done what she could for her son, for now, and she was with the man she loved. There wasn't much more she wanted out of life. Her career was going well . . . the show was a success . . . She looked up at Mel with a smile and he kissed her softly on the lips, amazed at the secret she had shared with him.

37

'Quiet . . . very quiet . . . light it up . . . cameras rolling . . . action, please!' The familiar sounds felt good to her. It was reassuring, like coming home, as Sabina went through her first scene with Jane. She was tired, and she hadn't rehearsed adequately but the scene went well and they did it in six takes, which wasn't too bad. The two women laughed for a moment afterwards.

'So you're knocked up this year, are you, Jess?' Sabina teased. 'That ought to give François a heart attack. Has anyone read the script to him?' She laughed and Jane grinned. It was news to all of them, one of the many surprises they'd been promised for the coming year.

Jane turned to Mel. 'Do I get to keep the baby?'

'Ask Zack. It's up to him. He's going to be torn between the two of you, and which one will he choose, the empire or the woman he loves and their child . . . tune in next week, folks.' Everyone laughed, and Jane went back to her dressing room where Zack was waiting for her, reading his lines for the next scene.

'How'd it go?'

'Pretty good. Did you know that I get pregnant this year?'

'That's interesting.' He glanced up from the script. 'How's Sabina?'

'She looks tired. She looks as though she had a rough time.'

'Did she say what it was?'

Jane shook her head. 'And I don't think she will. She keeps her private life to herself.'

'Not like the rest of us.' He grinned. Everyone knew about them that autumn, and about Gabby and Bill.

Jane poured herself a Coke, and sat down with a sigh. She was looking tired too. It was hard going back to work after their long holiday and it was still hot in New York, hotter than it had been in Los Angeles. 'What do you think of the new developments?'

'Interesting. They ought to keep the ratings up.' Gabby was going to shoot Bill, they'd been told, but not fatally. Jane always worried about that, about one of them getting cancelled from the show, but there seemed to be no threat of that at the moment.

'Personally, I'm kind of pleased about the story line.'

'Yeah.' He took a sip of her Coke. He was feeling relaxed. They had made love for hours the night before, and he was feeling pleased with life.

'It's going to make things a lot easier for me.'

'What is?'

'The pregnancy.'

'Whose pregnancy?' He looked confused, and she had an odd look in her eyes.

'Jessica's . . . and mine . . .' She spoke so softly that at first he only stared at her, and suddenly he grabbed her arm.

'What do you mean?'

She looked nervous suddenly. She had secretly bought two kits at the chemist the day before, and she had known anyway. 'I didn't know what to say . . . I think when we were in London . . .'

He was staring at her. 'Are you telling me, Jane Adams . . . do you mean . . . Jesus Christ . . .' He leapt to his feet and looked around, stunned, and then he looked down at her. 'You're pregnant?'

She nodded her head, suddenly terrified. Maybe he'd make her get rid of it . . . and there was the show to worry about. Mel could cancel her for getting pregnant out of wedlock.

'When did you find out?' Zack was staring at Jane.

'Yesterday.' Her lip trembled, fearing his reaction.

And then suddenly he beamed at her, and pulled her into his arms. 'Are you serious?'

'Yes.' There were tears in her eyes.

274

'My God . . .' His dream had come true. It wasn't too late. He looked at her as though she had wrought a miracle. 'My God . . . when? . . . I mean when is it due?'

'I guess the end of May, or maybe the very beginning of June.' She was still only a week late, but she had suspected it immediately. She had only been late three times in her life, and she'd been pregnant each time. 'It would work out fine with our shooting schedule, if Mel doesn't throw me off the show . . . and if . . . that is . . . it depends on you Zack.' Her voice was soft in the tiny dressing room, as someone knocked on the door and shouted, 'You're up next, Jane.'

'I'll be right out.' But she had to talk to Zack first. 'What do you want to do?'

'Are you kidding? Get married and have ten more.'

'What if they cancel me?' Her eyes were damp. He had said just what she wanted to hear.

'They won't. And if they do, so what? Isn't this more important to you?' He looked incensed that she should think otherwise, but the baby *was* much more important to her, and so was he. The show was only for a time, she had learned that once before, but their life together could be for the rest of their lives, and their baby. . .

'I want to keep it, Zack . . .' She was crying now and he held her tight.

'Of course you do. We'll get married right away, and talk to Mel. Hell, he might even think it's good for the show.'

She laughed through her tears. 'Are you sure? I don't want to push you into this.'

'Don't be an ass.' He stood up, feeling taller suddenly and twice the man he had before, and then he looked gently at her. 'I love you, Jane. Are you sure you want me . . . in spite of everything?'

'There is no "in spite of". I'm the luckiest woman alive.'

'Jane!' Someone was pounding on the door.

'I'll be right out.' She kissed him, and he held her tight and then she hurried out of her clothes and into her next change, as he watched, trying to imagine her six months

275

hence. He held the door open for her, and watched her lovingly in her next scene, and as she came off the set after four takes, he smiled at her. It was a look meant only for her, and they went back to her dressing room, talking quietly.

38

They talked to Mel that night at the Pierre, and he was stunned, but Jane was even more so when he congratulated them.

'Was this our idea or yours?'

'A little of both.' Zack laughed, and Jane looked faintly embarrassed as she explained that the baby was due at the end of their shooting schedule.

'I wouldn't have to screw anything up. . .'

'That's considerate of you,' he teased, but he didn't look furious, just a little bit amazed. 'Are you sure you'll feel up to working right till the end?'

'I don't see why not.' And then she had to ask him point blank. She had been worried about it all day, in spite of everything Zack said. 'You mean you won't fire me, Mel?'

'I should say not. Besides, to be really crass about it, the publicity people are going to have a ball with this. The viewers are going to fall even more in love with you. Every guy in the country is going to wish he'd knocked you up himself, and the women are going to feel all mushy about you. It's perfect for the show, but much more important than that' – he looked at them both – 'I suspect it's perfect for both of you.' He looked tenderly at them, holding hands like two kids. 'In fact, I kind of envy you.'

Jane looked relieved, and Mel ordered champagne. Zack asked him to be best man. Jane was going to call her kids and tell them only that they were getting married, and they thought they'd do it in the next two weeks. That way no one would be quite sure if she'd been pregnant beforehand. They had thought of everything, and after congratulating them both again, Mel told Sabina that night. And she was amused.

'How can she get knocked up at her age, unless she wanted to?'

'Maybe she did.' Mel was touched by the love he'd seen in their eyes.

'You know . . . I still can't figure Zack out . . .' She was lying on the couch, relaxing, happy to be back with Mel, and working again. She had called Anthony and he was doing well, and now she had someone to share it with. 'I could have sworn he was gay.'

'Guess you were wrong.' Mel grinned. 'I'd say you were.'

She shrugged. 'Guess so. Are you hungry yet?'

He was watching her carefully and he smiled. 'Yes . . . but not for room service . . . I had something else in mind first.' And she laughed as he approached, she threw back her head with the golden mane and held her arms out to him.

'What a good idea,' she purred.

'Isn't it though . . .' He picked her up with ease and carried her into the bedroom of his suite, and it was a long time before they called room service that night, and when they did, he ordered champagne and caviar and an omelette for both of them.

The next morning on the set Sabina was in grand form, and Jane looked like a Cheshire cat, laughing and whispering with Zack between scenes, so much so that the director had to tell them to be quiet more than once. Mel stood on the sidelines watching all of them. The ratings were extra-ordinary, and the show was a bigger success than even he had dreamed.

He was watching Sabina rehearse with two of her 'legal underlings' when Bill walked over to him with a sombre air.

'Something wrong?' Mel hadn't seen him look like that in months, and Bill looked into his eyes with concern.

'May I talk to you?'

'Sure.' It looked like trouble on the set, and he saw Gabby watching them. 'What's up, Bill? Can we talk here?' Bill nodded and held his breath as he saw Gabby approach. He had told her to stay away. He wanted to tell Mel himself, and they probably should have told him beforehand. He looked into the older man's eyes and decided to jump in.

'I don't know how you'll feel about this . . .'

'Some problem with the script?' He didn't understand and Bill looked consumed with guilt.

'No, sir.' He shook his head. 'Gabby and I got married last night.'

Mel looked at him for an instant and then started to laugh. He laughed so hard he cried. They were like children, all of them.

'I . . . Mel . . . we were worried you might be upset. . .'

'Now why would you think that?'

'Because I know when you hired me, you asked if I was single . . . and I lied to you. . .'

'You're not lying to me now, are you?'

Bill looked confused. 'Of course not. We just thought . . . we were afraid . . . Gabby didn't want the kind of big wedding her parents would have insisted on . . .'

'Are you happy?' Mel smiled beningly down at him, as Gabby walked up, relieved to see Mel smiling at Bill.

'Yes . . . I am . . .' He put an arm around his wife, and Mel looked at her.

'Are you happy, Gabrielle?'

'Yes, Mel.' She beamed up at him, and it was obvious that she had never been happier.

'Then my blessings on both of you . . . all of you . . .' He looked around, seeing Zack and Jane, and Sabina approaching them . . . 'I've never seen a group with more secrets than this . . . but may you be happy, always.' He leaned over and kissed Gabrielle on the cheek, as Sabina put her hands on her hips and pretended to snarl.

'Get your hands off her.' She grinned at Mel, and he slapped her behind and they walked away, leaving the newlyweds, as Mel explained, hoping they would somehow influence her. But it didn't really matter to him. He was happy with her as she was . . . with who she was . . . and as he told her about Gabby and Bill, she laughed and looked over her shoulder at them, with a wink for Gabrielle. And Gabby laughed and waved at her, as the production assistant called out.

'Stand-ins, stand-ins . . . take your places, please!'